my Star Crossed Summer

Publisher's Cataloging-in-Publication Data
Day, Lucy 1978-.
My Star-Crossed Summer: Jasmine Falls Love Stories/ Lucy Day.
p.____ cm.____
ISBN 978-1-947834-78-1 (Pbk) | ISBN 978-1-947834-77-4 (eBook)
1. Women—Fiction. 2. Love—Fiction. I. Title.
813'.6—dc23

Blue Crow Books

Published by Blue Crow Books,
a division of Faulkenberry Arts.
www.lucydayauthor.com
Cover Design + Illustration by Lauren Faulkenberry

MY STAR-CROSSED SUMMER

Jasmine Falls Love Stories, Book 4

LUCY DAY

Blue Crow Books

Also by Lucy Day

The Almost Lovebirds

Almost Definitely Never

One Sweet Holiday

Exclusive Bonus Content, Just for You!

Want more of Jasmine Falls? Join my author newsletter (it's always free) and get fun extras like bonus epilogues and my short novella **You Got This, Maggie Monroe.** It's a standalone story in the Jasmine Falls Love Stories series, and is not for sale anywhere—just available as a thank you to my newsletter subscribers. So go ahead—add a little something extra to your reading list. :)

Sign up and learn more at lucydayauthor.com.

*For everyone who's out there
looking for the glimmers.*

Chapter One

VICTORIA

This is it, I think. *This is how I die—utterly humiliated because of my mother.*

I've been saying for years that she was going to put me into an early grave, but mostly I was kidding.

But now, because of her, I'm ten feet up in the air and grasping a massive oak limb for dear life. My fingers are slipping as my legs dangle below me, the skirt of my traitorous knit dress rucked up around my waist as the moon shines above me like a spotlight.

Okay, fine. This is not entirely because of my mother. It's also because I'm a big fat chicken and refused to draw any more fire from her by walking out the front door like a woman with her dignity intact. But the walls of this house were closing in, and I was sick to death of her rubbing my nose in my mistakes, and those last words she said to me made me snap my champagne glass in half.

What you fail to grasp is that your bad decisions reflect badly on this whole family. I won't always be around to fix your mistakes.

Honestly, that woman was born on a high horse. But in the

Griffin house, you have to pick your battles. Sometimes, that means biting your tongue and climbing out the second-story window of your childhood bedroom.

Hanging by my fingertips, I grit my teeth and try once more to locate another limb with my foot, but it's no use. My legs swing in the air as the bark bites into my palms.

Awesome.

Laughter erupts inside the house and I freeze, certain that Mom's friends have spied me and are simultaneously clutching their pearls and whipping out their cell phones. This house, one of the oldest in Jasmine Falls, is a two-story Georgian with windows that stretch almost floor to ceiling—it's a regal home. A historic gem that has survived a dozen hurricanes, two fires, and plenty of parties as awful as this one. As a teenager, I slipped out this way a million times—stepped out onto this limb, walked it as easy as if it were a balance beam, and then shinnied down the trunk like a squirrel.

Tonight, though, I'm not so limber.

The din inside the house rises again, but it's only music and the usual gossip that always bubbles over once the champagne starts flowing. Tonight, my mother's fancy spring soiree just happens to coincide with the implosion of my career—and that means Mom's in damage-control mode. More than fifty people are crowded inside, and in the last hour, they've all heard my mother's version of how I cancelled my wedding, broke off my engagement, and left my lucrative job at a top-ranked real estate firm.

For the record, I stand by those decisions. Mom, however, thinks they represent a string of unforgivable failures—and a personal attack on her reputation. Elaine Griffin holds herself to an impossible standard of perfection: perfect job, perfect house, perfect marriage. So, of course she's always held my big sister

Gwen and me to that same standard. I know perfection is an illusion, but our mother might actually die—burst into flames like a vampire in sunlight—if her flawless facade ever fell and everyone in town saw she's just as imperfect as the rest of us.

That's why she cornered Sheila Jenkins to insist that I'd make an excellent addition to Sheila's real estate firm and would certainly bring some of my biggest clients with me. Mom's trying her best to spin the news about me leaving my job and ex-fiancé so that it resonates like fiery independence and not a Titanic-sized disaster.

Some days, it feels like both.

I wriggle like a worm on a hook, trying to get my skirt to fall down enough to cover my backside—because the Jasmine Falls rumor mill does not need to know what my lacy undies look like —but the dress is caught on a branch and won't budge.

Cursing, I struggle to walk my hands down the limb toward the trunk, but I'm losing my grip.

"Vic!" someone whisper-yells. "What the heck?"

In a blink, my hand slips and I yelp as I crash to the ground.

I land so hard in the grass that it rattles my teeth. My free fall was less than ten feet—but my backside will have an ugly bruise tomorrow.

My sister Gwen steps out of the shadows, her big blue eyes wide. "You okay there, champ?" she says.

I wince as she pulls me to my feet.

"How'd you know I was out here?" I ask.

She arches a brow. "I was hiding out in the study and saw your lily-white legs dangling out here in the moonlight. Thought you might need an extraction."

I grunt, brushing the grass from my dress. "Mom's dialed up to eleven. I'm done."

Gwen grabs my hand, pulling me into the back yard. "Come

on, before everyone comes out to see what crash-landed out here. Pretty sure they heard you clear across the county."

"You're hilarious." I grab my shoes and follow her toward the treehouse, our hiding spot since we were old enough to climb.

It's more like a deck than a house, with solid floors and waist-high rails. There's no roof or walls, but the dense trees hide us from view. Once we're up the ladder and sitting side-by-side on the floor, Gwen pulls a flask from somewhere in the folds of her dress and offers it to me.

"You're like a cartoon character with impossible pockets," I say. "What else do you have hiding in there?"

She shrugs. "All the essentials. Including Logan's favorite scotch."

"Can't hurt," I say, taking a big sip. "I feel like I've been hurled from a catapult."

Gwen's navy dress fans around her. She's effortlessly beautiful, all curves and soft edges. Her hair's cut in a cute bob that makes the curls extra bouncy—something my hair will never achieve. Tonight, I coaxed mine into waves, but as I run my fingers through it now, I pull out a couple of twigs.

"So what drove you to the emergency exit?" Gwen asks, sipping from the flask. "Usually, I'm the one who bails early."

"First Mom tried to get Sheila Jenkins to hire me—after telling her a masterful story about how Theo bullied me out of Rayanne's firm after I dumped him."

"Ugh," she groans.

"Agreed. I'd rather bathe in lava than work for Sheila Jenkins. Her sales record is amazing, but she's about as fun to be around as a nest of angry hornets that have been set on fire."

"Didn't her partner just leave?"

"Yep. Opened her own firm in Florida. And she's crushing

it." I take another sip of scotch, and it burns a path all the way to my belly. "Then Mom told Marcia Roberts that I dumped Theo because he left me—and I quote—unfulfilled."

She snorts. "Well, that's true. In a sense."

"She'll do anything to cover up my mistakes to save her precious reputation," I groan. "Theo's a jerk, but I don't love having Mom go into jackal mode and use the rumor mill to spread lies."

"If anyone deserves to see Mom reach her final form, it's Theo," Gwen says. "I'd argue he's getting precisely what he earned."

Gwen's accustomed to being the target of our mother's ire even more than I am. Mom expected both of us to be flawless: from hourglass figures and straight-As to impressive careers and trophy husbands. Gwen caught more scorn because she openly defied Mom's wishes, whereas I caved because it meant less fighting. When Gwen opened a bakery, I let Mom push me into real estate. When Gwen dated guys with tattoos and scruffy beards, I went out with the boring sons of Mom's friends just to keep the peace. Now that Gwen's dating Logan and running a booming business, some of the heat's off her. But that means it's squarely on me.

"That's how Mom works," Gwen says. "She thinks if she pulls enough strings, she can fix what's broken."

I snort. "Yeah. Right now, she thinks the broken thing is me."

"She's wrong," Gwen says, her blue eyes glittering.

"Maybe," I mutter. My breakup was no tragedy, and I refuse to play the sad, wounded woman—a shell of a human at age twenty-eight. Mom thought Theo was my perfect match, but that's because he shared her impossible standards for every part of his life—including me. And when I finally realized that Theo was resentful of my success and that his version of marriage meant me giving up my career—well, that made leaving him a no-brainer.

"Mom got me that job with Rayanne," I confess. "They were sorority sisters at Vanderbilt back in the day."

"But Rayanne kept you on because you're excellent at what you do. Mom had nothing to do with that part."

I shake my head. "It set a bad precedent." I'd let Mom pull those strings when I was twenty-three because I was struggling in a dead-end temp job and wanted to stop living off ramen noodles and grilled cheese sandwiches. Back then, I'd thought she was truly trying to help me, but now I know better. She was embarrassed that I wasn't making a name for myself fast enough. Mom's always been controlling of both me and Gwen, but I'd assumed it would stop when we were out of college.

I was dead wrong on that one.

"I never should have accepted her…help," I say, choking on the last word.

Gwen lifts a brow. "We both know how it would have gone if you hadn't. She'd rather die than stop holding us to her impossible standards." She smoothes a fold in her dress. "She thinks that molding you into a version of herself is going to make you a success and preserve her legacy."

"That is literally my worst nightmare."

She gives me a sad smile as the night birds twitter around us, the leaves rustling in the warm breeze. This is one of those perfect spring nights where the air's losing its chill and the stars shine a bit brighter. Everywhere you look, there are blossoming flowers and new leaves, and the whole world feels alive with new growth. Spring always makes me feel hopeful and tenacious, like I can tackle anything.

At least, it used to make me feel that way.

"She said she didn't raise me to be a quitter," I grumble. "Told me I run as soon as things get hard."

Gwen frowns. "Leaving a toxic relationship is not being a quitter. You know that."

"I told her I was doing what was best for me."

She points her finger at me. "That's exactly right. And don't ever forget it."

I pick at a tiny hole near the hem of my dress. "What Mom thinks she knows about us could fill an ocean."

Gwen snorts. "But what she actually knows might fill a teaspoon."

For example, Mom didn't know that Theo tried to mold me into his perfect image of a wife and constantly undermined me to preserve his massive ego. He hated that I outperformed him at Rayanne's and that I actually made friends with my clients. He was manipulative in that way that narcissists always are: they make you feel cherished one minute, like you're the best thing that happened to them. In the next, they're making you feel like a villain for having the audacity to not give in to their demands. He made me feel bad for standing up for myself and communicating my own needs—whether that was wanting to take a weekend trip to the coast by myself or disagreeing with him on how we should handle renovations of our house. The longer we were together, the more his resentment of me grew. Once I realized he was never going to change, I bailed.

And the job Mom thought was so great? Staying at Rayanne's firm made me feel comfortable (mostly) and meant I wasn't Mom's primary target anymore. But it meant that I had to keep working with Theo—and that was a hard no.

Once Theo was out of the picture, I felt free. Now I want to cut out all of the other parts of my life that are a mismatch, too.

"What's really going on with you?" Gwen says. "The Victoria

I know would stomp right over to Mom and tell her where to shove her spin before she dropped the mic and flounced out of that party *Real Housewives*-style."

I let out a heavy sigh because she's not wrong. Stifling my own needs has become my default, and I don't want that anymore.

"I've been wasting my life," I mutter. There's a hollowness in my chest that I can't explain, but I've been feeling it for months.

"Whoa," she says. "Big leap. Back up, sweetie."

I shake my head. "Mom's been trying to reframe all of my missteps to everyone here—and I gotta say, Gwennie, laying them all out like that just makes it super clear that I've been on the wrong path for a long time."

Like, since the second I let Mom get me that job with Rayanne's real estate firm.

Gwen sighs. "You're a force of nature. Don't let Mom convince you otherwise." She reaches over and taps her finger to my temple. "Don't let her in here. You'll have to burn a truckload of sage to get her out."

"You know the worst thing?" I say. "I don't think I even like real estate anymore. Maybe I never did."

She nods but doesn't look surprised.

"I'm good at it, but it doesn't bring me joy." I stretch my legs in front of me, feeling defeated. "I want what you have. I want to do something that truly makes me happy." I sigh, feeling this envy, this want, deep in my bones—and then instantly feel a wave of guilt because my sister deserves to be happy, and I love that she's built this amazing life for herself. "I want to be passionate about something, the way you are with the cafe. I want to do something that has purpose."

"Oh, honey," Gwen says.

"I just wish I knew what that something was."

She slides closer to me and places her hand over mine. "I have no doubt you'll find your happy," she says. She means well, but her words are a knife in my chest because I'm not sure of anything anymore. I feel like I've been doing everything wrong. I'm so far off my path, I can't even see it anymore.

"I've been looking at job listings everywhere since I left Rayanne's," I confess. "but nothing appeals to me. It's like I don't know myself the way I thought I did. I feel unmoored."

"To be fair, you've had a lot of upheaval in a short amount of time."

She's right, but it doesn't make me feel any better. When I broke off my engagement with Theo back in December, it blew up my whole life. I moved out of our house the very next day. A week later, I left my job with Rayanne, in part because Theo had convinced everyone in the office that I'd entered my villain era. He could be charming when he wanted, and he had all of our colleagues under his spell.

Theo didn't respect me, and he'd never truly seen me as his equal. He'd been threatened by my success and expected me to sacrifice my career for our marriage. It wasn't until I saw Gwen with her new boyfriend Logan that the truth really sank in. And that moment galvanized the fact that I wouldn't just be settling with Theo—I'd be sacrificing my identity and squeezing myself into this mold he'd made for me. Realizing that on the day of our wedding wasn't the best timing ever, but leaving him was my only option.

After the wedding debacle, I moved back into my house at the lake, next to Gwen. I'd been renting it to Logan, but once I broke things off with Theo, Logan ripped that lease in half and insisted I come back to my home. Gwen won the lottery with that guy, and I'd be lying if I said I wasn't a little jealous of that, too. Everything in Gwen's life seemed to be falling into place while mine felt like it had been blown to smithereens.

"I have to find a job soon," I mutter. "I'm burning through my savings."

"My offer still stands," she says matter-of-factly. "You can be the cafe's marketing strategist and social media wunderkind. Logan would pay you an obscene amount of money to do it."

"And I do appreciate it," I tell her. "But I can't let you do that. I have to do this on my own. I have to find what lights me up."

She nods in agreement. I could do the job she offered—easily. But I know it's not my path. I didn't blow up my life just to settle again.

That dwindling savings, though. It's a beast with big teeth.

"What about that job your friend Roxy called you about?" Gwen says.

I laugh. "Director of a kids' camp? Come on. I don't know what to do with kids."

"You don't give yourself enough credit. Kids would love you. Your skill set extends way beyond real estate and marketing."

"Please. I don't know the first thing about teaching kids. Mom's dead right on that one—I've got zero maternal genes."

She sips from the flask and frowns. "You need to stop letting other people define you, babe. Screw that noise."

"Scotch makes you sassy," I quip. But she's not wrong. The problem is, now that I've let go of everyone else's expectations of me, I don't recognize myself. I'm not sure what I want.

"Sometimes getting out of your comfort zone is the best way to shake something loose. No one ever grew from being comfortable. Ask me how I know." A chime splits the air, and she digs through the pocket of her dress to pull out her phone.

"It's not fair," I say. "You got all the curves and all the brains."

"One hundred percent false, and you know it."

"You're a good sister, Gwennie."

"Giddy up," she says, pulling me to my feet. "Logan's here to break us out for real. He's parked across the street."

"He really leans into the knight in shining armor thing," I tease.

The tiniest blush touches her cheeks. "He likes to be protective," she says. "Even though he knows I don't need rescue." She smirks, but I know she loves having a partner who makes her a priority.

I hope one day I'll have that, too.

But right now, it's time to make myself a priority. It's time to find my happy.

I just need to know where to look.

Chapter Two

Back at home, I change into my pajamas, pour myself a glass of wine, and collapse onto the couch. The lights are still on in Gwen's house next door, so I can see her moving around the kitchen with Logan. I love living next to my sister, but sometimes it feels like staring at the sun. She's got this great life doing what she loves, and now she's got Logan, who encourages her to shine even brighter. She's always been super talented at baking, immensely creative, and a whip-smart entrepreneur—even though she never would have described herself that way. Our mother was really good at making her doubt herself.

Once she met Logan, though, it was like she finally started to see herself the way the rest of her friends already did—like a total dynamo who can build whatever life she wants for herself. I'm so proud of her, and also friend-jealous. More than anything, I want to feel the contentment that she feels now. I want to go to bed each night happy with the knowledge that I'm doing something that makes the world a little brighter.

Gwen's words echo in the stillness: *No one ever grew from being comfortable.*

I need to be braver. Think bigger. Take a leap.

Pulling my phone from my pocket, I text Roxy. It's after eleven, but I'm feeling bold. And maybe desperate. Sometimes, the two overlap.

Hey, I write. **That job you told me about at the camp. Is it still available?**

Her notifications are turned off—probably because she's spending her Saturday night doing something fun and not falling out of trees with her skirt above her head. I should have taken the job when she offered, but it seemed like a bad fit. Me, in the wilderness. With kids. It sounded like one more thing I'd fail at. One more way to be humiliated.

Ever since Theo, I feel like I can't trust my gut anymore. I came so close to marrying a guy who undermined me, belittled me, and made me feel small because my parents had made me think that was normal behavior. I chased perfection because being wrong was bad, but being perfect meant being loved. So I spent years working endless hours in a job I didn't like because it felt like one I should be grateful to have. I'd fooled myself into thinking that I'd needed those things—worse, that I wanted them.

But I was wrong. What I wanted was for my mom to tell me I was good enough. That I could stop trying so hard and just enjoy my life. And now, after so many years of living the life someone else told me to live, I don't know who I am.

This job with Roxy still feels like a long shot, but when I think of how far Gwen's come in the last year, I can't help but think that maybe a long shot is exactly what I need to move forward.

I just hope it's not too late.

· · ·

WHEN MY PHONE rings for the sixth time, I grind my teeth so hard it's a miracle I don't crack a molar. My mother has already left me five voicemails, demanding to know why I left her party last night without saying goodbye—and without meeting Dan Sterling, another person she thought could somehow salvage my career.

Ugh.

Five voicemails, and it's not even ten in the morning.

I pick up the phone, ready to set up a new boundary that she'll delight in tearing down when I see that it's Roxy calling.

"Hey, stranger," I say in greeting. I wince as I climb off the bar stool at my kitchen island because crashing to the earth has indeed left one mighty bruise.

"Hey yourself," she says. "I didn't get your text until this morning."

"Yeah, about that," I say, biting my lip. "I was thinking more about that job you mentioned and thought maybe I was too quick to say no. Is it still open?"

She blows out a heavy breath. Roxy and I met right after college, when we were working at the same temp agency in Charleston. We were roommates for a couple of years until I moved back to Jasmine Falls. Hiding anything from her is impossible because she knows all of my tells, and she knows when I'm feeling desperate. With my bills piling up and my savings dwindling, I'm determined to get myself back on track.

And she knows that, too.

"I wish I could say yes," Roxy says. "I'd bring you on in a heartbeat, but they just filled that position with someone in-house."

My heart sinks. It feels like the universe is toying with me. I finally came around to see that it was offering me an opportunity only to have it snatched away.

"Surprised me, too," she grumbles. "You'd have been better." Her espresso machine whirs in the background. She still lives near the College of Charleston, where she's the director of a program for students interested in STEM. A few weeks ago, this job sounded like too much of a leap. Now it feels like a life raft.

"Is there anything else?" I ask.

"Not right away." She pauses, her spoon clinking as she stirs her coffee. "Except for a temp position that opened up, but I can't imagine you'd want—"

"Does it pay money?"

"Yes, but—"

"I'll take it."

She laughs. "Don't you want to know what it is first?"

"I'll make your coffee and handle your emails. No problem."

Roxy snorts. "My inbox would make you curl up and cry." She sips her coffee loudly and then says, "The open job is an activities director at one of the camp locations. Someone backed out last week. I was going to post the position tomorrow."

"Keep talking," I say. I'm not into tons of physical activities unless you count pacing in frustration and doing yoga every blue moon, but I can fake it.

"It's our astronomy camp near Pisgah," she says. "In the North Carolina mountains."

Deflated, I mutter, "I don't know anything about astronomy." I can fake a lot of things, but not physics. Unless their activities involve making model solar systems out of styrofoam balls and florist's wire, I'm out of luck.

"You wouldn't need to," she says. "That's the instructor's job. Each satellite camp has a partnership with us. They have dorms or cabins for sleeping quarters, plus classrooms, research facilities, and whatever else the kids need. They let us use their spaces for the three weeks that we're there, and we bring our own support staff—the instructors, the site director, and some admin and activities staff."

"So I'd be like a camp counselor?"

"Kind of," she says. "We have one male and female admin who stay in residence with the kids, and then plan and lead their non-academic activities. That's the open position. The woman I hired is a senior at NC State and got this summer internship studying sea turtles in the Caymans. I can't be too annoyed because that's a legit career move, and this woman loves sea turtles the way some girls love unicorns. Plus, who would say no to a summer in the Caribbean?" She slurps her coffee. "You're way overqualified for this job, and it doesn't pay anywhere close to what you're worth, or what you're used to. But if you want it, it's yours." She says that last part like she knows how dire my situation is.

I cringe, thinking that I'll likely be the oldest person there, with the possible exception of the instructor. Usually, these positions are filled by college students.

"Actually," she says, "there's a full-time version of this director job that's going to be posted later this summer. If you're interested, then this is a great way to get a leg up because they'll want to see some experience with kids. You could consider this session your trial period."

"I don't have to know anything about stars?"

"Nope."

"How old are the kids?"

"Seventh and eighth grade," she says. "They're great kids— thrilled to be there and geek out with each other at science camp. They're bright and well-behaved, and this is the highlight of their year. The most mischievous thing they'll do is build a moon rover out of roller skates and an old satellite dish."

Pacing in the kitchen, I think of the summer camps I went to as a kid. Swimming in the lake, roasting marshmallows, telling stories around a campfire. Do kids still do those things at camp? "Full disclosure, I'm not a natural with kids," I tell her, because truthfully, I never know what to do around them. "And you know I'm not outdoorsy, either." The original position I was interested in involved marketing strategy—not kids. What Roxy's describing is a million miles outside my comfort zone.

She laughs. "Babe, you can manage anyone. These kids will be a breeze. And the activities are just meant to get them some outside time. Low contact sports, hiking, canoeing, scavenger hunts—that sort of thing. You could do this in your sleep."

I bite my lip. When was the last time I went hiking? Working in real estate meant working some crazy hours—the only way I got my steps in was by doing back-to-back showings all day. "That sounds doable," I say at last, because I really need it to be.

"Plus, your counterpart is like the prince of the wilderness," Roxy says. "He's been working with us for a few years, and he's a total pro—and a super nice guy. You can tag team, and I'm sure he'll take on anything you're not comfortable doing. And the site is gorgeous—staff get a day off each week and have mornings off, so you'd have a little time to yourself. It'd be like a mountain retreat for you, too."

Lately, I've been feeling like I have more than enough time alone, but I keep that thought to myself. Some fresh air in a place that is not Jasmine Falls might give me the clarity that I need to figure out my next move. I can't even remember the last time I took an actual vacation, but this is more than that. This is a chance for discovery. A big leap. I need to embrace it and be brave.

Because *brave* is the only way forward.

"Okay," I tell her. "Let's do this."

"Super," she says. "I'll email you all the details. The camp starts June third."

"That's two weeks away."

"Is that a problem?"

"Nope," I tell her. "Not at all." Probably, the sooner I get out of here, the better.

When she ends the call, I flop back onto the couch and tell myself, *You got this, Griffin. You can do anything for three weeks.*

You can do hard things.

You can take big leaps.

I'll keep saying it until I believe it's true.

Chapter Three

NOAH

I knead the dough tenderly, just like they do on the bake-off. That show's one of my guilty pleasures, and watching it always makes me hungry. I'm no gifted baker, but somehow I've learned to make edible bread—and the rosemary garlic is my favorite.

Now that I finally have a day off and zero obligations, I'm prepared to bake this loaf, open a new bottle of my favorite bourbon, and watch the sunset over the inlet behind my house. I've spent the last two weeks doing last-minute planning for this year's summer camps, and the first one starts on Monday.

Today might be the last day off I have until September, so I plan to make it count.

I turn up the stereo because it's the Stones and "Sweet Virginia" is best sung at top volume, loud enough to rattle the glasses in the cabinet. Just as Mick and I hit the chorus, there's a pounding on the back door by the patio. I brush my hands off on my apron, leaving my loaf to proof one last time, and open the door.

My sister Hannah freezes, her hand poised to pound on the

door once more. Her brown curly hair is wild from the humidity, her blue eyes wide. Her cheeks are flushed, like she's been running. It's already hit ninety degrees in Charleston, which is a record for us.

"Hi," I say, but it comes out like a question.

"Why aren't you answering your phone?" she says.

"Kind of have my hands full."

She narrows her eyes, taking in my tee shirt and beat-up jeans, the fine dusting of flour that covers most of my skin.

"I need a favor," she says, just as her dog bursts through the door, nearly knocking me over as she tears through the kitchen, dragging her bright pink leash behind her. "Opal, sit!" Hannah hollers, and the big black and white sheepadoodle skids to a halt, teetering backward on her haunches as she stares at me, tongue lolling.

"Hannah, if you—"

"Jason and I had a fight," she says, "and I can't stay in that apartment one more minute. Can I please crash with you? Just for a day or two until these murderous thoughts pass and he gets his act together."

"Sure," I say, because I can never say no to my little sister. Even when she's still wasting her time with this Jason person, who always finds new ways to disappoint her.

Hannah's a genius coder, and she can obviously do so much better than this idiot just by randomly picking someone out of line down at the Music Farm one Friday night. But this is not my decision to make.

"Thank you," she says. "You really are the best. Is that bread you're baking?"

I turn just as she yells, "Opal, no! Down!"

Paws on the counter, Opal noses around the pastry mat toward a pile of chopped rosemary and half a garlic bulb that she would desperately like to taste. She stretches her tongue as far as she can to reach a stick of butter as Hannah claps her hands and rushes over to intervene.

"I'll just grab a few things from the car," she says, getting all four dog paws back on the floor before heading back out through the living room. Opal follows her, and when the front door slams shut, she comes racing back into the kitchen with my hiking boot in her mouth.

"Give me that," I say. She huffs and runs back into the living room, tail wagging.

Chase is her favorite game.

When I turn down the stereo, I hear my cell ringing. Roxy's name flashes on the screen, and I pick up just as I see the string of missed text messages, mostly from Hannah. My boss doesn't make a habit of calling me on weekends—except when camp season starts. Then all bets are off. There's always a last-minute crisis of some kind.

"Hey," I answer. "How's it going?"

"Good news," she says. "I found a replacement for the astronomy camp."

"Oh great," I answer. Probably a college kid with this short notice, but that's okay. Roxy's a good judge of character, and most of our college staff have worked out just fine.

The front door slams. From the living room, Hannah yells, "Opal, drop it! Now!"

"Have they done a camp with us before?" I ask.

"No," Roxy says. "But I know her, and I think you two will get along great. We go way back, actually. She's awesome."

Opal's claws clack on the hardwood as she flies through the kitchen, carrying my ruby ficus plant by the trunk, dirt falling in clumps behind her. She's yanked it right out of the pot and is delighted to show me.

"No!" I yell, lunging for the dog as the plant drops a leaf.

"What?" Roxy says.

"Sorry, not you," I say. Then I cover the speaker and yell, "Hannah, come handle your beast!"

I try to corner her as I tell Roxy, "Doodle drama. You were saying?"

"Her name's Victoria," Roxy says, just as I close in on Opal. She snorts with glee and darts under the kitchen table, dirt clods falling all around her. "She and I have been friends for years, and she was thinking of applying to this other job in admin. But she missed the deadline, so I talked her into filling in for Maura to get her on board. She'd be excellent to have with us full time, but for right now, we have her at the Blue Ridge site."

"Sounds good," I say, lunging for the dog. She gives a playful bark and skitters past me, my poor ficus wobbling in her teeth. I raised that plant from a sprig, and now it's about to be snapped in half by the world's cutest tornado.

"She's a great fit," Roxy says. "You'll like her."

Another crash comes from around the corner. "Sure thing," I tell her as I head into the living room, dreading what I'll find. Opal's just over a year old and tries to eat everything she can get her mouth on—the last time Hannah brought her over here, she ate two of my wool socks, three bananas, the first two chapters of *The Shining,* and half of my leather belt.

It made for an unpleasant evening.

"I'll let you go," Roxy says. "Just wanted to let you know you now have a full staff again."

"Thank you," I tell her. "I appreciate you doing that. Sophie and I would have managed, but having three makes everything so much easier." I tiptoe toward Opal, who's now lying on her back on my sofa, chewing on my boot while she gives me some overly dramatic side-eye. The ficus lies at her feet, a heap of soil on the sofa and another on the rug. The front door opens, and Hannah comes in with a rolling suitcase and a laptop bag, her eyes widening as I wave my arms at her and point to the disaster unfolding a few feet away.

"Of course," Roxy says. "I wouldn't leave you high and dry. Talk soon, okay?"

"You got it."

When I hang up, Hannah cringes. "Sorry," she says. "We did zoomies before we came in the house. I thought she'd just flop down and take a nap."

From the sofa, there's a loud urp. That doesn't bode well.

I rake my fingers through my hair and head back into the kitchen to open that top-shelf bourbon. And then I realize what Roxy said:

Victoria.

An old friend of mine.

It has to be a coincidence, right? This couldn't possibly be my Victoria.

Well. Not that she was ever really mine. We were best friends in college, but then I managed to wreck that beyond repair. So I never had the chance to tell her that I was completely in love with her. I shake my head to clear the thought because as often as I considered bumping into Victoria Griffin again, the odds of it being at a camp in the middle of nowhere are less than zero.

She's not a second chance I'll ever have.

Chapter Four

VICTORIA

Two weeks later, I'm driving to the Blue Ridge Astronomical Institute, a research facility that's on a mountaintop nestled deep in the National Forest. Approaching it feels like going into some secret government facility that isn't supposed to officially exist. Just a few hours' drive from Jasmine Falls, it's not truly in the middle of nowhere. Not completely. It's twenty minutes from the nearest town, but after winding up the mountain on a narrow two-lane road for what seemed like a hundred years, it feels like I'm in a remote location best suited for a horror movie.

When the road turned to gravel, I was certain I was lost—but then it emptied into a clearing with a cluster of buildings arranged like a tiny college campus. To my left is the ring of radio telescopes, all pointing in the same direction. One has a smiley face painted on the inside, grinning up toward whoever might be watching from above.

Another narrow paved road carries me past a group of 1950s-era buildings made from concrete and glass. At their center is a wide meadow with a small pond and a walking trail.

Two wood-shingle cabins are to my right, nestled in the evergreens.

My online snooping taught me that the institute has a dozen researchers who work here full time with state-of-the-art labs and observatories. Plus six radio telescopes that are the pride of the Southeast. When the cabins aren't being used by camps like the College of Charleston's, they're used by visiting scientists from around the world.

I park my small SUV next to one of the cabins, where there's a hand-painted welcome sign made of poster board taped to a folding table. A black pickup truck and a red mini Cooper are parked nearby, both covered in dust from the gravel road.

All around me is lush green: the trees, the grass, the broad-leafed shrubs. Massive evergreens seem to stretch a mile above the clusters of laurel and rhododendron at their feet. Jasmine Falls is in the Lowcountry, close enough to the coast to have Spanish moss in the trees and a hint of brine in the air. Here, the air is crisp and cool, not heavy and humid like it is back home. Overhead, one puffy cloud floats in a sky that's a striking shade of Carolina blue.

The buildings look dated, but the view behind them takes my breath away. Beyond the giant firs and pines, the mountains are undulating tones of blues and greens, as vast and serene as the ocean.

A rabbit hops out of the brush near me, just as the sun passes from behind a cloud and illuminates the bright green of the meadow.

"Okay, now you're just showing off," I say to the sky and head toward the nearest cabin. But I can't deny the spark of joy that warms my chest. The thrill of starting over.

"Hello," I call, stepping inside. There's a kitchenette and a lounge area by the front door, a long hallway extending beyond.

The interior looks like it hasn't seen an update in about fifty years, and smells musty in that way that old libraries do. The walls are a mix of dark paneling and off-white paint, and the chunky dorm-like furniture looks about as comfortable as granite.

"Oh, hi," a voice chirps. "You made it."

A young Black woman, twenty-two at most, strides toward me and extends her hand for me to shake. "I'm Sophie. The admin. You must be Victoria." She's a couple of inches taller than me, lean with bright eyes that crinkle at the corners when she flashes me a warm smile. "We're just getting settled in the office and going over some ideas for the week. Did you get lunch on the way? The cafeteria made us to-go boxes, so I have one for you, too." She shoves a handful of braids over her shoulder, and I note that several are purple. She has the cool-counselor vibe, big-time.

"Thank you," I say. "That'd be great."

"Your room's this way," she says, leading me down the hallway. "It's not fancy, but it's semi-private. You're at the one end of the building, and I'm on the other. In theory, that means we can keep a better eye on the kiddos."

"How long have you been doing this?" I ask.

She turns the corner and grins. "This is my third year as an admin. But I came to these camps as a student, years ago." She's practically glowing, like this is her happy place.

"Wow," I say, already feeling out of my depth. The hallway also looks like a dorm, with signs on the doors that have the campers' names written in marker, decorated with stickers and glitter. At the end of the hallway, Sophie stops at a door that has an identical sign with my name on it. She leads me inside, pointing out the basics—the bath, the switches for the lights over the bed, the baseboard heater under the window.

"Rustic, but cozy," she says. "I sleep like a baby here."

Rustic is a generous term. Fallout-shelter-chic is more like it.

"There's extra bedding in the closet here," Sophie says. "Plus some blankets. A first-aid kit's on the desk there, and a flashlight. It gets pitch-black out here at night, so don't go without your flashlight."

"Got it," I say.

"The kids start coming in tomorrow morning at eleven," she says. "Airport shuttles start rolling in earlier, but everyone should be here by five p.m. We'll have some informal activities tomorrow as the kids arrive and then orientation after dinner."

I check my phone for the time and see there's no service.

Sophie nods and says, "You won't get much of a signal out here. There's a landline in each cabin, and you're welcome to share that number with anyone who might need to reach you."

"Oh," I breathe. *Three weeks with no cell service?*

"It's amazing," she says, as if reading my horrified expression. "You can leave the whole world behind when you come here. Just us and the animals and the stars." She says this with absolute glee while my stomach clenches like a fist.

Sophie is clearly a Very Outdoorsy Person. Everything about her screams *wilderness,* from her navy camp-style shirt that has buttons everywhere—on the chest pockets, above the elbows, on little straps that hang below the rolled cuffs—to her sleek hiking pants that are a cross between leggings and cargo pants with zipper pockets on either side. She smells like citronella and has the kind of muscular thighs one earns by climbing over boulders and biking uphill.

Sophie looks right at home in this place. She doesn't seem one bit concerned about bears, rockslides, or falling into a nest of venomous snakes and not being able to use a cell phone to call for rescue.

I shift in my sandals, thinking that my knit skirt and tank top aren't the wisest choice in clothing. Sophie's wearing hiking boots that look like they could carry her right over Everest—and she's here as the lead admin. From what Roxy told me, Sophie's job is mostly mission control, keeping the whole operation running smoothly from behind the scenes.

"This session's going to be awesome," she says, and I do admire her enthusiasm. So far, this place's vibe is like *Friday the 13th* meets *Real Genius*, and I'm not sure which part of that is more unsettling. It's not hard to imagine these genius children pulling some A-level pranks on me—or to imagine any number of threatening creatures lurking out in the woods, waiting to jump out and eat me for dinner. Either way, I'm squarely out of my element, and the urge to run back to my car and drive down the mountain is strong.

But I won't do that because I can't let Roxy down. I keep my word, and I can do hard things. I've handled clients who were meaner than rabid raccoons, for heaven's sake—this should be a cinch. *It's only three weeks,* I tell myself. *You can do anything for three measly weeks.*

I take a deep breath, willing myself to relax. But everything in my chest stays wound tight like a spring that's ready to pop.

"Why don't you get your things inside and get settled," Sophie says. "And then we can all meet up to talk about tomorrow's orientation—say in twenty minutes?"

"Sounds great," I say, forcing myself to sound chipper.

She gives me a thumbs-up and heads back down the hallway, her boots thumping against the ancient linoleum.

Even her footsteps are confident.

I massage the knot forming near my shoulder, where it always appears when I'm anxious, and open the blinds at my window. My room is on the back side of the building, and because of the steep hillside below, I'm looking straight into the treetops. My new home is a box of wall-to-wall wood paneling that's just big enough to hold a dresser, a small desk, a single-sized bed, and a chair made from molded plastic. Made up with pale blue linens and a thin coverlet, the bed looks like it belongs in an old motel. And when I sit on it, the springs make an ungodly screeching sound. Far from fancy, but I've stayed in worse—mainly in college, when taking road trips with friends meant staying in the cheapest places we could find.

The tiny bathroom has plain white fixtures and dove-gray linoleum. The only spot of color is a set of mint-green towels that feel like sandpaper. But the room is clean, and there are even tiny hotel-sized bar soaps and a small vase with a cluster of laurel and honeysuckle. Someone's made an effort to make this room feel cozy—probably Sophie. After splashing some cold water on my face, I run my fingers through my hair to tame the frizz and head outside to unload my car.

As I open the back door and set my first bag on the ground, a deep voice says from behind me, "Hey there. Need a hand with those?"

When I turn towards the voice, I immediately feel like someone's knocked the wind out of me because—no. Just *no*.

My mouth falls open as the man standing in front of me arches a brow and puts his hands on his hips, staring at me as if he, too, can't believe his eyes. Finally, he speaks again in that familiar drawl that rumbles along my spine and turns my knees to jelly.

"Victoria," he says.

I blink a few times, stunned into silence, because this can't be. I know those warm hazel eyes, that tousled dark hair, and that roguish grin—they belong to someone I thought I'd never see again. My chest tightens, and my heart pounds so hard my ears tingle. Is it too late to climb back into my car and leave? I give myself a sharp pinch on the wrist because surely I'm dreaming.

Ouch. I rub the spot on my wrist where the skin is thin and tingling. Not dreaming.

"Noah," I wheeze, because no other words will come out. My brain is a tangle of thoughts, but none of them explain why Noah Valentine is standing three feet in front of me, on top of a mountain in one of the most remote parts of North Carolina.

I should have a better chance of being struck by lightning than to bump into this man again. And right now, I'm wishing a bolt would shoot down from this wide blue sky and knock me right off this mortal plane.

"It is you," he says. His brow furrows like he's not sure how to feel about this either. He shoves his hands into his jeans pockets and says, "It's good to see you again."

Is it, though? I feel like a bunny caught in headlights. How on earth can I get out of this situation? Spending three weeks with genius children in a research lab on a remote mountaintop is one thing, but staying here with Noah Valentine? That's a different thing entirely. This job doesn't come with hazard pay, but if Noah's here, it absolutely should—because this man wrecked me once, and I have no doubt he can do it again.

My eyes trace the long lines of his body and rest on his big hands, and my brain helpfully reminds me of the way they felt tangled in my hair and gripping my waist on the last night that we saw each other.

Suddenly, it's a hundred degrees on this mountain.

I haven't seen Noah since we were in college together—six years ago? Seven?—and already my heart's threatening to beat right out of my chest and flop around between our feet like a fish.

"Let me help you with that," he says, reaching for my bag.

His shoulders are wide, his thighs as big as tree trunks. The sleeves of his dark green shirt are rolled up to his elbows, revealing a small tattoo curling along the inside of his forearm. The wiry Noah that I knew before has been replaced by this man who's ripped everywhere, whose arm muscles flex in an almost torrid way as he lifts the bag—the heaviest one, with my shoes— and carries it inside the cabin. I try my best to ignore the snug fit of his jeans and his perfectly sculpted butt as I follow him inside.

Because of course Noah Valentine is somehow hotter than he was in college. By a degree of ten. Or maybe a thousand.

Stupefied, I try to think of anything to say to him, anything at all, but the words swirl around in my head like a tornado. None of it makes sense—not the words, not my thoughts, not the fact that he's on this mountain with me, looking as chiseled and confident as a stunt-double in the Thor movies.

Inside my room, he sets the bag by my bed and turns to catch me staring. His eyes, framed by thick, epic eyebrows that punctuate every word, still have that perpetually sleepy expression that makes him look like he just rolled out of bed.

I do not need to think of Noah Valentine in a bed, with rumpled hair and a lazy grin.

Nope.

"Thanks," I manage. All other words fly right out of my head.

A tiny smirk touches his lips as he takes the box that I'm clutching tight against my chest and sets it on the desk by the window. When he rests his hands on his hips, the movement drags my eyes exactly where they should not linger, and my mouth instantly goes dry.

I force my gaze back up, but that's no good either because now my brain is calculating just how delightful his beard stubble would feel against my skin—because unfortunately my body remembers that, too. He lifts one dark eyebrow as if he can read my mind and rakes a hand through his hair—short on the sides and long enough on top to stand up in every direction. He always did have an intense gaze, but now? It's smoldering.

And I'm a tinderbox.

"It's been a minute," he says, his voice more gravelly than I remember. "How have you been?"

He says this like it's not at all uncomfortable to be stuck in this tiny room, mere inches apart. Like he hasn't seen himself in a mirror lately and has no memory of the last time we were together. His voice is cool and even, but that furrow in his brow says he's just as taken aback as I am.

"Great," I say, because apparently I've been reduced to one-syllable words only.

"I can't believe it's really you." He offers a tiny smile, like he's not sure what to feel, either..

"Hey, Victoria," Sophie says, stepping into the doorway. "I've got your—oh. I see you've met Noah."

Noah gives her his full smile and says, "Just helping Victoria get her things inside."

Sophie turns to me and says, "One of the many reasons we love this guy. Always looking out for us."

I nod, expecting him to say more. Like how we know each other already, how we went to college together, how I ruined our friendship and smashed it to smithereens.

How I was over the moon for him and did the one thing that was guaranteed to drive us apart—and then never saw him again.

But instead, he gives me a quick glance and says, "I'll go get the last one from your car," and hurries out of the room like the building's on fire.

· · ·

ESCAPE WOULD BE SO EASY. Just climb into my car and drive as fast as possible down that winding mountain road, back to what's familiar and safe. In under a minute, I could high-tail it out of here, like I did when I took that awful telemarketing job in college. On that day, I'd made it through exactly three hours of "Dial and smile!" training before erupting into tears and fleeing on my lunch break, never to be seen again. Getting into my car now means beating that record because I've been on this mountain for less than forty-five minutes.

But I can't leave because I gave Roxy my word. And I need this job.

Plus, the whole point of this exercise is to prove to myself that I can take a leap and challenge myself to grow. And just like my Grandma June used to say, *Nothing worth having ever came easy.*

Besides, I've done scarier things than this.

Like for example, when Noah and I stayed in that creepy motel on our summer road trip after sophomore year. The Tinkerbell Motel had what some people would call *personality*—a bricked-up bathroom window, five deadbolt locks on the door, and gigantic neon signs that filled our room with so much bright pink light that it felt like we were inside a lava lamp. I'd barely slept a wink in that place, certain that we'd walked right into an episode of *The X-Files* and would end up featured on a murder podcast. Noah, however, had slept like a rock in the bed across from mine, the blissful slumber of a man not concerned about being chopped up into tiny pieces and fed to alligators in the adjacent reptile park. Shaking my head, I force that memory back down where it belongs, way down deep with all the other feelings I had for Noah Valentine.

Because I definitely shouldn't revisit any of those feelings now. Especially the ones that leave me weak-kneed.

Sophie fills me in on all things space camp as she and Noah give me a tour of the buildings: a research lab that looks like something NASA would have, a cafeteria with big floor-to-ceiling windows, an administrative building with offices and meeting spaces. Noah barely says a word as we walk, his face impossible to read. Is he annoyed that I'm here? Angry? Something else? He opens the door for us and avoids my gaze as Sophie leads me inside the admin building at the center of the campus. It's clearly the newest, with a high-ceilinged lobby and stairs that lead to offices above. A small library and conference room are tucked into one branch of the main floor, along with a lounge and kitchenette.

Sophie explains that we've been granted access to everything on the main floor, including a conference room to use as our office. Painted white and filled with modern Swedish-style furniture, it's the coziest room we've seen so far. When Sophie sits on the sofa, Noah and I sit in the chairs on either side of her. Already, it feels like we're opposing forces. Each time we make eye contact, he gives me a tight smile or averts his gaze like he's equal parts annoyed and flabbergasted.

Because they're old pros at this, Sophie and Noah have already created a schedule of activities for each day. Noah pulls out a three-inch binder that is no doubt his library for all things outdoorsy and kid-appropriate. He hands me a printout that immediately makes my stomach twist into knots.

"Most of this isn't set in stone," Noah says, leaning back in his chair. I try to ignore the line of his long legs, his full lips and sharp jaw. When he drags his fingers over his day-old beard stubble, I feel a tug low in my belly that is definitely not work appropriate.

What on earth is wrong with me?

His eyes dart to mine, and my heart leaps into my throat. I

shift my gaze back to the paper in front of me and will my eyeballs to stay right there on the activities list, between Frisbee golf and hiking trails.

"The weekend outings had to be booked in advance," he says, "the horseback riding, the canoeing, the camping and so forth. But the weekday afternoon and evening programs are totally flexible."

Sophie grins. "I get to go on these, too, right?"

"Of course," Noah says. He smiles at her so his dimples show, and lord have mercy, I forgot how those dimples make me forget about everything else in the whole world.

"I mean, technically the weekend trips are in your off-time," he tells her, "but you're welcome to come along."

Sophie nods enthusiastically, like she can't wait to gallop down one of these hillsides on horseback, and my heart pounds like a bass drum: *You're doomed. Doomed, doomed, doomed.*

When was the last time I rode a horse that wasn't on a carousel? When was the last time I slept on the *ground*? Noah and Sophie are getting more and more excited as they talk logistics, and it just underscores the reality that I'm going to be the one who falls off the side of the mountain or gets snatched up by a hungry bear. What was I thinking saying yes to this? I was prepared for making s'mores and singing horrendously off-key around a campfire, and hiking on a well-defined and oh-please-Jesus mostly flat trail—but what Noah's suggesting? I feel like a contestant on that reality show that plops a bunch of city people down blindfolded in the middle of a rainforest and then films them until they cry.

I'm an ugly crier.

I think I'm hiding all of these thoughts well until Noah stops and says, "You okay, Vic?"

Vic. No one calls me that now except my sister. Hearing it in

Noah's rumbling drawl snaps me back in time. Back to when he'd sling his arm over my shoulders and pull me close to tell me some goofy joke or a secret meant just for us. We'd been inseparable back then, and I'd thought we'd have that closeness forever.

You and me against the world, Vic, he used to say. And I felt that all the way down in my bones.

"Of course," I say. "Sounds amazing." I give him an exaggerated thumbs-up and immediately regret it because while it looks cute when Sophie does it, I probably look like a possum trying to hitchhike.

Smooth.

Noah lifts a brow, clearly skeptical.

Sophie gives me a sympathetic smile and glances at Noah, and I'm certain she can see straight through this act. She's a bonafide Very Outdoorsy Person, after all—just like he is—and those folks can spot an imposter faster than they can spot poison ivy in a thicket.

This is going to be the longest three weeks of my life.

"I've got the photo page up and running, too," Sophie says. Turning her laptop toward me, she explains that each day she'll post photos to document the kids' activities. "The parents love getting a peek at what everyone's up to in class and otherwise," she says. "It's great since we have spotty cell service and the kids have limited time to use the lounge phones."

Noah nods. "Sophie's in charge of wrangling photos, but if you want to use your cell and send her any, feel free."

"Will do." I look over Sophie's shoulder as she scrolls through the web page so I can see the setup.

"Password protected," she says. "It's only for staff, campers, and their parents."

"Great idea," I tell her, hoping that the parents won't immediately see me as an imposter, too.

"Hey, Victoria," Noah says, and part of me is sad to hear him drop the familiar nickname. "To be clear, you're welcome to hit me with any ideas you have for activities. I don't mean to leave you out of the planning." He gives me a polite smile, resting his big forearms on the table. How does one even get forearms that sculpted? He probably climbs sheer rock faces and rows himself upriver through rapids just for fun. "I pulled a lot of the weekday programs from our go-to list of things the kids have done in years past. Except for the trips that required reservations, everything else is negotiable. I just figured this would be a good place to start, and of course we'll see what the kids gravitate toward, too."

Bless his heart, Noah thinks I'm melting into the floor because I'm feeling left out of their planning. It hasn't dawned on him yet that I'm terrified of spending the night in the wilderness, in a tent that basically makes me a burrito for a bear. He doesn't realize that scaling mountains and riding horses and paddling down a river is light-years beyond my comfort zone.

And I'd really like to keep it that way. Because the last thing I need is to be humiliated in front of Noah. Again.

"No worries," I tell him, my voice entirely too chipper. "I appreciate you taking the reins here. I'm sure I'll think of some things to add once I meet the kids."

"Perfect," he says, and there's that tight smile again, the one that says he's seeing more than he lets on. The man's like a human lie detector and picks up on subtle cues that slip by most people—it's one of the many things that drew me to him all those years ago.

The way he's looking at me now, though, means he's not

having one bit of trouble seeing through my act. He knows as surely as I do that I'm in way over my head.

<h1 style="text-align:center">Chapter Five</h1>

NOAH

Victoria Griffin is the last person I'd ever expect to see in a place like this. And really, I never expected to see her again at all.

I can't decide if this is a dream come true or a nightmare.

But here she is, standing right in front of me, leaning against our rental car in a way that draws my eye directly to her delightfully round hip where her hand is firmly planted. Her lean legs still go on for miles, and I definitely don't need to be staring at them like this. I can't help myself, though, because Victoria looks like a goddess. She's curvier now, with a softness to her that's like stones polished smooth by a river. Her blonde hair's brighter, the chic shoulder-length cut drawing my eye straight to her collarbones. When she crosses her arms over her chest, I drag my gaze back up to her face, where her lips are pursed just enough to remind me of how they felt against mine.

When her stormy eyes drift over me, I feel like I've been knocked over by a rogue wave.

This camp is a sanctuary for me. It's a place where I can be myself, do the job I love, and be surrounded by cool kids that leave me feeling inspired. I don't have to think too hard about what I do here because this is the one place where all the pieces just come together naturally. There aren't many places where I feel like I belong. Here, I'm an integral part of the system.

But Victoria makes all of that more complicated. I know her—or rather, I used to—but how she'll affect this program is a mystery. How can she be both a known and unknown variable at the same time? She's Schrödinger's cat at summer camp, and my brain doesn't like this puzzle one bit.

My body, though. That's another story. It remembers her softness, her warmth, and I've already caught myself leaning closer to her twice, like a tide pulled by the moon.

I need to tear my gaze away from those pouty lips and focus on something neutral, like the grass between our feet. I don't need another thought experiment right now—I need to pull myself together and be a professional.

"Please tell me those aren't the only shoes you brought," I say, pointing to her hot pink sneakers. With hardly a scuff on them, they look like they can't handle terrain more rugged than a sidewalk.

Victoria narrows her eyes at me and says, "Of course not. I also have hiking sandals."

I groan because she's way out of her element here and still has a stubborn streak a mile wide. She's traded the skirt she was wearing earlier for jeans that might as well be painted on her body and a fleece that looks fresh off the rack. It'll be warm enough to get her through most nights here, but I'd be willing to bet my summer salary that she hasn't thought to bring a heavy-duty rain jacket or waterproof shoes. These mountains see mild temperatures in June, but at this altitude, the nights can dip into the forties and the rain can be torrential. I know you can't always judge a book by its cover, but Victoria looks about as at home in the outdoors as a deer would at your dinner party.

We climb into the SUV, and once she fastens her seat belt, I pull out of the parking lot and onto the narrow road that leads down the mountain into Laurel Creek—it's the nearest town, a twenty-minute drive if you're not stuck behind awestruck tourists. It's only quarter past six, but the sun's already dropped behind the ridge, turning the sky dark and the air chilly.

"You don't have a good pair of hiking boots?" I ask her, knowing what the answer will be.

"These will be fine," she says. "They're like walking on a cloud."

I grit my teeth. Those shoes don't have one bit of traction or ankle support. One wrong step on a slippery rock, and she'll land flat on her perfectly round backside and have a sprained ankle or worse. Most of the trails around here aren't difficult, but we like to challenge the kids enough so they leave here realizing they're a lot stronger than they thought they were. But even on the easy trails, this footwear won't do.

"What are we picking up in town?" she says, staring out the window. It's like she's determined to avoid talking to me about anything but the camp—understandable, since things ended so awkwardly for us before. But every time her big blue eyes lock on mine, I want to ask her a hundred questions that don't have anything to do with the kids or the summer session. Like, *why did we never talk after? How could we have given up so quickly? Why did you push me away?*

But I don't ask because her answers might make the next three weeks even more difficult. Some truths are better left buried.

So I focus on driving down the dark, winding road, trying to ignore how I can feel the warmth of her body all the way over here. How each time the breeze blows in through her open window, I can smell that sweet vanilla-citrusy smell that I'd think was a nice perfume if I didn't know it was one hundred percent Victoria.

The last time I smelled that scent, her hair was falling in my face, and her lips were moving against mine in a way that had nearly stopped my heart. A dozen thoughts were racing through my brain, but the only one that mattered was *hell yes, finally,* because I'd at last let myself have the one thing I'd been denying that I wanted for so long.

Victoria Griffin.

Holding her had felt amazing, electric, and terrifying. It was like trying to hold on to sunlight, and I'd been a complete idiot to let her go. I've thought about that night ten thousand times, and I can still close my eyes and feel the gentle pull of her lips and the warmth of her hands raking through my hair. Her soft curves had pressed into all of my hard edges, and it was no surprise that being with her felt so perfect—because with Vic, I always felt like I belonged.

The tires rumble in the loose gravel, yanking me back to the present. She squeaks with surprise, and I gently pull us off the shoulder and back onto the road.

I swallow hard, pushing that memory of kissing her aside because that's the last thought I need to have about Victoria right now.

But of course, that one is the most persistent.

"You okay over there?" she says, her hand gripping the dash.

"Thought I saw a deer," I mutter. "Sorry." My face is burning up, my heart hammering against my ribs so hard it hurts. Thank goodness it's already dark outside, so she can't see the effect she still has on me.

Her side-eye says that she knows full well there was no deer, but she just makes a little *Hmm* sound as she looks out the window, and that says everything.

"We mostly need some things for the afternoon sports," I tell her, steering my thoughts back to our errand. "Some frisbees and soccer balls, a few more first-aid kits, some extra toothbrushes and such, because somebody always forgets their toothbrush."

She snorts. "When I was a kid, I forgot my toothbrush every time I left home. Literally every time."

My brain oh-so-helpfully reminds me that she forgot it when we took that road trip in college, too. I ended up buying her a goofy kid's brush with a dinosaur on it as a joke, and a year later, I spotted it perched on the desk in her dorm room. She liked reminders of travel, she'd said, but even then, part of me hoped she was really keeping reminders of us.

"Laurel Creek's a tiny place," I tell her. "But there's a decent pizza restaurant, a grocery, and a general store with the basics. And a roller skating rink that's a straight-up time capsule from the 70s. You've never seen so much neon in one place, I guarantee it."

Her lip ticks up in a smile, making me wonder if she remembers that time we went skating in college. One of our friends rented the place out for a party, and I only went because Victoria was going. I could barely skate and kept crashing into her, but she always managed to keep me on my feet.

That's how it was with us, though. She always kept me grounded.

She flips on the radio and scrolls until the static clears. Otis Redding's crooning about his empty arms, and there's a tug deep in my chest that only makes me grip the steering wheel harder. Vic always had a soft spot for old soul. When I got a turntable sophomore year, she bought me a stack of old records for my birthday. I still have them all—even the Sam Cooke that skipped.

We drive without speaking the rest of the way down the mountain. Her fingers tap in time to the music, her gaze fixed somewhere in the distance with the evergreens. I want to ask her what she's thinking, but it seems too intrusive. She's finally starting to relax around me, and I don't want to push my luck.

The last time I laid eyes on Victoria, I was twenty-one—a junior at the College of Charleston. She was twenty, and we'd become fast friends. She was hilarious and brilliant and shared my love of campy old horror movies and punk-ska bands. We saw each other every day back then, even though we rarely had classes together. After a few months, I started falling for her—hard—but kept telling myself she was off-limits because I didn't want to ruin our friendship. College was difficult because I felt weird around most people. Everyone called me a loner, but really I was just slow to open up to people I barely knew. I was more comfortable out hiking in the woods than making small talk with people who seemed to only hang out with me until someone more interesting came along. But Victoria didn't shrug me off like most others did. She made me feel seen right from the get-go. She never indicated she had romantic feelings for me at all—until that one night that blew everything apart. I've had a lot of regrets in my life, but that night might be the biggest. If I had a time machine and could only use it once, I'd send myself right back to that spring break at the beach house, drag my sorry younger self into the surf, and talk some sense into him.

"How long have you been doing this?" she asks. We're headed through town now, where most of the businesses have closed for the night. For a second, I think she means how long have I been wishing I could turn back time, but she's talking about the summer camp, of course.

It's misting rain as I pull into the parking lot of the store. It does that a lot here—in summer, the storms can come out of nowhere and soak you to the bone. "Off and on after college," I say, and when I wince at that last word, I steal a glance at her. She's biting her lip like she's been yanked back in time, too.

Is she thinking about that same night, on the beach under the stars? Is she wishing things had gone differently, or that it had never happened at all? Maybe she hasn't thought about us for one second since that night. Maybe that's why she seems so uncomfortable now.

Or maybe she remembers how good we were together, too.

"Not this site in particular," I say, hoping to skim right over *college* because we don't need to touch that memory with a ten-foot pole. At least not here, like this, crammed into a giant boat of an SUV that's about to hold a bunch of kids we're charged with helping to see the wonders of western North Carolina and all the stars that hang above it. The adult thing to do is address the giant elephant that's squeezed into the car with us, but right now, that thought is nauseating.

I don't want to make the next three weeks awkward for Victoria. So I'll keep my mouth shut and follow her lead. If she doesn't bring up what happened all those years ago, then I won't either.

"I was a teaching assistant first, at the home campus in Charleston," I explain. "And then I did an admin job like Sophie for a couple of years, and they offered me this position. I did biology camps down in Beaufort and the Outer Banks and have been at this site twice. It's a good one." I tack on that last part because she still looks uneasy, like she's considering taking the keys and driving this vehicle at the speed of light until this mountain is a tiny dot in her rearview mirror.

She nods as we get out of the car and head into the store.

"Lots of experience, then." Her tiny frown tells me that detail is more troublesome to her than reassuring.

I shrug. "It's a pretty easy gig. Make sure everyone has fun, respects each other and the site, and make sure they all come home with ten fingers and toes each night after all the hiking and rafting and whatnot."

She falls into step next to me, her brows pinched together as if she's thinking hard.

"Why are you here?" I ask her. "You hate nature."

"I don't hate nature," she says. "Maybe I wanted to challenge myself. To do something new. Different. Is that so strange?"

As we step inside the store and under the bright fluorescent lights, I see her cheeks are flushed. I want to snatch my words out of the air and shove them into my pocket because obviously I don't know her that well anymore. And I really don't need to talk about our past. If I'm going to make it through this session, then she needs to be Victoria, a charming stranger and colleague —not the woman who stole my heart before she strode out of my life and slammed the door behind her.

Her jaw clenches as she grabs a shopping cart and heads down the first aisle. "That's not who I am anymore," she says, her tone clipped. "I needed a change."

"A change from what?"

"Everything." Her tone is matter-of-fact, and the deep furrow in her brow suggests she doesn't like this line of questioning one bit. There's a wound there that I shouldn't poke, even though I'm curious what brought her here, doing a job that's usually done by college students like Sophie.

And six years ago, she wouldn't go in the woods with me unless she lost a bet.

She steers the cart toward the center aisle and says, "What's first on the list?"

"First-aid kits," I say, wishing there was one big enough to patch us back together. The next few weeks are going to be brutal if we can't figure out a way to be around each other without feeling like we're two live wires trying not to cross.

Vic pulls two kinds of first-aid kits from the shelf and holds them up for me to examine. When I nod, she plops them into the cart and continues down the aisle, and I try hard to focus on the list instead of the mesmerizing sway of her hips and the tension that seems to have settled in her shoulders again—likely because of me.

Before long, the cart's nearly full. After we get through the checkout line and pile everything into the back of the car, she starts to get in the passenger side.

"One more thing," I tell her.

She freezes, her hand on the door handle, and gives me a wary look.

"Hiking boots," I say. "For you."

Her brow lifts in that way that means she thinks she doesn't need any help.

"Come on. The outfitters over there will have what you need."

"I told you, these are fine," she insists.

"Fine for running around in the grass," I say. "Maybe. But if you go hiking in those, it's a safety hazard and I'm not going to let you put yourself in danger. Plus, the amount of paperwork we have to fill out for an injury would make your head explode."

She narrows those big blue eyes at me, and I know she wants to argue because she always hated it when I tried to boss her around—even when I so obviously knew better, in times such as now. But then she sighs and says, "Point taken. You win."

Not yet, but I'm working on it.

Inside the store, I lead her to the aisle with the hiking boots. There are only a dozen styles to choose from, but these are quality brands that will do the job.

She pulls a boot from the rack with soles thick enough to walk through lava. When she looks at the price sticker, her face scrunches up like she's bitten into a lemon.

"A good pair will last you for years," I tell her.

She frowns. "The next three weeks will likely be the most wear they ever get."

I point to a few that are tough and not too expensive, and she tries them on with minimal complaint.

At last, she settles on a tan pair with green laces and says, "These aren't terrible."

"Hang on." I can tell by the way the toes bend as she walks that the fit's not right. The snap in each step says they're too big. I pull another pair from the shelf and motion for her to sit in the chair at the end of the aisle. "Humor me."

She slips off the too-large pair, and I undo the laces of the smaller boot. When she reaches for it, I kneel in front of her and reach for her foot.

As I cup her heel in my hand, she sucks in a breath. When her teeth sink into her full bottom lip, it sends a tingle from my chest all the way to my hairline. Being on my knees in front of Vic is waking up a whole bunch of feelings that I thought were gone forever.

Willing all my tingly parts to stand down, I force my gaze away from her perfect lips and back to the boots.

"You have to lace them up the right way so you get the support," I say, holding the shoe as she slips her foot inside. I place her foot on my thigh and tug the laces tight, starting near the toes. When I get to her ankle, I pull the laces gently, showing her how to tighten them just right. "If they slip too much, you'll get blisters," I tell her. "And you want them snug enough to support your ankle. I'll do this one looser so you see what I mean."

As I tie the other one, I try hard to ignore the heat that washes through me when her foot presses against my thigh. When she stands to test them, her gaze falls so heavy on mine that I feel it deep in my belly. It would be so easy to close this space between us—two steps would do it—and then I could slide my hands along her cheeks and kiss her the way I should have all those years ago.

But I can't. Because I have to earn her trust again.

After taking a few steps, she nods—though the furrow in her brow tells me she doesn't want to drop a hundred and fifty dollars on them.

"You'll thank me when you're still upright after a full day of walking and your toes are warm and dry, Vic."

She considers that for a moment and then says, "Fair enough," with a tight little smile that nearly unravels me. She stumbles a little as she pulls them off and grabs my shoulder to right herself. A current zips along my skin, up to my ears and down to my toes. So much for those old feelings going away, because my body has decided that it very much likes being in close proximity to Victoria. Like a reflex, I drop my hand on her hip to steady her.

That was us back then—our relationship in a nutshell. Something about her was always drawing me closer, and it never occurred to me that I was flying too close to the sun.

Her eyes widen for a split second, and she yanks her hand from my shoulder like she's touched a hot stovetop.

I try to swallow those feelings because I cannot feel this way about Victoria Griffin. I cannot feel all of this *want*. She broke my heart once, and she can do it again.

If we're going to survive the next three weeks together, I need to not fall apart at the seams every time she looks at me. I need to hold myself together.

ON THE DRIVE BACK, Victoria's quiet, as if deep in thought. The moon is nearly full, but it still feels like we're inside an ink bottle because the thirty-foot evergreens block out the light. That's what I love about this place, though—it feels like you're on the edge of the world, yet somehow connected to everything. The forest seems ancient, the sky above infinite, and it feels like even though I'm a tiny, insignificant human, I can make a difference with these kids for just a little while and know that what I do matters.

That's the feeling that's most important to me. But tonight, a little voice inside my head comes out of the depths to ask: *But is it? Is that what's most important to you right now?*

When Victoria finally speaks again, it's to ask me more about what to expect from the kids this week. She seems uncomfortable in the silence between us, which makes me wonder exactly what's rolling around in her head. Usually, her face is a dead giveaway for her feelings—she used to joke that she had no control over her expressions and was incapable of hiding her emotions. But she's wrong about that. Eighty percent of the time, her face is easy to read. Other times, she's completely stone-faced. When I first met her, I thought she hated me—but then she cracked a smile as wide as the ocean, and I knew right then that she was someone I needed in my life.

I just didn't realize how much.

Gravel crunches under the tires as we wend our way up the narrow road to the institute, and each turn winds something in my chest tighter and tighter. It feels so strange being this close to her again—like my heart's pulling me closer to her and my head's pushing us apart. She's doing her friendly chatter now, which she always did when she was extra nervous with other people, but never with me. It makes me feel like a stranger, and that feeling is way worse than the knot that's been in my stomach since this afternoon.

When I park next to the office, I switch off the engine and turn toward her. I can't keep up this charade any longer, pretending that our history isn't lurking around us like a storm cloud.

"So listen," I say. "I think we should clear the air." I keep my tone warm and friendly, though the words feel ragged in my mouth. "I expect you have some mixed feelings about being here together, given how things ended between us."

That furrow in her brow deepens. I've hit a nerve, but there's no backing out now.

"Given how things ended," she repeats, turning to face me. "That's one way to say it."

My whole body tenses when I see the flash of hurt in her eyes. "How would you say it?"

She blinks at me for a moment, like she's deciding whether she can tell me off and still keep her job. "You completely ghosted me," she says. "Vanished like Houdini. Or D.B. Cooper. Poof!"

"You kissed me like the world was ending and then bolted," I counter. "You wouldn't even talk to me after."

"I needed to clear my head," she says, exasperated. "I made myself so vulnerable with you. And felt like I'd made the worst mistake and I didn't know how to fix it." She crosses her arms over her chest as if she's holding herself together. "I was humiliated, and then you disappeared from the face of the earth. With your *girlfriend* that you kept secret from me."

"That was a serious error in judgment," I tell her. "And for what it's worth, she ditched me in Amsterdam when she met some Swedish guy with a platinum credit card and cheekbones that could cut glass."

"Are you trying to make me feel sorry for you?" she asks, her cheeks flaming.

"Not for a minute," I insist. "Just wanted you to know that karma kicked me square in the balls, and I definitely deserved it." My attempt at levity is failing because she looks like she wants to hurl those new boots right at my head. "There's a lot I regret about that string of decisions," I say. "But mostly, I regret not being honest with you. And not trying harder to fix things between us."

She narrows her eyes, but that hard line of her lips softens. "You stopped texting me," she says with a shrug. "I figured you lived happily ever after and forgot about me."

"Not even close." I slide my hand over hers, and to my surprise, she doesn't pull it away. "I could never forget about you. I didn't try to get in touch anymore because I thought that's what you wanted." I swallow hard, thinking of that night on the beach, that kiss that turned the whole world on its side—and that text she sent weeks later that read *All good things come to an end, N—leave me be.*

There were some other words, but those are the ones that feel tattooed on my heart.

"I never meant to hurt you, Vic. I thought you wanted me to stay away."

"I just wanted my best friend back," she says, and I feel gutted.

"I'm sorry," I tell her, squeezing her hand. "For all of it. Being oblivious, keeping my feelings hidden, not trying harder to make it up to you." I give her a small shrug. "Your last words to me just felt so final. I was trying to do what you asked."

Puzzled, she cocks her head to the side. "What do you mean?"

"That last text you sent me, telling me to leave you alone. I took you at your word when you said you didn't want to see me again."

Her brows pinch together. "I never said that."

"You did, though." There's no way I'm misremembering because at the time, those words were like a knife plunged into my chest. It had seemed so unlike her to cut me off so easily, but there was no mistaking her words—eventually, I convinced myself that there was no way to fix what I'd broken. "I thought if I gave you some space, you might get in touch again when you were ready. But you never did. I just figured I didn't matter to you anymore. And maybe I deserve that. But I will do anything to make all that up to you."

"But I—" She shakes her head, pulling her hand away from mine. She looks like she wants to say more, but she's quiet for a long moment. When she finally turns back to me, her eyes are glassy. "You know what? It doesn't matter now. We have a job to do. I think it's best for everyone if we keep our past in the past and focus on making sure the kids have a good time here." Her tone is cool. She's building that wall up between us again.

Now I feel like I've made a mistake and shouldn't have poked this wound.

Why do I always make everything between us worse?

"We're adults," she goes on. "And people with complicated histories work together all the time. I can handle being colleagues for three weeks if you can."

Something about the word *colleague* makes me want to choke.

It's so cold and clinical, the opposite of how we used to be with each other. Back then, I broke her trust—I see that now. It's a tricky thing, earning back someone's trust when you've lost it. But that's what I have to do—because I'm not that scared twenty-one-year-old anymore.

"Pretend you don't know me," she says, her tone icy.

"What?"

"I think it's best," she says. "For the sake of camp, we have no history. We've never met before today."

"That's a bit extreme, don't you think?"

"No." She reaches for the door handle and gives me a look of disappointment that could burn a hole in my chest. "You said you'd do anything. This is what I'm asking."

I study her face for a long moment, but she's unreadable. "If that's what you want," I say at last.

She nods once and climbs out of the car.

My pulse pounds in my ears because I never thought I'd see Victoria again, and of course it would happen like this: here, in a camp full of kids, where she's my co-worker and I have to be a no-nonsense role model and be on my best behavior—when all I really want to do is pick up where we left off and kiss her until we're both seeing stars.

But clearly, she doesn't want that.

These three weeks are going to be the death of me.

Chapter Six

VICTORIA

You're not sharing," Noah says, teasing. He inches closer with his spoon, a wicked gleam in his eye. It's spring break of our senior year in college, and we're on the beach behind the house we're sharing with some friends. Six of us have spent the week crammed into this little barrier-island bungalow that I'm pretty sure belongs to someone's grandmother, based on all the doilies and floral upholstery. Our friends went back inside hours ago, so now it's just me and Noah, under a thin blanket next to the dying campfire, eating the special combo of shave-ice and gelato that's only made in one special food truck down by the boardwalk.

"The whole point of us not getting the same flavor was so we could double the culinary adventure," he says, his brow lifting.

"But I like this one better," I say, nearing the bottom of the cup.

Mischief flashes in his eyes as he leans closer, his fingers wiggling.

"Don't you dare," I warn. "Stop right there, Valentine."

He grins and then pounces, his fingers tickling just below my ribs, where he knows I'm most ticklish.

Squealing, I hold fast to the gelato and try to wriggle out of his grasp. It's no use because he's stronger, faster, and more determined. That, and I don't hate the feel of his hands on me, even when he's tickling me mercilessly.

He lunges for the cup, and I topple backwards into the sand, still laughing as he falls on top of me, his arms caging me in. His hair's wild from the ocean and the wind, his hazel eyes glittering in the light from the campfire. As he reaches over my head to pluck the cup from my hand, he says, "Uh-oh, what are you going to do now, Griffin?"

When his weight shifts, I take that moment to roll us over—but I put way too much effort into it because we roll twice, and Noah gasps in surprise. When we stop, he's on his back in the sand, and I'm draped over him like a blanket. Sand is sticking to my bare legs, and now Noah's laughing too. My hips are pinned against his, and I can feel his heartbeat pounding against my chest. We touch all the time—his arm slung around my shoulders, a hug when we say goodnight—but this is different. Noah's my best friend, but over the last few months, I've caught all the feelings—big time. I've wanted to tell him how I feel so often, but each time convince myself that I should wait for some sign that he feels the same way. He's the closest friend I've ever had, and I don't want to ruin everything between us.

But feeling his whole body here beneath me, seeing that teasing glint in his eyes, my body just wants *more*. And it's done listening to reason.

He lifts the cup into the air, victorious. "Got it," he says, a little out of breath. And when his eyebrow lifts and that sexy smirk appears, I lose what's left of my control.

I close the few inches between us and kiss him gently at first, but when his teeth scrape against my lips and I feel his hand rest in the small of my back, it lights a fire inside me. He groans as I kiss him harder, tangling my hands in his hair. I've imagined how this might happen a thousand different ways, and this is better than all of them. Noah's lips are soft but firm, and when his teeth catch my bottom lip, I'm certain my heart will explode.

It's heaven.

I'm gasping when I break the kiss, and then Noah's hands are on my wrists, gently pulling my hands from his hair and resting them on his chest. My heart's banging against my ribs, and my body is desperate to feel more of his skin against mine—all I can think is, *Why did I wait so long?* I move to kiss him again, but when his brows pinch together and his lips part, my heart sinks.

"Vic," he whispers. "We shouldn't. I can't—" He pauses, as if choosing his words carefully, and gives my hands a gentle squeeze.

I freeze. This is the worst-case scenario—the outcome I've feared most. I wish a giant wave would wash over us and carry me out to sea so I don't have to hear the next words out of his mouth.

"It's not you." He swallows hard and whispers, "I mean, there's someone else."

Nope, I stand corrected. *This* is the worst-case scenario.

"What? Who?" I blurt. "How?" My calculations never included *someone else*. Because he's never indicated that *someone else* exists. Noah and I don't have secrets.

Well. Mostly.

He sighs. "Samantha. We went to high school together. A while back, we started chatting online, and it's become this weird long-distance thing." He shrugs. "It just sort of... happened. We reconnected over winter break, and she's been bugging me to take this backpacking trip with her this summer—"

"Oh my god!" I cry. "You have a secret girlfriend?" The air whooshes out of my lungs. Noah has a *secret girlfriend.* He's kept this fact from me. On purpose. "I can't believe you didn't tell me," I say.

"Not a secret," he says, frowning. "It's just new."

Right now, it feels like there's a dagger lodged in my chest, but I can't tell which hurts worse: the fact that Noah has a *girlfriend* or the fact that he hid her from me.

Or the fact that they've made plans together. Post-graduation plans.

"I honestly didn't know how to tell you without it being awkward," he says. "And it just never came up."

I feel sick. "But we tell each other everything."

He lifts a brow. "Do we?"

My cheeks burn at the pointed question, and now I can't get away from him fast enough. Because yes, I've been keeping my feelings secret, too. "Sorry," I tell him. "I just got caught up in the moment. Nothing more." But that's a lie. I've wanted this for so many months now and was just afraid to tell him. Afraid he wouldn't feel the same.

Afraid he'd look at me the way he is now, with this exact pained expression as he crushed my heart. Because he doesn't share my feelings.

And he never will.

I scramble off of him, but he catches my hand. "Wait," he says. "Don't go."

"I definitely should go," I tell him, because I'm about two seconds away from falling apart. Can you die from humiliation? I think yes. And I have no one to blame but myself because I waited too long to say something—*do* something. And now I've missed my chance. Because now he has Samantha, and they have plans.

And the way he's looking at me now—with *pity*—I can't take it.

My throat feels like it's closing up. There's no undoing this moment. There's no going back to how we were before.

"Please, Vic," he says, getting to his feet to follow me. "Don't leave like this. Just talk to me."

But I'm already walking back toward the beach house, the sand biting at my bare feet, my lip still tingling from that kiss that—for one moment—cracked my heart wide open.

"DID YOU HEAR ME, VICTORIA?" Sophie's voice yanks me back to the present where there is no beach, no Noah, and no heart-stopping kiss. It's just Sophie and me sitting at a table on the far side of the cafeteria, her big binder of plans resting between us.

"Sorry," I say, my voice raspy. "Didn't sleep that well. I'm listening." I reach for my coffee and take a big gulp. It tastes like actual dirt, but it'll have to do.

Sophie arches her brow. "Not a morning person," she says with a teasing grin. "Noted."

"I'll be better in a couple of days. Promise." I shake my head, trying to knock those memories of Noah out of my brain. It's been ages since I thought about that night on the beach, but the conversation we had last night has made the memory come back vivid and fierce. I feel like I'm blushing all the way down to my new boots, and my body shivers as if he's just stepped away and left me cold.

Get it together, I scold myself. I can't think about Noah's strong hands or his fiery kisses, and I sure as heck shouldn't be dreaming about him. If compartmentalizing were a sport, I'd have a wall full of gold medals. Now I need to shove all of these feelings for Noah into a neat little box, as far from my summer camp box as possible.

As if summoned by my scorching memory, Noah strides over to our table, carrying a mug of coffee and a bagel. Dressed in dark jeans and a button-up green shirt that seem tailor-made for him, he's the epitome of mountain-man cool. When he sits in the chair across from me, I try to ignore his rumpled hair and scruffy jaw, willing myself to forget how they once felt against my skin.

My body, though, does not want to forget. It wants to catalogue every detail all over again and then play that memory on an endless loop like some lovesick fool.

He bites into the bagel and then licks a bit of cream cheese from his thumb, his eyes flicking to mine. He holds my gaze with an intensity that makes me wonder if he's somehow able to read my mind. A furious blush races to the tips of my ears, and I chug more of my horrible coffee to distract myself from the flick of his tongue.

Pretending we don't know each other is one thing. Pretending our past never happened is impossible—and my brain seems to want to remind me of that every chance it gets.

As much as I regret the way our friendship ended, I don't regret everything that came before. I don't want to forget how Noah once made me feel so seen. So valued. So loved. Everything that I didn't have growing up Griffin.

I would, however, like to wipe everything that happened post-kiss from my memory because that moment was the first and only time that I felt like I wasn't enough for him.

And that feeling was the worst part of the whole debacle, by far.

Reaching for my toast, I shove all thoughts of Noah's lips and tongue way down deep, where they belong. Down in the fossil record, a million miles from here. Roxy doesn't have a lot of rules for this camp, but canoodling with your co-workers definitely breaks at least two of them—that's front and center in the *staff rules* section of the camp manual, highlighted for extra emphasis. Not that there's any chance of canoodling with Noah. That ship sailed a long time ago. Then it crashed into rocks and sank to the bottom of the ocean.

There is no more Noah and Victoria, and never will be again. So he really needs to stop looking at me like I'm a puzzle he wants to solve.

And he needs to stop licking his thumb.

"As of right now, all flights are on schedule," Sophie says, pen tapping on the table. She has a checklist for everything, including today's airport runs. "Half the kids' flights will be in by noon, and the rest by three. If anyone gets delayed, I can make the third run and let y'all stay here." Her welcome strategy is simple: she'll stay on site to greet the kids who arrive by car while Noah and I shuttle campers from the airport. We'll drive separately, a couple of hours apart, and have all the kids back by four-thirty this afternoon. Then it's dinner, orientation, and a night of goofy icebreakers and games to get the kids settled. This packed schedule should be enough to occupy my brain and leave it no space to devote to Noah and his smoldering gazes and lopsided smiles.

But *should* rarely happens the way I want it to.

"I think you and I should go together," Noah tells me, sipping his coffee. "That way, I can help you as the kids arrive. We'll load up your vehicle, and you can bring the first group back. I'll hang back with the late arrivals."

"You don't have to do that," I say. "That's like three extra hours at the airport for you."

He shrugs. "It's okay. It can be a lot the first time."

And now I understand—he thinks I need supervision because I can't handle wrangling half a dozen kids on my own. Heat blooms in my cheeks again.

"Good idea," Sophie says. "The airport's small, but sometimes collecting the kiddos is like its own little scavenger hunt." She looks at me and says, "Never hurts to have backup."

I stab my fork into my omelet and muster up a smile. "Of course. Never say no to backup."

Noah checks his watch—he's one of the few men my age on this earth who still wears one that simply tells time—and lifts a brow. "We should take off in thirty. Meet you by the cars?"

"Sounds good," I say, tamping down my frustration, reminding myself that Sophie and Noah have worked together before. They trust each other. I'm the wildcard here, the one who has to prove herself.

So that's exactly what I'll do. I'll ace this transport duty and make Noah feel like a doofus for hovering over me like a helicopter parent.

"Pro-tip? Take a book and some snacks," Sophie tells me. "There's always at least one delay."

"Roger that," I answer.

Noah stands abruptly, grabbing his travel mug and avoiding my gaze entirely. I was just about to leave myself, but I decide to wait five minutes so we're not walking out together and forced into idle chatter or deafening silence, pretending we haven't made this awkwardness between us worse. As he leaves, I push my eggs around my plate while Sophie tells me about the icebreakers that she's putting together for tonight. And I desperately try to forget how

Noah's thick lashes give his eyes a dreamy look—and how his intense gaze makes it feel like we're the last two people on earth.

———

"HOW DOES one kid have that many bags?" I ask.

Noah grunts, raking a hand through his unruly hair. "I've seen worse." He seems crabby now that we're alone, probably because he's had a whole night to process the fact that he's stuck with me for the next three weeks.

Across the way in the baggage claim, Derrick, a lanky boy with bright red hair and a million freckles, is pulling a fourth big duffle bag from the conveyor belt. He's already checked in with us, but he didn't mention bringing the entire contents of his home with him. He slings a big red bag over his shoulder and stumbles under the weight.

"Did he pack a moon rover in that thing?" I ask.

Noah snorts. "It wouldn't surprise me if he did. Come on. Let's put him out of his misery." He grabs the nearest luggage cart, and we head over to where the kid's mountain of bags are teetering on the edge of collapse.

Derrick unzips the largest duffle and riffles through it until he pulls out a dark blue ball cap that he shoves onto his head. When Noah and I approach, he crams the clothes back into his bag. By some miracle, it zips closed again.

"Ursa Major," I say to him. "Cool."

He blinks at me for a moment and then seems to realize that I'm talking about his hat. Tiny stars are stitched onto it, a faint outline of a bear stitched around them.

"It's lucky," he says. "I thought I shouldn't wear it on the plane since I lose stuff a lot."

"Wouldn't want you to lose that one," I say, and he gives me a tiny smile.

Once we pile Derrick's entire life onto the cart, two young girls spot us from across the room and wave. Noah and I are both wearing our official neon blue staff tee shirts, so it's easy for the campers to spot us.

The good thing about an airport this small is that the limited flights mean there's a smaller window of arrival times, and all incoming children are funneled into this small baggage claim with only two conveyor belts. The bad news is that there is no kiosk with decent coffee, and Noah and I are stuck together like sardines.

Soon, we're a cluster of six, waiting on five more. In the row of seats across from us, the kids have moved past their introductions and started passing phones and iPads around. The two girls, Layla and Priya, met each other on their flight from Atlanta. They've been giggling and playing some game on their phones together ever since. Meanwhile, Derrick and Ethan are sharing earbuds and watching something on an iPad screen that has them completely entranced.

"The next flight has been delayed an hour," Noah says, checking his phone. "You want to go ahead and take this group back?"

"I don't mind waiting for one more," I tell him. The plan was for me to take five kids and leave him four, mostly in case someone else packs like Derrick.

"I'm not worried," he says. "I think your vehicle's going to be loaded to the gills anyway." He eyes the pile of luggage like he's solving a math problem, but it feels like the real calculation is how to get me out of here quickly.

"Good thing you sprang for the roof racks on the rentals," I say.

"No kidding. Bungee cords have become my new best friend." He stands then and rounds up the four kids to tell them the plan. With them, he's back to being warm, friendly Noah.

I hate that he feels like he can't be that warm and friendly with me—but technically, he's doing exactly as I asked, pretending we're strangers who have never shared intimate moments that made the world wobble on its axis.

"LOOK AT THAT," Noah says. "We didn't even need the bungee cords." He'd stashed a set in each vehicle, though, just in case. Because that's Noah—always prepared.

The Tahoe I'm driving is crammed tight. Luckily, no one else brought as many bags as Derrick, but it was still a challenge to get them all wedged into the back. When my four passengers are strapped in, with Priya riding shotgun, Noah gives me a little salute and strides back inside the door to baggage claim to wait for the rest of the flights to arrive.

"Everybody ready?" I ask.

I'm met with a couple of nods and two raised thumbs from the back seat. Derrick and Ethan are in the seat right behind me, and Layla's in the very back with her pink rolling suitcase strapped in beside her.

Next to me, Priya's scrolling on her phone. She has deep brown skin and curly hair that's raven-black, cut just above her shoulders. A cherry-red streak peeks through at the bottom, the same color as her tee shirt. "Can we put on music?" she asks.

"Sure," I say, pulling out of the parking lot. "If you can figure out how to—"

Before I can finish the thought, she's plugged her phone into the console with a short pink cord, her fingers tapping against the touchscreen on the dash.

"Fair enough," I mutter, merging onto the highway.

The kids are mostly quiet, chattering about which other camps they've been to, which class they're taking at ours. Before long, we're halfway through the playlist that Priya's humming along to, and I'm turning off the main highway and thinking that maybe I've been worried over nothing. My car's full of kids who seem friendly and happy to be headed up the mountain. I've got Roxy in my corner, a job that could shake me out of my funk.

Things could be a lot worse. And they have been.

It's nearly two o'clock, and Noah should be leaving just after three-thirty, when the last flight arrives. We'll all get back in time for the kids to unload their bags and meet their roommates before orientation and dinner.

"Do you work at a lot of camps like this?" Priya asks.

"Actually, it's my first one," I tell her. "I mean, aside from ones I went to as a kid."

She nods. "This is my first astronomy camp."

"Mine too."

"I don't know much about astronomy," she says, her voice lower. "I was supposed to go to marine biology camp, but it got canceled. My mom thought I'd like this place better anyway. She used to teach astrophysics at the University of Mumbai, but now she teaches at Cal Tech."

"Wow," I tell her. "That's impressive."

She nods. "Astronomy's cool and all, but I really wanted to swim with some dolphins. Mom thinks that's silly, though. She's glad that camp was canceled." She says this all matter-of-factly, with only a hint of emotion. I can't help but see a little of myself in her because her mom sounds a lot like mine.

"I don't know much about astronomy either," I say. "So it'll be an adventure for us both."

Priya smiles. "I like adventure. I can't wait for our camping trip."

From the back of the car, Layla hollers, "Hey, turn it up! This is my favorite!"

As Priya turns the music up, she and Layla belt out the chorus to a Taylor Swift song that will no doubt be their summer anthem.

Ethan and Derrick nod along, still staring at the iPad they're sharing.

Just as Layla hits her last "Uh-huh, that's right," the car bounces as it hits a pothole the size of a moon crater. I grit my teeth, gripping the wheel tighter as the kids shriek and laugh. We're on a two-lane highway with pasture on one side and woods on the other, and this road looks like it hasn't been re-paved in thirty years.

A loud rumbling fills the air, and I brake gently, hoping the sound is just part of the next song on Priya's playlist. But the *thwack-thwack-thwack* that follows makes my stomach sink.

"What's that?" Priya says, her eyes wide.

"It's okay," I say calmly, "But I think we have a flat."

I slow down, easing off the road, while a chorus of questions erupt from the back seats—suddenly everyone has something to say, and the phones aren't nearly as interesting as why I'm pulling onto the grassy shoulder.

"Y'all hang tight a minute," I tell them. "I just need to check something on the car."

Fingers crossed, I climb out and walk towards the back, telling myself I'm just being extra cautious and imagining the worst case scenario.

Except that I'm not, because the rear passenger tire is flat as a pancake.

On our side of the road is a wide-open meadow, full of knee-high weeds and wildflowers. On the other is dense forest with the mountains looming beyond. Thirty yards away, a ramshackle barn sits across the field near the tree line. It's the only man-made thing out here, aside from the telephone poles that look like they've been here for a hundred years.

Once all the kids are out of the car, I haul the bags out of the back because of course, the spare tire is in the compartment below, under ten thousand pounds of Derrick's luggage.

"Can't you call like, roadside assistance?" Derrick says. He shoves his hair from his eyes, and for a moment, it stands straight up.

"That'll take too long out here," I say. "I don't want you to miss the evening activities." I stop short of telling him that we're in the middle of nowhere, a solid hour from even a Starbucks. Laurel Creek isn't far, but it's Sunday, and that means the whole town's closed.

"Besides," I tell them. "It's just a flat. An easy fix."

They look at me with varying degrees of doubt etched into their faces.

"So today you learn a new life skill," I quip, digging the jack out of the side compartment.

"My dad had a flat when we went to the beach last summer," Ethan says. He's all lanky limbs and sharp angles, with a mop of sandy blond hair that keeps falling in his eyes. "But he just kicked it a bunch of times and called a tow truck."

I sigh, lifting the spare tire from the floor compartment. I haven't changed a flat since college, but I'm hoping all the steps come back to me once I get my hands dirty.

A car zips past us, the only one I've seen since we pulled over. "I need all of you to stay there in the shade, okay?" I point them towards the grassy area between the shoulder and the tree line, several yards from the car. "You can help me by watching for traffic."

"On it!" Layla sings. Everything about her screams bright energy, from her electric blue shirt and pink shorts to the perky top note of her voice. Her dark brown hair is cut right below her ears, her bangs falling in her eyes. She skips toward the clearing with the other kids at her heels, far enough from the road that I won't worry about them.

The memory of how to do this comes back to me as I remove all the bolts from the hubcap, just like Dad taught me when I first learned to drive. My hair's falling in my face, and my tee shirt is sticking to me, but I manage to assemble the jack and remove the tire without too much difficulty. Meanwhile, the kids sit in a semicircle, a couple of them staring intently at the road.

"Car!" Priya shouts, pointing in the opposite direction.

I give her a thumbs-up and move the spare tire over and slip it into place. After some fussing, the bolts are tight and the tire is secure. I double-check everything and then put the jack and the bad tire into the floor compartment.

I give myself a mental high-five and call out, "Okay guys! Let's load up."

They help me pile the luggage back into the car as I brush a bit of dirt from my eye. The next time I look up, I only count three kids.

"Hey, where's Derrick?" I ask.

Layla says, "He was here a minute ago."

My stomach drops to the ground. I look all around us, down the road, across the meadow, over by the big oak with the pool of shade.

There's no sign of him.

My throat starts to close up, but I force out a yell anyway.

"Derrick!" I holler. It's a strangled cry, but I pull myself together because the last thing these kids need is to see me panic.

I call his name again, and the other kids do, too, and my heart is pounding like a jackhammer. It's been less than three hours, and I've somehow lost a kid? When there were only four to begin with? A hundred terrifying thoughts race through my brain. I will never forgive myself if I don't find him in the next ten seconds.

I bet Noah Valentine never lost a kid out here. He probably never even loses his car keys.

My eyes rest on the barn at the edge of the field, and I bite my lip.

"Hey, there he is," Ethan says, pointing in the opposite direction, toward the trees.

I follow his gaze, and sure enough, Derrick is shuffling out of the tree line like he's just out for a stroll.

"Derrick!" I call, trying not to sound like I'm screaming "FIRE!" to save a whole city from an inferno, and wave him over to us.

He jogs over to the group, and I ask, "Where the heck were you?"

He blinks at me and shrugs. "I had to pee," he says, as if Occam's Razor should have led me to that answer first.

A ten-ton boulder has been lifted off my chest. But that was also the closest call ever and just more evidence that coming here was the worst idea that ever popped into my brain.

I can barely keep a cactus alive—what made me think I could be in charge of tiny humans?

"Okay," I tell them, keeping my voice calm. I take a deep breath because they are fine, and no one is lost forever, and this is on me. "First rule of camp: use the buddy system. When we're in unfamiliar places, you always take someone with you. Don't go away from the group all by yourself. Deal?"

"Even to pee?" Ethan says.

"Yes."

They all nod in agreement. Even Ethan, despite the eye-roll.

"Sorry," Derrick says, staring between his shoes.

"It's okay," I tell him. "You didn't know that rule yet. But now we all do, and we'll always make sure there's someone with us, agreed?"

"Yeah, dude," Ethan says to Derrick. "What if there was a bear out there? Or a mountain lion?" He pauses and grins. "Or Bigfoot?"

Derrick's eyes widen, and he looks at me. "There's mountain lions here?"

"No," Priya says, frowning. "They don't live on the east coast."

"But there are bears," Layla says. Her eyes twinkle like she's hoping to see one.

"Correct," I say, "So, buddy system."

They pile back into the car, debating the likelihood of seeing Bigfoot while I check my phone. There's a text from Sophie asking how things are going with a string of smiley-face emojis.

I quickly reply: **All good! Headed back now.**

She sends me a thumbs-up immediately, no doubt answering texts from her laptop, since the service on the mountain is so spotty.

Once we're back on the road, Priya starts the music again and hums along while Derrick and Ethan compare their knowledge of North American cryptids.

"You can't prove that Bigfoot *doesn't* exist, though," Ethan says. "Logically, you can't prove the absence of something."

"Sure you can," Derrick says. "We can prove that Bigfoot is not in this car."

"You can gather data to indicate that something doesn't exist in a certain set of conditions," Ethan argues. "He might not be present in this car, at this moment—but we can't say he doesn't exist anywhere on the planet or in the multiverse."

Derrick groans.

"It's the scientific method, dude," Ethan says.

"Sort of," Priya says.

I glance at the car's GPS as the dot that is us shifts over into the uncharted green of the map. Our blue dot hovers in that mysterious space in between where we are and where we should be until the glitch finally corrects itself after the next turn.

Never has a map felt so accurate for my life.

WHEN WE PULL up to the institute, the kids start firing questions at me, curious about every detail of this place. Their faces are plastered to the windows as they take in the big radio telescopes, the towering evergreens, the wide blue sky.

They're full of excited chatter now, and I'm still humming with adrenaline from our roadside adventure. Because it's nearly five now, the kids will just barely have time to get their bags into their rooms before orientation starts.

I park by the cabins and haul the luggage out double-time, telling them to meet back right here in fifteen minutes. When they've all disappeared into the cabins, I collapse against the car and lay my hands on the roof, trying to force some air back into my lungs and slow my hammering heart.

"Hey," Noah says from behind me, and that one word is enough to startle me so much that my knees wobble.

I turn, giving him my nothing-to-see-here face. "Hi," I say, my tone way too chipper. "How's it going?"

"How are you just now getting back?" he says, his brow furrowed. "Is everything okay?" His eyes rake over me—slower than necessary—taking in my messy hair, my dirty tee shirt and jeans. A blush creeps into my cheeks as his eyes lift up to mine.

"Flat tire," I answer, hoping I don't have to admit to also losing a child.

His eyebrows shoot up. "Why didn't you call me?"

"That seemed unnecessary," I say with a shrug. "It wasn't hard to change."

"We paid for roadside assistance, you know. With the rentals." He plants his hands on his hips and frowns. Even his scowl is sexy.

"I figured that would take too long," I answer. "It wasn't a big deal." Plus, I really wanted to solve that problem on my own and not call for rescue. But I keep that thought to myself.

"You're allowed to ask for help, you know." He lifts a brow. "You don't have to do everything yourself."

I make a show of leaning past him, searching the horizon.

"What?" he says, turning around.

"I'm just looking for that big white horse of yours."

He lets out a heavy sigh, clearly exasperated. "As the site director, it's my job to make sure that you're safe and have all the help you need." His eyes bore into mine, pinning me to this spot, and my heart does a little somersault because protective Noah is *hot*. Like surface-of-the-sun hot. "Next time, call me," he says, his voice gravelly. "We look out for each other here. Buddy system, remember?"

"Fine," I tell him, holding my hands up in surrender. "Next time I'll call you."

He frowns as if he doesn't believe me.

"Cross my heart," I say, drawing an invisible X over my chest. His eyes track the movement, and when they drift back up to mine, they're filled with something that looks a lot like want.

It's the same look he'd had all those years ago, right before I kissed him on that moonlit beach in Charleston.

He seems to realize that fact at the precise moment that I do and tears his gaze away from mine as a blush touches the tips of his ears.

"Orientation in five," he says, and is gone before the memory fades.

Chapter Seven

Victoria is going to unravel me. It's bad enough that she's here demanding all of my attention without even trying. But the way she looks at me with those wide blue eyes, as if she can't decide whether to punch me in the gut or kiss me until I forget my name—that's going to be a problem.

Because I really want it to be the latter. As soon as humanly possible.

The kids are hyper-focused during orientation, giving Sophie their full attention as she explains what everyone can expect from their camp experience. I'm hyper-focused because I can't tear my eyes away from Victoria's delicate neck, where a smudge of grease lies just below her ear, a swipe perhaps made by her fingers as she was changing that flat tire. There's just one empty seat between us in the auditorium, and she draws my gaze like a magnet—just like she always has. She's wearing a clean shirt now, her hair pulled back into a ponytail that swings every time she moves her head. When she tucks a stray lock of hair behind her ear, I spot another smudge on her cheekbone that I'm dying to reach over and wipe away with my thumb.

I hate that she didn't call me for help. She's perfectly capable of changing a tire, but having a bunch of kids around like this can make even the simplest task more difficult because you have to keep one eye on them all the time. It's like having a box full of kittens that keep crawling out and scurrying off the second you look away. Plus, I know the roads around here and I wouldn't want to change a flat on any of them. It's all blind curves and narrow shoulders on this mountain, and I don't like to think of her putting herself in danger.

More than that, I hate the idea that she feels uncomfortable asking me for help.

I drag my fingers through my hair, trying to set aside all those unsettling thoughts. Probably, she didn't call me because she was embarrassed. I need her to know that she can trust me and depend on me to help her when she needs it. She's always been independent and never liked asking for my help—whether it was to fix a busted radiator in her car or pay her electric bill when it was overdue—so I shouldn't expect her to ask for it now.

Now she's twirling the end of her ponytail in her fingers, and that smear of grease is taunting me. Helpless to tear my gaze away, I study the line of her neck, that elegant curve where it meets her shoulder, and then think of how it would feel to kiss her there, to drag my lips down to her collarbone as I push the collar of that shirt aside and undo the buttons with my teeth.

She coughs, and I look up to meet her eyes.

Busted.

I tap my fingers on my neck, in the approximate area where her smudge is. She lifts a brow and then catches on, rubbing her skin and frowning when she sees the grease on her hand. Her cheeks turn pink, as if she's disappointed that the smudge is what held my gaze. She rubs her hand on her dark jeans, where the knees show some dirt, and turns her attention back to the stage.

Sophie introduces the two instructors, Dr. Cassie and Dr. Sanjay, both of whom insist the kids call them by their first names. Dr. Cassie, a petite blond woman from the University of New Mexico, was here last year and has this endless energy that we'd all love to bottle for ourselves. Dr. Sanjay is new to us—a doctoral student at the University of Virginia, he interned with NASA down in Cape Canaveral. He towers over Dr. Cassie, but his big blue-framed glasses and orange sneakers give him an approachable yet nerdy vibe that the kids will no doubt love. In between space puns, he tells them about how during his internship, he experienced zero gravity just long enough to make him puke.

The kids groan and laugh. Already, he and Dr. Cassie are their heroes.

"I think that's the closest I'll come to being an astronaut," Dr. Sanjay says. "Does anyone here want to travel to space?"

Hands shoot into the air as the kids shout excitedly.

As he and Dr. Cassie take turns at the microphone, I keep my eyes fixed on them, where there's zero chance of staring at Victoria and her lovely collarbones. I can't for the life of me figure out how she ended up here—what are the chances that we'd ever cross paths again? And the chances of meeting her in a summer camp for kids? It seems more likely that I'd win the lottery. But here she sits, somehow even more beautiful than she was in college, turning my world upside down all over again.

ON THE DAY WE MET, I knew two things for certain: one, that Victoria was not like any other girl I'd met before, and two, that I had to find a way to spend more time with her.

We collided at a Halloween party freshman year. My roommates were throwing a huge bash, and our house was overflowing with people, most of whom I'd never met. Our tiny backyard was beyond capacity, so I'd escaped to the upstairs balcony because it was the only space left where I could sit still without being elbowed in the kidney.

My cousin Ray had insisted I wear a costume, but I'd refused to wear anything that wasn't inside my closet already because I didn't want to be at that stupid party at all. Exasperated, he'd dug through my clothes until he found a white tee shirt, jeans, and my beat-up motorcycle jacket. "Looks like you're either Danny Zuko or Wolverine," he said, tossing my old harness boots at me. "Take your pick."

The choice was obvious.

Hours later, I escaped to the balcony and had been out there less than twenty minutes when a woman came bursting through the skinny French doors connecting to Ray's bedroom. The glass panes rattled as she fumbled with the doors, which never wanted to come together just right. When they finally banged shut, she leaned against them and let out an adorable irritated grunt.

Cheers and shouts erupted below us, where someone was doing yet another keg stand.

"Hi," I said. It seemed a greeting would make the moment less awkward since I was sitting a few feet away from her in a corner, deep in the shadow of a palmetto.

"Sweet baby cheeses," she said, holding a hand to her chest. "You scared the daylights out of me."

"Said the bull in the china shop. I could barely hear the music over that clatter."

She cocked her head and pursed her lips, fixing me with a curious stare. Long blond hair fell in waves past her shoulders.

Her emerald-green dress hugged her curves and flared out at the bottom like a mermaid's tail. Atop her head sat a crown made of flowers and two small deer-like antlers. Ethereal and lovely, she was like something from a fairy tale—and entirely out of place at a raucous party like this one.

"Well, in a moment, this bull will be out of your way." She nudged past me and peered over the iron railing, studying the line of the roof as she reached for the trellis that was overgrown with ivy and lord knows what else.

"Easy there, Rapunzel," I said. "That thing's historic. And likely teeming with tetanus."

"Rapunzel brought the prince *up*," she said, slipping off her green heels. "I'm looking for a way down."

"Don't even think about that trellis. It's entirely decorative and not one bit practical."

She turned and fixed me with her stare, her plump lip caught between her teeth.

"Who are you hiding from?" I asked, suddenly overwhelmed with the urge to protect her. Hopefully, whoever she was trying to outrun wasn't twice my size, but I could easily see myself making all kinds of bad decisions for this girl.

She snorted. "You've been out here longer than I have. Who are *you* hiding from?"

"Everyone."

Her brow lifted, her attention fully on me.

"I don't love these parties," I grumbled. Being packed in a house with people I didn't know or especially like was the worst.

"Then why did you come?"

"I live here."

She smirked. "So the unlikely hero is also the unlikely host. That tracks." She waved her hand in front of her in a small circle, as if to emphasize my whole ensemble, from the leather jacket to the jeans and beat-up boots.

I fought back a grin, shoving a hand into the pocket of my jacket. "Does it count as a costume if it's your normal clothes?"

"So you always dress like low-profile Wolverine? Interesting." That devilish twinkle in her eye was quickly becoming one of my favorite things about her. The corner of her lip ticked upward as she said, "Not that it isn't a good look for you."

"Thank you. And wood nymph is a good look for you."

She grinned as she sat in the empty wire-framed chair next to me. Her dress filled what little space was left between us. "I'm a party animal," she deadpanned. "Get it?" She squirmed in the chair, no doubt trying to adjust the dress so she could breathe properly. "It was my roommate's idea—genius, I know. Plus, I get to wear this old bridesmaid's dress one more time, so I feel like I got my money's worth."

"That explains the antlers," I said. "Very clever."

"That hair is very clever," she said, motioning toward my head.

"The hair is what makes the costume. Without it, I'm just a surly guy in a rad leather jacket."

"And three-day-old beard scruff."

"I grew it special."

She pursed her lips again and fixed me with an ice-blue gaze that made my heart hammer in my chest. "I admire that level of commitment."

"Some things are worth committing to one hundred percent," I said.

"That must have taken a startling amount of aerosol." She reached over to pat the top of my hair like it was a shy puppy, and I decided right then that I liked her more than anyone I'd met on campus.

"Egg whites," I said.

"Clever *and* eco-friendly." Her eyes held mine for a moment that could have been two seconds or an eternity.

Then she pulled a small flask from somewhere in her cleavage and unscrewed the cap. After taking a quick sip, she offered it to me like a goddess passing me ambrosia.

The whiskey danced on my tongue and burned a trail straight down my chest. When I handed the flask back to her, her fingers brushed over mine and sent an electric current zipping along my skin. She was so close that I could see a faint spray of freckles over her cheeks—real ones that were under the bits of makeup that were painted on like the soft brown and white spots on a fawn.

"I'm Noah," I said.

"Victoria," she said, her eyes glittering. "Nice digs."

"This is my uncle's house. Lucky for us, he only wants enough rent to cover the mortgage." It was a typical row house, two stories with three tiny bedrooms, big windows, a claw-foot tub, and not a single plumb wall or level floor. Charlestonians called that *character*.

"Nice of him," she said.

I nodded. "Still takes four of us to pay it, and part of the deal is that we fix it up while we live here. We spent last summer painting every square inch of this place."

"Sounds like your uncle might be coming out on the better end of that deal."

"Oh, we've totally been had," I quipped. "I'm pretty sure it's haunted, but at least it's close to campus."

"And down the street from the best bakery in town."

"That totally makes up for the haunting."

Her eyes sparkled when she smiled, and I felt some invisible thread drawing me closer.

Downstairs, the music shifted to something with enough bass to rattle the floorboards. It was warmer than usual, and a rare breeze kept lifting her hair in a mesmerizing way.

"You never said why you were running," I said, holding her gaze.

She took another quick drink before shoving the flask back into the bodice of her dress. "I slapped a dude downstairs dressed like James Bond, and he didn't take it well. Figured it was time to split."

"I'm sure he deserved it."

Her brow arched. "Sure did."

A crash came from inside the bedroom, followed by a loud pop and laughter. One peek through the French doors showed me exactly what I did not want to see: Ray and a young woman fumbling their way toward his bed. Her costume consisted of a bunch of purple balloons strategically attached to her body like a cluster of grapes. And Ray, dressed as Elvis in the early years, was trying clumsily to pop them with his teeth.

"Okay," I told my wood nymph, taking her hand. "Time to beat feet. Unless you want to spend all night on this balcony. Ray can be laser-focused when he wants to be."

She squeaked with surprise as I pulled open the narrow doors and led her inside.

"Don't mind us," I hollered, striding past the bed. "Just passing through."

Ray paid us zero attention, too focused on which balloon to pop next. His lady friend giggled and ran a hand through her dark hair, knocking her leaf-and-stem hat askew.

"Great costume!" Victoria yelled to her as we scurried through the bedroom and out into the hallway.

"This way," I told her. "Secret stairs."

We hurried through the hall, down the narrow back stairs of the house, and squeezed past the crowd in the kitchen to escape through the side door into the alley.

When we were finally alone, she said, "Whew. It pays to put your trust in the reluctant hero."

"I'm no one's hero," I told her, which was the absolute truth.

"I'm hungry," she said. "How do you feel about waffles?"

From that moment on, we were inseparable. Since she was a marketing major and I studied English, our classes never intersected—except for those times we took electives like "Life of the Geologic Past" because learning about dinosaurs sounded like a fun time.

Spoiler alert: it was. It also inspired us to dress like a pterodactyl and dimetrodon the following Halloween and gave us both nightmares about how a meteor large enough to cause the next great extinction was long overdue.

We saw each other every day, even if it was just to scarf greasy take-out and watch woefully bad movies so we could snort with laughter. Vic was funny, down to earth, and easy to talk to. For my introverted self, that was a big deal because I had a hard time letting people get close to me. Plus, college had just reinforced the fact that I was the guy people hung around with when their only other option was being alone. People talked to me only until someone more interesting came along. But Victoria wasn't like those other people, and she didn't leave. Soon, she became one of the few people I could be comfortable around, and we had fun together. She seemed to like me just as I was, quirks and all—and I was hopelessly in love with her. But I also knew that I might never have another friend like her, so I shoved those other feelings into a neat little box in the corner of my heart and swore that I'd never cross that line unless she made it clear she wanted me to. There was just too much we stood to lose, and I couldn't bear to lose Victoria.

But then I made one stupid move and lost her anyway.

"HEY, MOON UNIT," Vic says, "Ready to come back to Earth and break some ice?" She's standing next to me, bumping her knee against my thigh. The last of the kids are leaving the auditorium, and clearly I stopped paying attention sometime after Dr. Sanjay made his joke about tossing his cookies during space camp.

"Yeah," I tell her, swallowing hard.

"You look beat," she says. "You gonna make it?"

I try to ignore the curve of her hip that is now just inches from my face. I'd love nothing more than to pull her down onto my lap and show her how much I've missed her and precisely how I'd like to make that up to her, but for now, I have to settle for boring work-appropriate words instead.

"Long day," I tell her. "It's just catching up with me, I guess."

She lifts a brow like she doesn't believe that for a second, but she doesn't press me.

"Let's go catch up with the kiddos," she says. "Before they decide to run this camp without us."

I follow her out and then move quickly to her side because walking behind her allows me to admire how even her tee shirts and jeans seem to be tailor-made to emphasize her lovely curves. My brain doesn't need any more help cataloguing the most stunning things about Victoria right now.

We catch up with the kids and head back over to one of the meeting rooms in the admin building. I've nearly put her out of my mind as we start in on the games and icebreakers, the usual way we get the kids to open up a little and get to know each other.

Soon Victoria and Sophie are laughing and cheering as the kids holler out guesses in a heated round of charades. When Vic does her adorable snort-laugh, it fills me with an ache that nearly buckles my knees. Why can't I just put her out of my mind for an hour and focus on what I'm here to do?

Pretend we're strangers, she said. Obviously, she's not interested in being anything other than co-workers.

When we take a break and switch to the next game, Sophie plops down next to me and says, "Hey, are you okay?" Her brows are pinched together with concern, and for a moment, I'm convinced she can read all of my thoughts like a book.

"Sure," I tell her. "Super."

"Your creepy Patrick Bateman smile says otherwise," she says, arching a brow. She always teases me about slapping on an *American Psycho* fake smile when I want to pretend something isn't bothering me. My sister Hannah says the same thing, so it must be true.

"All good," I say, trying for a real smile. And I am. I'm good. I can deal with being on top of a mountain with Victoria for three weeks.

Really.

"I'm around if you want to talk about it later," Sophie says and heads back to the games.

I keep repeating my words like a mantra until free time is over and it's lights out in the cabins. And then I stand in front of the tiny mirror in my room and tell myself again: *Everything is fine. You've got this.*

But the words still feel like a lie.

And when I smile to reassure myself, it's another Bateman smile.

I am so screwed.

Chapter Eight

VICTORIA

I'm fine," I tell Gwen. "Really." My sister's so quiet on the other end of the line that I have to check to make sure she's still there.

"I'm here," she says. "I just don't believe you."

"Okay. I'll *be* fine." I keep my voice low because it's after 11 p.m., lights out for the kids. I'm using the landline in the lounge, curled up by the window in one of the dorm-style chairs that's just as uncomfortable as it looks. I'm pretty sure there's solid rock under this cheap, scratchy upholstery, but it fits the whole woodsy-cabin-meets-doomsday-bunker vibe they have going here.

"But you're there with *Noah* Noah?" Gwen says. "As in the first guy you were hopelessly in love with?"

"Hopelessly is a stretch."

"Agree to disagree," she says. "And then he broke your heart."

"I can't argue with that. But I think he didn't mean to."

"You were devastated," she says. "In pieces. He doesn't get a pass for that."

"We talked it over, and I see now that there was some miscommunication on both sides. He thought I never wanted to see him again." I breathe out a heavy sigh. "I don't know where he got that idea, but now I wish I'd tried reaching out again."

There's another long pause—the kind that means my sister's thinking hard. Or hiding something.

"What is it?" I say.

"Nothing." There's a clatter of dishes in the background. "How did you not know he'd be there on staff?"

"Roxy didn't send me anyone's names. Some of the staff work together every year, but a lot of new people show up, too. I think unless you already know someone you're working with, you don't meet your staff until you get to camp. Plus, I never told her about Noah."

"I've got to say, if it were me, I'd have jumped back in my car and floored it down the mountain. I couldn't work with any of my exes."

"I thought about it," I mutter. "But I didn't want to run this time. In the last year, I've fled my fiancé, my job, and all of Jasmine Falls."

And years ago, I ran from Noah after kissing him hard enough to make me see stars.

"Technically, you ditched an arrogant, manipulative jerk, and just in time," she says. Unlike our mother, Gwen has never made me feel guilty about making that decision.

"Sometimes I'm afraid Mom might be right," I tell her. "That I always run when things get hard."

"Ugh," she groans. "Things Mom is right about include which shade of green we can wear with our skin tone, when to send a thank-you note, and how to mix a proper martini. They don't include your decisions about when to stop doing something that no longer aligns with what you want from life."

"Wow, that's—"

"Super accurate?" she interrupts. "Yeah, I've been thinking about that for a while. I've also learned that walking away and giving up are not the same thing."

"Sometimes that annoying little voice in my head still likes to tell me that they *are* the same, and I'm a big fat chicken."

"Tell that voice to take a hike," she says. "It's courtesy of Mom, and it's a big fat liar. Contrary to what we've been told for most of our lives, we get to reject what doesn't serve us. We're never obligated to go down a path that someone else pulls us onto."

"I like that idea."

"Good," she chirps. "Then put it into practice."

"Bossy pants," I tell her.

"It's because I love you," she says. "Now I have to go because there's a hot, lonely Scot in my bed."

I snort. "Love you more, Gwennie."

"Call me anytime, okay?"

After we hang up, I head back to my room. A wave of giggles erupts from one of the rooms near mine, but otherwise, it's quiet. After taking a quick shower, I put on my tee shirt and sleep shorts and climb under the covers. My bed is by the window, so the moonlight slices through the room and casts everything in a soothing blue light. I tell my brain to let these old mistakes go and to stop thinking about Noah, but that just means that his face is the last thing I picture as I fall asleep.

<hr>

MY BRAIN IS STRUGGLING to make sense of the noise I'm hearing. It's like the crinkle of a candy bar wrapper or the crunching of a peanut shell. But that's impossible because I'm alone in this room—or at least I should be.

The room is dark as a cave, no longer filled with moonlight. It takes me a minute to remember that I'm in a tiny bed in a cabin in the mountains, and not in my house by the lake. My brain leaps to high alert, and all at once, I'm certain that this is *Friday the 13th* and some weirdo in a hockey mask is lurking in the shadows, waiting to do me in so my story can end up on the next true crime podcast.

Stop, I tell myself. It's probably a limb scratching against the window since I'm basically up in the treetops here.

But the crunching noise starts again. I'm not imagining it.

I fumble for the lamp on the bedside table. When the light flashes on, I squint and survey the room, looking for the source of the noise. And I find it at the foot of my bed.

A mouse is perched on the blanket by my feet, sitting up on its haunches, its beady black eyes fixed on me. It's holding a half-eaten peanut butter cracker in its paws, nose twitching as if daring me to say something about it.

"Gah!" I shriek, scrambling back towards the headboard. I hate the idea of a tiny creature scurrying up my pant leg or diving into my sleeve while I'm helpless in slumber. Ugh. This is not the kind of nature I signed up for.

I expect it to run away and disappear into a hole in the wall, like any self-respecting critter at the bottom of the food chain. Instead, it holds its ground and stares me dead in the eye while it gobbles up the last half of my cracker.

I ease myself off the bed, trying not to startle the mouse, because I can see tiny wheels turning in that furry little brain, and it looks like it could cause some mayhem if it wanted. Based on that diabolical glint in its eye, it's definitely planning to crawl over my face as soon as I fall back asleep.

I scramble to find anything that I might use to trap it—a jar, a box, a paper bag—but there's nothing in this sparse room that can be used to catch a rogue mouse. When I reach the desk, the mouse springs from the corner of the bed and zips across the room, right towards me, fast as lightning. I climb on top of the desk chair so it can't run over my bare feet, and it dives into the empty sneaker I left by the door.

"Ha!" I whisper-yell. I grab my pillow from the bed, yank the case free, and tiptoe over to the shoe. In one swift motion, I sweep both the sneaker and mouse into the pillowcase. Then I shove my feet into my fuzzy slippers and hurry out the door.

I'm halfway across the parking lot, headed for I don't even know where when I hear a twig snap. I freeze, turning slowly as my heart leaps into my throat. That snap sounded like it was under the foot of a huge animal—a catamount? A bear? Some beastly thing with big teeth and ghastly claws and an appetite for young wayward women in fuzzy slippers who don't know what to do with their lives anymore.

Noah's voice comes out of the shadows. "Leaving under cover of darkness?" he says.

I startle, feeling the hair on my neck stand up. "Holy shirtsleeves," I breathe. "Lurk much?"

He smirks, walking over from his spot under a big evergreen. His thin tee shirt strains across his shoulders, and his plaid pajama pants hang low on his hips. If he ever wanted a career change, he could model loungewear like this and probably retire at forty. Because even in an old tee shirt and flannel, Noah Valentine is drop-dead stunning.

"Should I even ask what you're doing with that?" he asks. His hair's standing up in every direction, and his big eyes look even wider in the moonlight.

"I caught a mouse in my room," I reply, trying hard to ignore the faint outline of taut muscle I can see through that thin shirt. "He was helping himself to my snacks."

"The audacity," Noah says, his voice a low rumble.

He looks delicious with all that wild hair and scruff—and I'd sell my soul at the crossroads just to have him kiss me again, whispering my name as he tugs my hair and slides his stubbled cheek over my skin. But this is not a thought that needs to be planted in my mind before I go back to sleep because my dreams are vivid enough already, and my subconscious is a shameless, starving beast.

"They were very good snacks," I say.

"I'm sure they're delicious," he says, his gaze dropping to my lips.

A tornado of butterflies swirl in my chest. *No*, I think. *Focus*.

Carefully, I empty the pillowcase next to a sprawling rhododendron. When the mouse scurries into the underbrush, I retrieve my shoe and turn back to Noah.

"What are you doing out here?" I ask him.

He shrugs. "Couldn't sleep. Sometimes taking a walk helps."

I almost tease him about leaving the kids unsupervised, but I know Noah won't stay out long, and he won't be out of earshot because he's a responsible man and he cares about people's safety. It's his thing. He's a protector, and it's one of the many traits I always appreciated about him. His "walk" was probably no farther than thirty yards from these cabins, and with those Thor-like thighs of his, he can no doubt make it back to his room in three seconds flat.

He looks tired, like he needs to sleep but can't. Is it because I'm here?

"Don't let me keep you up," I tell him. "That's all the excitement I have planned for tonight. Disaster averted."

He smirks as his eyes drift over me, and I realize with horror that I'm wearing my old threadbare Stevie Nicks tee shirt and boxer shorts that are about three nights away from falling apart at the seams. And my goofy fuzzy pink slippers. I hadn't expected to encounter another human as I dashed out into the night and had only been thinking of removing the mouse in the fastest way possible. But it's chilly out here, and these clothes are far from modest. I clutch the empty pillowcase to my chest and blurt, "Okay then, good night."

"Come on," he says, nodding towards the cabins. "I'll walk you back. Wouldn't want you to have any other close encounters."

He matches my stride back to the entrance to the girls' cabin, raking his hand through his hair like something's on his mind.

I feel a tug in my chest because that's typical Noah. Making sure I get in safely, even though I was within a stone's throw of the cabin.

He can play that grumpy card all he wants, but I see him. Under all that muscle and furrowed brow is still a big softie who wants to make sure everyone around him is okay and knows that he has their back.

I didn't realize how much I'd missed having someone in my life who made me feel that way. Because other than my sister, no one else truly has.

He pauses by the picnic table that's situated just a few feet from the cabins. "Can I ask you something?" he says. "Why are you really here?"

"You mean out in the woods, doing a job you think I'm completely unqualified to do?"

He frowns. "That's not what I think at all. If anything, you're overqualified. When Roxy told me she'd hired a replacement, I was expecting another Sophie."

I snort. "Exactly. Another super outdoorsy person who can do all this nature stuff in her sleep. The opposite of me."

"No," he says. "I meant a college student."

I sigh, sitting down at the picnic table. "I just blew up my career," I tell him. "My whole life, really. And now I'm looking for what's next. I thought doing something completely different would help shake something loose and give me some perspective."

"What did you do?" He sits next to me, leaving just a few inches of space between us. "For work, I mean."

"Real estate."

"Interesting," he says. "I wouldn't have guessed that."

I choke back a laugh. "Young Me wouldn't have either. I sort of fell into it—when my mother pushed me."

"Oh," he says, and that tone tells me he remembers plenty about my mom and the endless pressure she put on me to aim higher and be better, lest her reputation be tarnished by my mediocre actions.

"At the time, I was in an entry-level marketing job that my mother thought was beneath me—or, more accurately, beneath *her*. She acted like she was doing me a big favor by pulling these strings and getting me hired as an assistant in her friend's top-notch firm." I cringe at the memory of her telling me she'd set this up and fixed the problem—like I was incapable of finding my own way. "I couldn't say no because that would be like throwing gasoline on a fire. To her, it would mean I was being lazy, ungrateful, unambitious, or worse. I knew she'd never let it go and keep using it against me until I did what she wanted."

"Vic," he says, shaking his head. "I'm sorry. That wasn't fair to you."

"Then the pressure was on—I had to be flawless because if I wasn't, then Mom would take it personally, like I was trying to ruin her reputation. There was no way I could leave the firm because that would mean I wasn't *grateful* for Mom's intervention. But that's how she is—any favor or gift comes with serious strings. I felt like I had to stay, so I got my real estate license." I shrug. "Turns out I was good at it, but I didn't love it."

His knee brushes against mine, and I know I should pull away, but I don't.

"I felt like I was successful," I confess. "I was making good money, climbing the ladder, and doing all the things my parents expected of me. I had a nice home, a savings account, and was getting married—you know, all the things that feel like success. Pretty soon, I was just coasting along on autopilot. But I felt empty." My chest loosens as the words come out—Gwen's the only other person I've ever said these things to.

It feels good to finally let these feelings out.

"You got married?" he says, his brows pinching together.

"Nope. Wrecked that, too." I force out a smile. "But actually, that was for the best. Even though I left him at the altar and fueled the town gossip mill for the next three years, the real tragedy would have been going through with it."

Noah rakes a hand through his hair. The look that passes over his face looks like relief, and my heart flutters in my chest.

"I let myself believe we were good together, but now I see that I was settling. Truth be told, I was just afraid that something better wasn't out there." I shrug, feeling like a dam has burst and all these truths can finally emerge. "I told myself that what I had was good, but I was just so wrapped up in everyone else's expectations that I couldn't see how lost I'd become. And now sometimes I feel like I don't know who I am because of that."

He nods, resting his hands on his knees. "You shouldn't let other people's expectations run your life."

I nod, listening to the chirping crickets and the calls of the night birds. Something about being here makes me feel free, and Noah is still so easy to talk to. It's like he sees parts of me that I can't always see so clearly. "Sometimes that's easier said than done," I tell him.

His brow lifts. "I know."

"It probably sounds silly to you," I tell him. "But Roxy thought I'd be a good fit for another position that's coming up later this year. This was a way to get my foot in the door, even though it's totally out of my comfort zone."

"Doesn't sound silly." He shakes his head, shifting so his knee's pressed against mine again, grounding me. "But you know, my mom told me once that other people's thoughts about you are none of your business. So why bother worrying about them? At the time, that concept blew my mind. But then I understood what she was saying. People are going to feel the way they feel, but don't let that undermine how *you* feel about yourself and your dreams."

I stare at him for a long moment, feeling once again like Noah Valentine can see right through me. Right into the deep corners of my heart where all the fears lie. It's both comforting and unsettling, and the truth is that no one has ever made me feel seen the way that Noah does.

"What about you?" I ask. "How'd you land here?"

He's close enough that I can see his unfairly full lashes, the faint freckles high on his cheeks.

Frowning, he leans back against the top of the picnic table. "The short version is that after graduation, when Samantha dropped me like a hot potato, I decided to finish that backpacking trip on my own. That led me to a group that was sort of like Outward Bound, and then I found this program." He shrugs. "I just decided I was going to be open to whatever happened next, and things clicked into place."

"That's an incredibly mature response to being dropped like a hot potato."

His lip curves in a hint of a smile. "I wasn't so mature about it at the time. In the moment, it felt like she was following the pattern."

"What do you mean?"

Another shrug. "I'm never the most interesting guy," he says. "I'm the guy people talk to until someone more intriguing comes along."

"Noah," I breathe. "That's not true."

His sidelong look is the only argument he offers.

"I'm sorry that happened," I say. "The hot potato part, that is."

"Are you?" His brow lifts.

"Well, maybe not. Since everything seems to have worked out all right." I give his shoulder a nudge. "We have to have some rough patches to appreciate the good things, right?" I gesture toward the cabins, the towering firs that encircle us. "And anyway, you seem to have found your happy place."

His eyes meet mine, and something tugs tight in my chest. Then he smiles and says, "I have no doubt you'll find yours, too. You always could do anything you set your mind to."

"Except salsa dancing. I will forever be terrible at that."

He laughs because he clearly hasn't forgotten the time I insisted we join the ballroom dancing club during our junior year. I stomped on his feet no fewer than one thousand times and gave him a black eye when I flailed my arms during an over-energetic swing lesson.

"It's okay to not be amazing at everything," he says. "If you don't fail, then you can't grow."

"You make that sound so simple." Failure wasn't an option in the Griffin household. Failure meant embarrassment. Shame.

Weakness. Logically, I know that's not true—but for decades, my parents made me feel like it was.

"Our feelings make it complicated," he says.

Right. Feelings. Like the tingly ones surfacing now. The ones I have to keep locked down because this is Noah, my colleague, practically my supervisor.

He's completely off-limits, but I don't want him to be. And all that stuff I said about pretending we don't have a history? I don't want that, either.

"I should turn in," I blurt, jumping to my feet.

"Yeah," he says, following me the last few feet to the cabin. "We should try again."

I know he's talking about sleep, but a tiny part of me lights up at the idea of us trying again for real—to be friends, or something more.

With Noah, I always wanted more—even when it wrecked us.

"Good night, Noah," I whisper, opening the door.

"Night, Vic," he says, his voice gravelly. "Sleep tight." His gaze drops to my slippers, and just as he turns back toward the boys' cabin, I see a hint of a smile.

Chapter Nine

VICTORIA

Three days later, I've made it clear to everyone on this mountain that sports are not my superpower.

Today's afternoon game is ultimate Frisbee, which as a concept sounds easy enough and potentially fun—if you're a kid who likes to run around at warp speed and not a twenty-nine-year-old woman who has zero hand-eye coordination and gets winded after running thirty yards. We're twenty minutes into the afternoon game, and already I'm wheezing and have been smacked in the face by a Frisbee. Twice. But I'm going to rally because that's the point of this whole camp adventure: I'm supposed to be proving to myself that I can thrive outside my comfort zone. I can do more than I give myself credit for.

Frisbee, though, might be my undoing. I feel like one of those inflatable air dancers that wiggle around to get your attention at car dealerships—completely goofy and bending at all the wrong angles.

I definitely do not want anyone's attention. I'd prefer to rally from the sidelines.

Half the kids love this game and ask to play it every

afternoon—but a few of them are hanging out on the fringe of the action, moving only when it's necessary to get out of the way of the players who are intent on winning this game. Sophie's on my team, and Noah's on the other. Sophie, trying to keep me from feeling excluded, tosses the Frisbee to me every chance she gets—and keeps saying, "You'll get the hang of it," every time I drop it. Or bat it out of the air when it flies anywhere near my face.

Bless her heart for throwing all that optimism my way. She's like an endless well of affirmations—but what I want her to do is pretend I'm not here so I can stop looking like a goofball. I offered to stay safely on the sidelines and take photos to share on the website, but she gave me this speech about how important it was to bond with the kids and play with them, and then I just felt like a jerk for trying to weasel out of the game.

Noah, of course, is the complete opposite of me. If you were to send your kid to camp and put in an order to the universe for the coolest camp counselor it could manifest, Noah is who you'd get. With the kids, he turns into this big scruffy teddy bear with a movie-star smile that draws them in closer, like plants leaning toward a sunbeam. He's like their easygoing big brother, telling them stories about how he went backpacking in Maine, swam with dolphins in the Virgin Islands, or trekked through the Rockies and met some amazing forest dweller who changed his perspective on life.

It's completely adorable, and yes—I'm a little jealous. Noah and Sophie are like the cool aunt and uncle at the reunion, and I'm the weirdo cousin that no one wants to stand next to for too long in the buffet line.

Every word Noah says keeps the kids riveted, their eyes sparkling with delight. When I talk to them, I bumble through questions about their favorite class, their hometown, their favorite hobby. Sometimes, I get a blank stare, but I see the eye rolls that pass between them when they think I'm not looking. It reminds me too much of high school and how I was never quite cool enough to fit in with the popular girls. How I constantly felt like a chameleon and needed to change myself to fit in with whichever crowd I was with that day. The kids here tolerate me, but they seem excited to hang out with Sophie and Noah. It's just one more way that I feel completely out of place here.

Today, though, I've pulled out all the stops. I'm cheering my team on, giving high-fives galore, and doing everything I can to channel Sophie's energy so the kids like hanging out with me, too.

When I trip over my own foot after missing yet another pass, I roll back up to my feet and throw my hands up in victory. Layla and Priya give me sympathetic smiles and giggle as they chase the Frisbee on the next play.

Across the field, Noah gives me a questioning look, and I respond with an exaggerated smile and a big thumbs-up. He smirks as he shakes his head, and I try to ignore the way the muscles in his forearms ripple as he rakes his hands through his sweaty hair. I'm not sure when forearms became my catnip, but from this point forward, all others will be measured against his.

Probably, all others will fall short.

Half of my problem today might be that Sporty Noah takes my breath away. Today, he showed up in soccer shorts and a vintage Queen tee shirt, a blue 1980s-era sweatband wrapped around his head like this was the most serious game in the history of games. He got the kids all pumped up to have fun and went over the ground rules (no tackling, no tripping, no trash talking) before dividing us into teams.

He's gone to great lengths to research different ways to assign kids to teams so that no one is choosing and no one has that sucky feeling of getting picked last. Today, it was "All people born between January 1 and June 10 are Team Noah, and everyone born between June 11 and Dec 31 are Team Sophie." Yesterday, it was those who have more than one sibling and those who do not. Each day, he makes it seem like this is a system he's just thought of on the fly, a not-quite random way to change up the teams and keep them even.

When he first explained this system to me, it tugged at something in my heart so hard that it almost made me tear up. He shrugged it off like it was the simplest idea on earth and not a super sneaky way of making sure no kid felt like they weren't wanted on a team.

It's no surprise that these kids love Noah. They ask him questions all during the evening, hang with him at mealtimes, and seek him out when there's downtime, too. They're like a bunch of little asteroids orbiting their sun.

"I'm on to you," Sophie says, giving me a playful nudge.

"What?" The word comes out like a squawk. She's caught me drooling over Noah, and now it's game over.

"This whole clumsy act," she says with a smile. "It's totally working. Some of the kids are self-conscious about sports, but you're taking the pressure off. It's sweet."

"It's no act," I say. "I'm truly this bad at sports."

She smiles. "You're good with the kids, though. We're really lucky to have you here." She claps me on the shoulder and then jogs back over to where the action is.

The tightness in my chest loosens. *Good. Lucky.*

Ethan tosses the Frisbee to Noah, a wobbly throw that he all but dives for. Noah's right by the end zone, but instead of running across the line, he tosses the Frisbee to Layla, who's just ten feet away. She catches it and dodges another kid as she bolts across the line and scores.

Together, she and Noah do a funny end-zone dance that earns cheers from the kids and a laugh from Sophie. Noah rips the sweatband from his head and shoots it across the goal line like it's a rubber band, then gives us some finger-guns. It's both the dorkiest and sweetest display I've seen in ages.

Noah slaps Layla a high-five, and she grins like she's won a trip to Disney World. My heart just grew three sizes, and I am in so much trouble.

Sometimes when we encounter people from our past, they don't live up to our memories of them, and we realize that we're better off with just the memories. Sometimes, though, the opposite is true. I know that we're the sum of all of our experiences, and I wouldn't be who I am without mine. But when I look at Noah, and this big-hearted man he's become, I wonder how different my life might be if I'd done a few things differently.

Starting with not walking away from him on that beach.

The kids take their places as the Frisbee's thrown into play again, whizzing across the meadow in a bright orange blur. Noah hangs back as his team chases the play, and when he lifts his shirt to wipe the sweat from his brow, time stands still. My eyes track the long lines of his body, and I stare far too long at his ridiculously chiseled abs. My mouth goes dry as I allow myself one moment to fully appreciate those hard edges and solid lines that will haunt me for the next decade.

Noah's focused on the kids, and I can't tear my gaze away as he runs a hand through his hair, back and forth, back and forth, leaving it standing up in all directions. He stretches one arm over his head, revealing another tattoo peeking out of his shirt sleeve. His bicep looks like cut marble, and I know I should follow the sound of my teammates' voices, but my feet are rooted to the earth because despite all the natural beauty out here, Noah Valentine is still the most captivating thing on this mountain.

He places his big hands on his hips, which makes his arms flex in a delightful way that tugs at something low in my belly. Then he turns toward me and his brow arches as his lips curl into a hint of a smile. My heart drops to my feet because he's definitely caught me staring—and then his mouth falls open at the same instant that pain shoots through my temple and the world wobbles on its axis.

"I TOLD you to pass it to me, instead," Derrick says, matter-of-factly. He's deadly serious about winning Frisbee games.

Someone snorts back a laugh, but all I see is Noah's face, backlit by the golden afternoon sun, the sky a brilliant blue behind him. His stubble's grown out today, reddish in this light, and his eyes are a deep green-brown. He's so close I can see little flecks of gold in them. I'd forgotten the way they change color in the light.

"Good job, Tyrone," a kid says. Ethan, I think. "Death by Frisbee."

Tyrone has a good arm.

"Don't be ridiculous," Priya says. "No one's dying from a Frisbee strike."

But in this moment, that idea doesn't feel so ridiculous, because I might as well have cartoon stars circling above my head and it feels like a rock is poking into my liver.

"Are you okay?" Noah says, kneeling next to me. His brows are pinched with concern, but all I can think about is how my body is tingling all over because he seems to be hovering above me, his face close enough to touch.

That's when I realize I'm lying on my back in the grass, the kids huddled around me, eyes wide like this is another opportunity for them to collect some data to analyze. Is there an equation that calculates one's level of mortification over time and what that might mean for her overall success in life? I hear a few chuckles, but most of the kids have the decency not to laugh. Probably, this strikes them as more pitiful than funny, and that idea hurts a whole lot worse.

"Come on, y'all," Sophie says, clapping her hands. "Let's give her some air and take a water break." She tucks her phone into her back pocket, and I say a silent prayer that she didn't capture that moment in a photo for the web page.

Noah lifts a brow. He really does have epic eyebrows—he might keep his thoughts close to the vest, but those eyebrows make whatever emotion he's feeling front and center. "How do you feel?" he says, his voice doing that sexy-rumble thing that makes me feel like a match being struck.

"Aside from feeling like an idiot?" I say.

"Harsh, Griffin." He smiles, revealing that deadly dimple. "I think that means you're okay." He moves his index finger back and forth in front of my face and stares intently into my eyes as I track the movement. He's probably just putting his first-aid merit badge to good use and not using this as an excuse to spend time with me.

Probably.

He holds one hand out toward me, then slips his other behind my shoulder and helps me to sit up. His eyes are still heavy on mine, his palm warm on my back. I shiver when he lets me go.

"Dizzy?" he asks.

"No," I say after a moment. "I'm fine. The Frisbee just caught me by surprise. Again." He frowns as if to say he's in total agreement there. Everything about this week has taken me by surprise—especially him.

Gently, he brushes my hair from my face and says, "Come with me and I'll do something about that cut."

When I touch my left eyebrow, my fingertips come away red. That explains the stinging pain that's coming from somewhere above my brow.

"In case it's not evident yet, I should tell you that sports are not my strong suit," I tell him. "Probably should have told you that on Day One."

He pulls me to my feet. "Don't sweat it. We all land in the dirt from time to time. It's how you know you're playing the game."

"Not sure I agree with that a hundred percent, but I appreciate the sentiment."

Another tiny smile. One that says we'll agree to disagree.

Holding my arm in a firm grip, he walks me out of the meadow, where Sophie's transitioned to referee as the kids finish the game.

"I have a first aid kit in my room," he says, leading me into the boys' cabin. It's the mirror image of the girls' cabin, but this one smells like sweaty old socks and middle school boys. Thankfully, Noah's room smells like cedar and cloves, and there's not a single dirty sock in sight. Just like mine, it has the same dresser, desk, and chair. The space is tidy, his clothes hanging neatly in the closet and his bed made. I spot two pairs of hiking boots in the closet, a notebook on his desk with a couple of sci-fi novels, and a reed diffuser that's no doubt the source of the heavenly smell. This is the room of a man who knew what he was getting into—someone who knows how to prepare.

He pulls a first-aid kit from his bottom dresser drawer and motions for me to sit on the bed. When he sits next to me, I'm yanked back in time to that night at the beach house, when we sat together by the campfire under the stars. Something in my chest coils tight at the thought, and I swallow hard, trying to forget about how his hands felt around my waist, how his lips felt on my neck as he pulled me tight against his chest, so close that I could feel his heartbeat against my skin.

He tears open a sterilizing wipe and pushes my hair behind my ear before he gently swipes it over my eyebrow. I wince at the cool touch.

"I'll try to be gentle," he says. "It doesn't look deep."

He carefully cleans the wound and then applies some antiseptic with a cotton swab. His fingers are whisper-light, his eyes flicking to mine every few moments. At this distance, I can fully appreciate his long lashes, the way his lips pinch together when he's concentrating hard. I hadn't exactly forgotten these details about Noah, but I hadn't let myself think about them— and that's not quite the same thing.

I wince as his fingers brush over my brow, so delicate.

"Sorry," he breathes. "It stings a little."

What also stings is that memory of him that has never quite slipped away. And worse, this feeling that I'm failing at every part of my life and can't even manage to do summer camp right. That critical voice in my head grows louder and more insistent, and before I know it, I'm choking back a sob.

"Vic?" he says, his hand frozen in mid-air. "Are you hurt somewhere else?" His voice is so calm, so soothing, and I want to tell him that I hurt everywhere, down to the deepest crevices of my heart.

"I'm fine," I mutter, but the words come out sounding strangled and weak. But that's what Griffins do. We roll along chanting *Everything's fine,* even when the world's burning down around us. Because to admit things are not fine is to confront all the difficult, uncomfortable feelings—like hurt, regret, and fear.

And that's another hard truth I've gotten used to evading.

"Victoria," he whispers. "Tell me what's wrong. Let me help."

I brush the tears away, avoiding his gaze. "I really want to not suck at this."

"Frisbee?" He gives me a tiny smile, the kind he always used to make me feel better.

"All of it," I sigh. "I've made so many mistakes lately, and I've wasted so much time. I don't want to keep feeling like a failure." When I think of the time I wasted with Theo and with a job I didn't like, it makes me wish I'd stood up for what I wanted. That nagging voice in my head has kept immaculate records of every mistake I've ever made, and now they're washing over me like a tidal wave. Before I know it, I'm telling Noah more about my near-marriage and my unfulfilling job—all the ugly details I'd left out when we talked before.

It's only when Noah's big hand touches my shoulder that I realize I'm shaking all over. My brain is buzzing, and my skin feels too tight, but Noah's hand is like an anchor, and when he moves it in a tiny circle, the warmth spreads across my back and into my chest, and it becomes easier to breathe.

"Vic," he says. "You're not a failure."

I let out an unladylike snort. His gentle hand is the only thing keeping me from crumbling into pieces. "This was supposed to be easy," I tell him. "Help kids have fun at camp. How am I failing at that, too?"

"You're not," he says, and there's that warm smile again. The one that says everything's going to be okay, no matter how it feels right now. "So Frisbee's not your jam. That doesn't mean you're failing."

"You make this look so effortless," I tell him, a little envious of how he seems so perfectly suited to this role, this place. "You've so clearly found where you belong, and I thought that by now I would have found that, too."

He shrugs. "I've been doing this a long time. But my first summer was a disaster."

"It was not. You forget that I know when you're lying. You have a tell."

He shakes his head, biting back a smile as he dabs more ointment on my brow and tears open a tiny bandage. "During my first summer, at the New Mexico camp, I planned a day trip with horseback riding. First, my horse threw me into the biggest cactus I've ever seen, and I spent the rest of the day pulling spines out of places I won't even mention. Then I realized I'd left all of our food and water behind, so we had to cut the trip short and go raid the nearest gas station—thirty miles down the road—for snacks. And let me tell you, feeding kids beef jerky and peanut butter cups is hands-down the worst decision one can make on a road trip." He grimaces. "The next day, I made two kids cry, and one went home early. I thought for sure I'd get fired. But then Roxy told me the same thing I'm telling you."

When he leans in closer to examine the cut, his knee presses into mine, and he doesn't pull away. Then his eyes flick to mine as he lifts a brow, as if daring me to argue. "We all have to find our rhythm, Vic. No one's perfect, so we shouldn't beat ourselves up for that. We just need to be excellent to each other and leave the world a little better than we found it."

"Did you just quote *Bill and Ted's Excellent Adventure* to me?"

He shrugs. "It's sound advice, and I will die on that hill."

I snort out a laugh because I've missed this feeling so much—being able to relax and be my goofy weirdo self without worry about who's watching and judging my actions against some impossible standard.

Noah smiles—a real one that makes his dimples pop and his eyes crinkle at the corners, and it's like feeling sunlight on my face. When his eyes meet mine, there's a flicker of something that tugs deep in my ribcage, and another chunk of that wall between us crumbles.

I stay still, feeling the heat from his knee burning into my thigh, his fingers warm on my brow. Before I can stop myself, the words spill out. "Have you ever thought about that night on the beach? I mean, before I showed up here?"

He pauses, brows raised in surprise. When he meets my gaze again, his eyes are stormy gray-green. "Lots of times."

It would be so easy to lean over and kiss him right now and turn all of this hurt into something else entirely. "Did you miss me?"

His voice is gravelly. "You first this time."

"Yes," I whisper.

He leans closer, his gaze dropping to my lips. My heart leaps into my throat.

"Same," he says. "So much."

He reaches up, and my body hums, waiting for his touch. He tugs a blade of grass from my hair, his thumb grazing my cheek.

Heat blooms in my chest. He's just a breath away, and I'm about to combust. It would be so easy to kiss him, and no one would ever have to know.

No more pretending.

I move closer until we're only a breath apart. His hand rests on my thigh, and that small touch breaks the last of my resolve. When his eyes lock on mine, he dips his head—an invitation— and I'm a goner. In a blink, my hand is in his hair, and my lips press against his gently at first. He's still for a moment, but then I catch his bottom lip in my teeth, and he makes a low sound, deep in his throat that makes those butterflies swirl in my ribcage like a hurricane. His tongue parts my lips, and I know I should stop this—but this is *Noah,* and it just feels so right.

A door slams down the hall, and Noah jumps back as if he's been zapped with a cattle prod. We both leap from the bed at the sound of the boys' voices as they come closer, their sneakers squeaking on the tile. Noah glances toward his half-open door, his eyebrows shooting up to his hairline.

"I should go," I tell him, just as he says, "I think you're all set," and eases away from me. It's a tiny movement, but says everything.

Clearing my throat, I say, "I'm sorry. I shouldn't have... brought up ancient history."

His lip curves into a sad smile. "It's okay."

"We can't," I whisper.

His brow lifts. "I know."

Willing my heart to go back to its normal rhythm, I take a deep breath, pushing all of the feelings I stupidly brought to the surface back down again.

"I'm going to go," I tell him, even though leaving him is the last thing I want and my feet feel rooted to this spot.

His gaze pins me in place. "Yeah."

I head for the door and pause. "I had a thought. Before I ate dirt."

He busies himself closing the first-aid kit. When he glances up at me, there's a hunger there that nearly unravels me.

"What's that?" he says, his voice low.

"What if we had a second activity each day for the kids? We could offer a sporty-sport like Frisbee, and then also something that's a little less... contact."

"A sporty-sport?" he says lightly, and just like that, my teasing Noah is back.

"We could do yoga, or dancing, or just walk one of the easy trails around the property." I shrug. "Some of the kids were hanging on the sidelines, looking like they'd rather be at the dentist than standing out on that field. I remember that feeling as a kid—playing sports was agony if you felt like you were terrible at it."

"You want to lead the alternate activity?" he says.

"Given my record with the sporty-sports, I think that's the safest solution."

He smiles. "That's a great idea. Make a list of what you want to offer, and I'll add it to our schedule. We can start tomorrow."

"Thanks for patching me up," I tell him.

"Of course," he says.

When I open the door to leave, he says, "One more thing."

I turn and find him looking at me intently. His gaze drops to the floor between his feet—another tell—and when he looks up at me again, his smile is a little more than friendly. "I'm really glad you're here, Vic."

I wait for him to say more, but he doesn't. Despite my slip-up, he's back to being my colleague now, the nice guy who put me back together after a bad spill and is trying so hard to make me feel welcome. As I slip out the door and head down the hall, I try to imagine what else he wanted to say—because when Noah looks down at his feet, it means he's reconsidering. He's shoving down a thought he thinks he shouldn't share.

And now, despite my better instincts, I'm dying to know what precisely that thought might be.

Chapter Ten

NOAH

I've been kidding myself. All week, I've been telling myself that I can get along just fine with Vic as my colleague.

But that's a total lie.

I kept telling myself that lie as we ate meals together in the cafeteria, as we played games with the kids in the evening, and as we planned new activities in the afternoons. I told myself that lie as she laughed her musical laugh when she caught me staring at her across the table at breakfast while I was half-asleep and hungover from the wild dreams about her that had me tossing and turning all night. (Did you know that you can have a hangover from an intensely vivid dream? Neither did I.) Victoria Griffin swept onto this mountain like a summer storm that makes everything brighter and takes your breath away when the clouds break. And she's going to leave me wrecked.

Ever since the Great Frisbee Incident, it takes everything in me not to cup her cheeks in my hands and kiss her senseless every time I see her. The longing in her eyes tells me she wants that, too—which makes me feel both better and worse. Better, because I'm not alone in feeling this churning want, this *need*—

but worse because now I'm going to feel this torturous ache every time we're in a room together.

And heaven help me, that ache is going to make me combust and leave a little Noah-shaped pile of ash at her feet.

Friends. Colleagues. That's what we can be for each other right now. But what I want is so much more.

"Shoot," Victoria says, glancing at her phone. "We're going to miss lunch."

"Will we though?" I ask her. "Will we really *miss* corn dogs and tater tots?"

We drove into Laurel Creek after breakfast this morning to get some supplies for the kiddos, and somehow, it's already noon. I shove our shopping bags into the back of the Tahoe and shut the back door.

"Fair point," she says, her lip lifting in a sly smile. "I spy a bakery over there that I'll bet can do way better than corn dogs."

She points to a building on Main Street that's painted yellow and has a giant sign over the door that's shaped like a bright pink and white cupcake. No name—just a cupcake. A couple of bistro tables are set up on the sidewalk next to a wrought-iron bench and waist-high flower boxes overflowing with pansies and daisies. This street is like a living ad for small-town mountain getaways, packed with boutique shops and blissful-looking tourists.

"Come on," she says, linking her arm in mine and practically dragging me across the street. "Tasty treats await."

I follow, relishing the warmth of her hand on my bicep. It's a glimpse of how we could be together if the camp rules didn't apply.

A bell above the door jingles as we step inside. The space is filled with retro-style tables and vinyl chairs that look like they came straight from a 1950s-era diner. Two upholstered chairs are set up by the front window, and the walls are covered in colorful paintings and fiber art that are no doubt made by local artists. Half the tables are full with families who look like they're in vacation mode, the others occupied by people with laptops.

Victoria makes a beeline to the back, where there's a coffee bar and a pastry case a mile long.

"Would it be wrong to take a stash of contraband back to my cabin?" she asks, her eyes roaming over the endless trays of treats. Somewhere between the blackberry pie and the apple fritters, my stomach has started rumbling loud enough to shake the foundation.

"I won't tell," I answer. "But you might make lots of raccoon friends."

"Actually," she says, eyes glittering, "I'd rather order a bunch of those for the dance on the last night. What do you think?" She points to the far end of the pastry case, where there are cookies decorated like rockets, complete with rivets and bright orange flames coming out the back.

"I think the kids would go nuts," I reply. "As if they don't already have enough reasons to love you." My breath hitches over the last two words, but she doesn't seem to notice.

"Done," she says with a grin, and the next thing I know, she's talking to the owner about airbrushing sugar cookies to look like planets and discussing the group's food allergies.

We order two deli sandwiches and a mix of pastries, including a couple for Sophie. When a family of four abandons the table by the window, Victoria swoops in like a hawk to claim it, grinning as she slides across the vinyl booth. Being with her like this, out in the world that doesn't revolve around camp and kids, feels so familiar and natural. Victoria always did put me at ease, but she also made even the most mundane activities seem exciting. Something tugs at my chest when I realize that in just a couple of weeks, I'll be back in the real world like this—but she won't be with me.

I've missed her more than I realized.

She opens her big purse to make room for our take-home pastries and pulls out her wallet, an e-reader, and a dog-eared copy of *Ready Player One*.

"I must be the last person on earth who hasn't read that book," I tell her. "I keep meaning to because it's been recommended to me no less than a thousand times."

Her eyes widen as she clutches the paperback to her chest. "You haven't yet? Noah, you'd love it. A treasure hunt, 1980s game lore, a brilliant misfit kid." She thrusts it toward me and says, "I dare you to read the first two chapters and not be hooked. It's one of my favorites."

I take the book from her, because how can I say no to all of that? Plus, I love the idea of having something of Victoria's, even if only for a short time. When I turn it over to read the back cover copy, I see a sticker that has Vic's name and address under the words *This book belongs to*.

"Lose your books often?" I ask her.

She shrugs. "I like to make it easy for the important things to find their way back to me. Plus, my sister makes a sport of stealing my books."

"I'll guard it with my life."

She smiles as I lay the book next to me in the booth.

"So how did you end up doing all the outdoorsy stuff?" she asks. "Last time I saw you, you were dead set on teaching English Lit and writing novels."

"Yeah, that didn't go the way I planned." I shrug. "But I've always liked being outdoors. My dad used to take me camping when I was a kid—it's one of the few things we did together. He and my mom got divorced when I was ten, and my dad wasn't around much after that." I take a bite of my sandwich, which has amazing aioli that I'll definitely try to replicate someday. "He was always flaky, but after they split up, I only saw him once or twice a year. He always wanted to go camping, probably because he didn't have much money. I loved it, though, because I got to go hiking and fishing and sleep under the stars. It felt like an adventure."

"You never told me much about him," Vic says. "Back then." And she's right. We didn't talk much about our parents. I knew that hers were overbearing and critical of her every move, and she'd rather eat tin foil than talk about how they made her feel. She knew that my dad was absent for ninety-seven percent of the year and that my mom did everything she could to make up for it. But the rest we seldom mentioned.

I nod. "There wasn't much to tell. I always felt like he left me and my mom because he traded up. He married a woman fifteen years younger than him and had two kids with her, and then I never saw him. It made me think that somehow we weren't good enough for him, and I thought I'd done something wrong that made him leave. It wasn't something I wanted to think about, let alone talk about."

"Oh, Noah," she says. "I'm so sorry that happened. But I can promise you, it's nothing you did. That's all on him."

"I realize that now," I tell her, feeling that familiar sting behind my heart that I always feel when I think about my dad. "But for a long time, it felt like he was choosing these other people over us—except when he took me on those trips. Those were the times where I felt close to him, like I still mattered."

She reaches over and lays her hand over mine. "We don't have to talk about this," she whispers. "I didn't mean to pry."

"It's okay," I tell her, swallowing a lump in my throat. "You aren't."

"It was definitely *not* okay," she says, her brow lifting.

"Yeah, but each time I get outside, I make a little more peace with it, and I feel a little more okay. Things were always strained with my dad, but those camping trips were the times when it felt easy. I loved that we could drive out from the city and feel like we were a million miles from everyone else. It was just the two of us, and things almost felt normal. We were just two guys with backpacks and an old army tent, watching birds and roasting hot dogs over a campfire." I pause, feeling that deep-seated ache, and try not to push it away like I have so many times before. It feels safe to feel it now, here with Victoria. "I loved the ease of being out there and enjoying the solitude. It was like all the noise in the world, all the noise inside my head—just melted away. I didn't feel anxious and small when I was in nature. I felt part of something bigger, like I belonged."

Beneath the table, Victoria's foot brushes against mine. It's what she used to do back in college, when I started to feel anxious, just to let me know she was there, grounding me to the earth. It was always a discreet hand on my shoulder blade, her palm on my knee. But sometimes, I wanted her to be less discreet —I wanted her to show the whole world that we were connected in this way that I never felt with anyone else.

"Dad wasn't one for great advice," I tell her. "But he did teach me to look for the glimmers—those tiny flickers of joy that expand when you focus on them. The more you look for them, the more you find them, and pretty soon, you see them everywhere. And it reminds me that even though there's a lot of bad in the world, there's a lot of good, too."

When I look back at Vic, there are tears in her eyes. "I wish I'd known these things sooner," she says. "About you."

"Hey, it worked out," I tell her. "I found something I love. And no matter how flaky my dad is, or what mistakes he made, I found it thanks to him." I shrug, feeling that tightness in my chest loosen just a little. "Things are still strained, and I might always feel hurt by the way he left us. But it's strange—every time I do one of these camps and see a kid light up at the foot of a waterfall or laugh with their whole body by a campfire, I feel like a little piece of me gets mended."

She gets up from the table and slides into the booth next to me. Before I can say anything more, she throws her arms around me and pulls me into a tight hug, resting her chin on my shoulder. "There's no trading up from you, Noah," she says. "For the record." She squeezes me tight, her chest pressed against mine, and I want to stay like this forever. What I didn't tell her was that the only other time I felt like I truly belonged was with her.

"Thank you," I say.

My phone buzzes on the table, and when I look over, I see Sophie's name on the screen.

"Take it," Vic says. "I'm going to grab us coffees for the road. And maybe just a couple more of those brownies because, sweet baby cheeses, this place is magic."

BY THE TIME we get back to the institute, it's nearly time for afternoon activities. Victoria's idea to split up for outdoor time was a good one because she was right—I'd been ignoring the likelihood that some kids didn't enjoy the "sporty-sports," as she called them. When we'd offered them a choice each day, six of the kids had opted to go with Victoria and do her low-contact activity, which ranged from them teaching each other dance moves to her leading the group in yoga.

After finishing up today's Frisbee game with my group, I

head back over to the cabins and halfway there stop dead in my tracks. Vic's still doing yoga with her kids, going over our allotted time. She's on her feet, guiding the group as they stretch themselves into pretzels, and it takes every shred of my willpower not to openly stare at her. Lit by the afternoon sun, she's smiling in that sweet, satisfied way that tugs at something deep in my chest. Her hair's pulled up in a messy bun, and she's wearing a tank top and leggings that hug her body, clearly designed for the sole purpose of stopping my heart. I slip behind a big loblolly pine because apparently I'm a creeper now, and watch her as she talks to the kids, coaching them through a deep breath and a liquid movement that takes them from what I recognize as a downward dog into a lying-down pose that gives them all blissed-out smiles. All long lines and tempting curves, Victoria moves as smooth and slow as a river. Her melodic voice drifts over to where I'm standing and warms me like a sunbeam. She says she feels out of place here, but at moments like this, it seems she fits in just fine. She's like that last piece of the puzzle —the one that looks like it can't possibly fit, but when it slips into place, the whole picture makes sense.

When she smiles at the group and brings her hands together —*namaste*—the kids all slowly stand. Derrick clambers to his feet, and now I see why he's ditched Frisbee for yoga—because Priya's on the mat next to him, and he's been following her like a puppy for the last three days. As the kids leave, Layla stops to ask Victoria about a certain stretch. Vic, facing her, spreads her feet wider than hip distance apart and stretches to the side—her right arm goes to her right foot, her left into the air, and it's as graceful as a ballet. Layla does the same, wobbling a little, and Vic reaches out to steady her. She's better with these kids than she thinks she is—she's got a knack for putting them at ease.

Layla grabs a sweatshirt and then heads off toward the

cabins. Victoria stays put for a minute and then tucks her tank top into her leggings. She raises her hands over her head as if she's stretching but then dives toward the ground in a cartwheel, her hands planted firmly in the grass as her long legs knife through the air. Her landing's not perfect, but her smile is—she topples onto the grass and then lies on her back, lacing her hands behind her head as she grins up at the sky. She laughs, and the sound makes my heart squeeze like a fist.

Finally, she looks like she's adjusted to being here. But more than that, she looks calm, like she's not concerned about what anyone else thinks of her, and she's not worried about meeting anyone's expectations—she's just letting herself *be*.

I'm walking towards her before I even realize it, drawn to her like that first night we met on the balcony.

"Hey," I say, sitting next to her on the grass. "Looks like your group had a good session."

She opens her eyes, shielding them from the sun with her hand. "They're getting the hang of it. Fast learners."

"It also looks like someone has a little crush."

"What?" she says, her brow arching.

"Derrick," I say. "He's stuck to Priya like glue."

"Right. That explains a few things. Like why she was wearing his cap yesterday."

"Happens every session," I say. "By the end of week one, there's at least ten camp crushes in full effect."

"Aww," she coos. "So cute."

I shrug. "The magic of summer camp. Time moves faster, and emotions run higher. Instalove."

"Oh, is that what it is?" she teases.

"I mean, I guess it could be the altitude. Thin air does some weird stuff to you."

She smacks my arm playfully. "The air's not that thin up

here, Valentine." The warmth from her hand sends a current of heat straight through my chest, coiling around each rib.

I wish I could hold it there forever.

"Good call, by the way," I tell her. "On the new activities."

"There's plenty more where that one came from," she says with a smile.

"I have no doubt about that." Climbing to my feet, I brush the grass from my shirt, and her eyes track the movement.

"You want a hand setting up the lounge before dinner?" She wiggles her toes in the grass as a cloud passes overhead. She looks perfectly content in this moment, like a cat in a sunbeam.

"Nah, I got it," I tell her. "Take a break. You look like you found your happy place."

She stretches her arms behind her head and says, "I'm getting there."

And I have no doubt about that, either. But a growing part of me is hoping that somehow, when this camp is over, her happy place could include me.

Chapter Eleven

VICTORIA

By Friday, I'm finding my rhythm. Today it's one foot in front of the other, on a loop trail that feels like it's been entirely uphill for a thousand miles. Noah's leading our group, Sophie's somewhere in the middle, and I'm at the back, cursing myself for letting my gym membership lapse. I offered to take this spot so I have an excuse to walk more slowly and hang back with the kids who aren't charging ahead like little mountain goats.

The joke's on me, though, because these kids are itching to get to the waterfall, and I'm struggling to keep up with the slowest of the bunch. Keeping my eyes on the trail to watch for roots and snakes means I've hardly been able to take in the details of my surroundings. We're on a densely wooded trail that cuts through evergreens and mountain laurel, and all I want is to stop long enough to soak it all up: I want to trace my fingers over the leaves and touch the big pale pink blossoms. I want to stand in the stillness and listen to the birds twittering in the branches and picture the bright colors of their feathers. I want to close my eyes and feel the dappled sunlight filtering through the canopy and falling on my face. But we're moving so fast that all I can focus on is the dirt trail in front of me, the space between my feet and the kids up ahead.

Probably, this is an apt metaphor for my lack of work-life balance.

My focus has been too narrow. I've been too preoccupied with moving forward, being productive, and making progress—what do those ideas even mean anymore? My work with Rayanne's realty firm was so fast and frenzied that I forgot how to be unhurried and still. For years, I was focused on building my career: being better and faster than everyone around me, and now those years are a blur.

When did I stop paying attention to all the bits of beauty around me?

I stop by a huge rhododendron with magenta flowers as big as my hands. Tracing the broad leaf with my fingers, I'm mesmerized by the tiny veins in the leaves. The blossom is silk-soft, and when I tip it towards me, I find a sleeping bumblebee inside, at the very center of the blossom. Its body is dusted in yellow pollen, and I move the flower back gently, so I don't wake it. It's a surprising delight—one of Noah's glimmers—something I'd never have noticed in my regular life.

And then a tiny voice in my head says, *What if this* was *your regular life?*

Further down the trail, a whistle pierces the air. I jog towards the sound to catch up with the group, and once I'm around a curve in the trail, I see the kids have all stopped. Noah, towering over them, zeroes in on me and cocks his head to the side in a question: *You doing okay?*

Aside from my burning calves and the stitch in my side, I'm great. So I give him a wave and a thumbs-up that says, *All good.*

"Okay," he says to the group, "we're almost to the falls. Remember to watch for slippery rocks."

Sophie leads them onward while Noah waits for me to catch up. His eyes drift to my feet and then back up to my face as if he's looking for any outward signs of distress. I'm certain he can hear the pounding of my heart from ten paces, even as I plant my hands on my hips and inhale slow and deep. I'm breathless from the hike, but also from this feeling of wonder—and a persistent thought that I've been chasing the wrong kind of success.

And the wrong kind of meaning.

That pursuit hasn't felt right for a long time, but I've been afraid to admit it. Because, at best, it means I've wasted my time and effort. At worst, it means I've been sacrificing what's most important to me because of someone else's expectations.

Both feel like a loss.

"You all right?" he asks. His hair's standing out every which way, his eyes curious. It's such a simple question, but it has a complicated answer.

"Sure," I tell him, because now's not the moment to explain my existential crisis. "Just wanted to stop for a minute. It's been a while since I saw a place with zero concrete."

That lazy smile pulls at his lips, and now my heart's pounding for a different reason. Ever since we kissed, I've been trying to keep more distance between us. Because as much as I'd like to do that again, we can't.

My brain has gone over the logic of this line we've drawn a thousand times, but my body's having none of it.

"It's not far," he says, nodding in the direction the kids went. "And it's totally worth the screaming quads."

I swallow hard because I do not need to think about Noah's

muscular thighs and powerful glutes and the masterful way they propel him up this mountain.

Nope.

He leads me onward, and I keep his pace as we climb rustic steps made from packed dirt and railroad ties. The trail turns downhill again where there's a drop-off to a clearing, the waterfall just beyond. The sound of crashing water fills my ears, and Noah holds out his hand to help me down.

I hesitate, but only for a second. The downward part of the trail is steep and rocky, and I don't trust myself to not slip. I take his hand, and his fingers squeeze as he gently guides me to where he stands solidly on the earth.

His eyes meet mine, and my breath hitches as I try to focus on my feet and not the firm grip of his hand. Then my foot slips on a loose rock, and I instinctively reach out to him. Noah steps forward, placing his other hand on my hip to steady me. "I've got you," he says, his voice a deep rumble.

Heat rushes through me as he lowers me to the ground. And then I'm just a breath away from him, the toes of our boots touching and my whole body pressed against his. Somehow, both of his hands are on my hips, and my hands rest on his chest. When I look up at him, his pupils widen, and a blush races from my cheeks down to my collarbones.

"Thanks," I say, and the word whooshes out in a way that's entirely too breathy. My heart's pounding from trying to keep his quick pace going uphill, and I know I should put more space between us, but I can't.

Or rather, I don't want to.

His eyes darken to a deep green, and I know he feels it too— the invisible thread that tugs us closer.

"Anytime," he says.

As he glances over his shoulder at the clearing where the kids are gathered, his hands tighten, and my entire body hums in response. It's only then that I notice the fifty-foot waterfall behind him—because as gorgeous as that rushing water is, it still has nothing on Noah Valentine.

Turning back to me, he whispers, "Come on. The falls are the best part."

Debatable, I think. Because this part—right here—is tough to beat.

I follow him to a quiet pool near the waterfall, encircled by rocks. A wooden footbridge stretches across the stream, and the kids have fanned out into groups to explore. Some are on the bridge with Sophie, some are gathered on the rocks, and a few have taken their shoes off to wade in the shallow pool.

"Derrick caught a chipmunk!" Layla sings, because she apparently lives every day like she's in a high school musical. She's impossible to miss out here, in her bright red top and yellow shorts, aqua socks pulled to her knees. Her wardrobe is like a rainbow—in fact, I don't think I've ever seen so many colors on one person.

Noah turns toward the pool, where Derrick's crouched by the rocks with Priya. He waves at us with one hand, the chipmunk peeking out of the other.

"Careful," Sophie calls to Derrick. "They can get bitey."

Noah lets out a weary sigh and gives me a look that says, *We'll continue this later*, before jogging off to join the kids gathered around Derrick.

Still reeling from being held in Noah's firm grip, I inhale deeply, taking in the beauty of the falls. I count to four with each breath to calm my racing heart because one minute with Noah has turned it into a powder keg.

When I close my eyes, I listen to the twittering birds and feel the cool air drifting from the water. I can't recall the last time I felt this kind of calm, and I'm so glad that I took this risk and came here. I can't help but wonder what other moments like this I've missed out on just because I spent so much time focused on doing what other people expected of me. My parents, Theo, my friends—even Gwen sometimes. I've been so wrapped up in making the people around me happy—and proud of my accomplishments—that I lost track of what I really wanted.

And who I truly am.

Out here, though, all the noise in my head dies down. I see why Noah likes it so much, and I see that it's good for me, too.

When I open my eyes, Derrick is crouching next to Noah, releasing the chipmunk into the brush.

"Godspeed, little doodle," Noah says, giving a tiny salute. This man is like a young, hot, Mister Rogers of the wilderness, and my heart feels like it might crack in half—because everyone deserves to have a Noah in their life, sparking their curiosity and inspiring them to grow.

And I want him back in mine.

I don't know exactly where I'm headed, and I don't yet know what I want. But what I *need* is to feel like I'm doing something that matters. And that I'm making decisions that align with my purpose and not what others think is right for me.

I've spent too much of my life trying to please other people, and today, I'm taking the first step in leaving that behind. I pluck a stone from the pool, a green-tinted one that's worn smooth by the current. As I close my fist around it, I etch this moment into my memory and then tuck it into the pocket of my shorts.

AFTER HAVING snacks and stowing their trash in their backpacks ("Pack it in, pack it out," Noah reminded them), the kids are taking their last few minutes to snap photos with their new friends.

Overhead, big puffy clouds have passed over the sun. I hadn't even noticed the sky darkening, but an ominous gray cloud is sweeping in from the direction we came.

"We should head back," Noah says, gathering everyone up. He usually only has to speak two words, and the kids snap to attention like he's the Pied Piper. He's always had that effect on people, though, even when we were in college. He always claimed to be an introvert, spooked by large groups of people, but he drew people to him just the same. His quiet confidence makes you feel at ease, like you're simultaneously safe with him and also about to embark on the adventure of a lifetime—if you're willing to follow.

And if he invites you to come along.

After we met on that balcony, he chose me—and it made me feel like I was special. Worthy of his attention and his friendship. And that just made it harder when graduation rolled around and he *didn't* choose me.

But it wasn't just *harder*—it was the worst feeling in the world.

The kids all grab their designated buddy, and we do our head count before heading back onto the trail. Ethan and Priya are right by Noah's side, trying to emulate his confidence and ease.

"The good news," Sophie tells me, "is that it's mostly downhill from here."

She winks and then practically skips ahead down the trail, the most eager kids following close behind her. She's like a little wood sprite in her hiking shorts and tank top, her hair somehow still styled into flawless braids in this wretched humidity. She seems to be perfectly at home in this place, like all the cute woodland animals and the blossoming flowers, which for a second makes me feel like an imposter again.

But then I wonder: was she naturally like this, completely at home in nature, or was it an acquired skill? And then: could I acquire it, too?

This time, I end up in the middle of the group, with three kids behind me and Noah following in the back. We've moved about a hundred yards when that dark cloud splits open and the rain starts to fall. The kids up ahead giggle, and one of the boys behind me grumbles. It's Jacob from Cleveland, who so far has groused about everything from the altitude and the lunch menu to our choice of board games in the evening.

"Just the usual shower," Noah tells him. "You know what they say around here? If you don't like the weather, wait twenty minutes."

Jacob lets out a heavy sigh, and I can tell he feels out of his element, too. At least two of the kids said they'd never been in a mountain climate before, and that's partly why these outings were planned. The kids are here to learn about supernovas and Mars rovers, but Noah was quick to tell me that it's just as important that they learn a little about the world here outside the lab, too.

It's good training, giving them opportunities to look for those glimmers, he said during our last planning meeting. And the way his brow arched told me, *It's good for you, too.*

The rain falls heavier as we walk, pattering on the big rhododendron leaves in a calming way that would put me to sleep if I was lying in my cabin. I catch myself smiling, even though the rain has plastered my hair to my face and my arms are chilly from the cooling air. The kids talk quietly as we walk, focused on the sights and sounds of the trail. Up ahead, there's a gasp and some giggles—Priya and Layla have flushed a rabbit out of the brush, and I see the flash of its cotton-white tail as it skitters under a fallen tree.

Thunder rumbles overhead. This is one of those summer storms that comes out of nowhere, so fast that the clouds don't fully block the sun. The leaves on the trees sparkle with raindrops, and I try to remember the last time I was caught in the rain—in a place that wasn't a parking lot. The three kids behind scurry around me to catch up with the rest of the group, leaving me to fall back with Noah as another low rumble of thunder rolls overhead.

"Should have brought my rain jacket," he says, walking beside me and matching my stride. His shirt's stuck to his chest now, almost completely soaked. Mine probably is, too. My eyes catch on the defined muscles of his shoulders and biceps, and I tear my gaze away.

Another glimmer, I think. Once you start looking for them, you really do see them everywhere.

He rakes a hand through his hair, shaking out some water, and droplets hit my arm. Something in my chest pulls at the thought—these tiny drops of rain that have touched his skin and are now touching mine. A part of him that's now a part of me.

I want more of our parts to overlap. I want to know everything that's happened to him since I left him on that beach outside of Charleston. I want to know all of his secret feelings. And most of all, I want to know what he's thinking about us now.

We're headed downhill, the trail sloppy from the rain. My feet feel less sure, and I'm back to staring at the ground, choosing my steps carefully as I mind the growing space between us and the kids. When we come to a small creek that's rushing from the rain, Noah walks right through with no hesitation—two big steps and he's on the other side. It's only a few inches deep, but I try to dodge the loose rocks and aim for the shallow spots.

"Let's catch up," he says, and even though I know he's talking about the kids, my brain snaps right back to that last night we saw each other before everything blew apart. My chest tightens as I remember straddling his lap on the beach, trying to communicate all of my bottled-up feelings in one fiery kiss. We'd been building toward that moment for so long—it's easy to see in retrospect, but it was impossible to see at the time. That moment had felt inevitable but also clumsy, in that way that collisions so often do. Kissing Noah had been thrilling and terrifying, and then when he'd clasped my hands and pulled away from me, I'd panicked.

There's someone else, he'd said. It was the one variable I hadn't considered, and it blindsided me.

It also hurt like a punch to the kidney.

After that night, I avoided him completely. Part of me had hoped that he'd choose me instead. He'd tell me that he felt the same and would break up with Samantha and spend the summer with me.

But that didn't happen. He and Samantha left for their backpacking trip the week after graduation. He posted endless photos of them hiking in Ireland, playing with puffins in Scotland, and swimming in an ocean that was an impossible blue.

He texted me a few times and sent a photo of himself posing with an adorable Shetland pony in a knitted sweater. It was charming and hilarious—one hundred percent Noah—and it broke my heart in half.

I wanted to call him and tell him, *Choose me. Pick me.*

But that seemed unlikely. Samantha was tall and model-gorgeous with big doe eyes and a warm smile. She had perfect skin, perfect hair, and had graduated summa cum laude—every time I scrolled through her social media channels, I felt more inadequate.

And in every picture she posted of them together, she and Noah looked like they were head over heels for each other.

When Gwen had scraped me off the floor for the tenth time, she grabbed my phone and unfollowed both Samantha's and Noah's accounts. *I love you too much to watch you torment yourself like this*, she'd said, and part of me was grateful.

I should have just talked to Noah—I see that now. But back on that beach, I didn't know how to explain what I was feeling and what that meant for us. And afterward, I was too embarrassed to try. We knew how to do a lot of things together, but we didn't know how to talk about our feelings for each other. I was terrified that my words would ruin our friendship— instead, I wrecked it by holding them in.

I won't make that mistake again. I touch the smooth stone in my pocket, just to remind me of this new promise, too.

When we're past the creek, he slips his hand into the crook of my arm and starts to jog slowly. My body follows his without a thought because it remembers that Noah's safe. My feet fall into rhythm next to his as his fingers tighten on my arm—just enough to let me know that he's there, he's got me—and we quickly close the gap and catch up with the group.

A growing part of me, though, would like to be out here alone. Just the two of us. Catching up for real. Saying those things we should have said a long time ago. I want to know why he let me go so easily and why he never reached out again after Samantha left him. I want to tell him why I panicked and how sorry I am for shutting him out.

But how do I tell him that now, without dragging all of that hurt back to the surface? Talking to him here seems like a very bad idea—the worst, actually. Because that conversation could either help us mend this terrible break, or it could blow up like one of those mega black holes that the kids learned about this week. And those things are seriously brutal. Like, swallow the galaxy and rip a hole in space-time brutal.

I really don't want my talk with Noah to rip a hole in space-time.

But sometimes the scary move is the right one, that voice in my head whispers. And it's right, I know—but knowing it's the right move doesn't make it any easier.

When we finally make it to the parking area, the rain has slowed to a drizzle, the sun shining bright again. Soaked to the skin, I cross my arms over my chest, thankful that I wore a loose tee shirt and hoodie, but wishing I'd brought a rain jacket, too. When we unlock the vehicles, the kids all pile inside. They're laughing now, chattering as they climb over each other, taking the rain in stride. Tonight's game night, and they're already deciding who will team up at which game. Sophie opens the back of her van and starts passing out bottled water from a cooler, and even though I'm cold and drenched, I see why Noah does this every summer. For the first time in ages, I feel like I belong—and am a part of something that matters.

Noah rakes his hand through his wet hair, pushing it out of his eyes. Then he gives me a long look that I can't quite decipher, and I feel the heat of his hands on my hips again. His gaze drops to my lips for one brief moment, so fast that I wonder if I imagined it.

But I definitely didn't. When his eyes flick back to mine, they're back to that deep shade of green that will haunt me until the end of time. I'm pinned in place by this look that's heavy with longing, and I want so badly to pull him into my arms and kiss him until we're both breathless.

A squeal and a giggle erupt from somewhere behind us, and then the moment's gone.

"You two ready?" Sophie says, and my heart flutters in my chest like a bird. "Or you want to stay out here and get wetter?"

More chatter and laughter ripple over us. Noah smirks as he turns back to me and nods toward the cars. It's a look that says, *Come on, we're in this together,* and it's precisely the message I needed to see.

Chapter Twelve

NOAH

I'm still reeling from yesterday's hike. More specifically, from Victoria falling against me in a way that pressed every inch of her body against mine and filled my brain with a dozen thoughts that I definitely should not be having because *we are work colleagues*. I repeat that last part over and over in my mind, but it's no use. When her hands landed on my chest and she looked up at me through those fluttering lashes, it took every ounce of my self-control not to wrap her in my arms and kiss her senseless.

My brain has been oh-so-helpfully playing that moment on an endless loop—all through dinner yesterday, all through game night last night.

And all through my dreams until daybreak.

I was still thinking about her at breakfast when I accidentally poured orange juice into my coffee.

"Hey there," Sophie says, watching me as I sit down with my second attempt at coffee. "Your sister called again." She slips me a note that says, *Hannah says Need proof of life, please.*

"Thanks," I tell her.

"You doing okay there?" She raises a brow.

"Sure. Just had trouble sleeping."

"Your shirt's on inside-out," she says, sipping her tea.

When I glance down, I see the rough seams of the tee, the tag sticking out from the side. As I grumble into my coffee, Sophie smirks. Rarely has she seen me out of sorts. Today, I feel like I've been completely dismantled and then put back together—but missing a couple of pieces.

"Man, the owls were loud last night," she says, popping a strawberry into her mouth. "They kept waking me up, too. They're frisky this time of year."

"Right," I said. "The owls. Frisky."

The door behind us opens, and Victoria drifts in like a breeze, wearing hiking pants and a tank top, her hair pinned up in some kind of loose knot that's just begging to be let down. She smiles at us as she heads toward the breakfast bar, and my heart hammers against my ribs.

"I should call Hannah before our meeting," I tell Sophie. "I'll see you in a few."

I'm out the door before Victoria makes it to the table with her breakfast, hoping that if I move fast enough, I can outrun the memory of how right it had felt yesterday when she'd let me catch her and hold her close.

By the time I make it to the cell phone tree—the one spot on this campus where we get a clear signal—I'm almost thinking straight again. When I position myself just right under the fir's massive limbs, I call Hannah, and she answers on the third ring.

"Everything okay?" I ask her.

"It's about time, brother," she quips. "How's camp going? I thought when you didn't call me back that you'd been snatched up by a Bigfoot."

"It's way worse than that," I mutter, pacing under the tree.

She snort-laughs. "Did you finally get a little bunch of little wild things? It was only a matter of time before your run with all the sweet little geniuses ended. The odds can't always be in your favor."

"No kidding," I grumble, thinking the odds are never in my favor. For the first time ever, I'm unable to sleep here, but it's got nothing to do with the kids. Or the frisky owls. "But whatever. It's fine."

"What's wrong?" she says, and I can imagine her eyes narrowing the way they do when she smells trouble. "Something's awry."

"Awry? Are you Benoit Blanc now?"

"Your voice gets that cute little hiccup in it when you're lying. And when you're stressed."

"I'm not lying, and I'm not stressed." I cringe because I hear the little waver in my voice that says otherwise.

"Want to try that again?" she drawls. "Once more with feeling?"

"Okay, I might be a little stressed," I tell her.

"You've done this camp for a million years," she says. "It's like your paradise. What's so different this time?"

Pacing under the tree, I mumble, "Victoria's here."

There's a long pause, filled with the crackle of a cell signal that's bouncing along the mountain tops, all the way over to Hannah's neighborhood in Charleston.

"Wait," she says. "Victoria from college? The one that got away?" Her voice is getting higher in pitch, her words running together like they do when she's excited.

I bite my lip before I argue with *the one that got away* because we've had this conversation, and Hannah always wins no matter how much evidence I produce. So instead, I just say, "The same."

Hannah lets out a squeal that makes my ears ring as she

nears a pitch that only dogs can hear. A flock of crows burst from the limbs above me, squawking in alarm, and I hold the cell phone away from my ear and check to make sure I'm still alone out here in the clearing.

"Noah!" she yells. "What are the chances? That's amazing!"

"It's terrible," I say. "I can't focus on anything. I keep catching myself spacing out." I leave out the specifics, like how my brain goes straight to thinking of Victoria's perfect lips and long legs and contagious laugh because my sister doesn't need to know those details. "The kids are going to think I'm distracted," I grumble. "And I am!"

"Awwww," she says, and I can tell from that syrupy sound that she's clutching her hand over her chest like one of the *Bridgerton* ladies who's just spotted the new most eligible duke and is already picturing their happy-ever-after. Hannah insisted I watch all the episodes with her, so I know how these things work. Heart-eyes are contagious.

I also know that shutting down all my thoughts about Victoria is impossible. We're barely one week into the session, and I'm coming undone.

"You're in your very own second-chance romance!" Hannah cries, and we're back to making my ears ring. "I always liked her. I was so sad when things ended between you two."

"Hannah," I scoff. "It's not that. Not even close." But the words sound false even to my ears because this weird, tangled feeling in my chest feels a lot like hope.

Hope that we might try again.

She hums and says, "That's what they all say in act one." Then her voice drops an octave, and she says, "But you need to put your fence-mending pants on because you broke her heart."

"Hey, whose side are you on here?"

She huffs. "It was obvious to everyone—except you, for some

reason—that Victoria was completely in love with you. Big-time."

"It was?" I always knew she liked me—maybe loved me in the way that good friends do. But it wasn't until she kissed me on that beach that I ever let myself believe it could be more. But then she acted like it had been a mistake, and that was far easier to believe.

Hannah groans, and I can practically hear her eye roll. *"Noah,"* she drawls. "She went on trips with you. She gave you birthday presents. She came home with you to meet us for my birthday that year."

"We were best friends," I tell her. "That's what best friends do."

She sighs. "And then she finally got up the courage to kiss you, and you left the country with another girl."

I never should have told Hannah all of those details.

"You broke her heart, dummy," she says. "But now you get to fix it." I can hear her typing on a keyboard, which means she's at work. "So what's your big romantic gesture going to be?"

"Hannah," I plead. "I can't think about that right now. We're working together. I'm practically her supervisor."

"Oooooh," she says. "Forbidden love is the best."

"Stop. Go back to your dukes and duchesses. Forget I said anything."

"You can do it, my dude. I believe in you."

I smash my palm against my forehead. It was a mistake to mention Victoria, but it slipped out like a piece of gossip at the grocery store. Hannah makes it impossible to hide anything from her. Why she went into IT instead of espionage is beyond me.

"How is she even there?" Hannah says. "Is she one of the instructors?"

"No, she's on staff. Like me." I relay only the broad strokes that Vic's told me about wanting to try something new and taking this job on a whim. The rest I keep to myself because it's not my story to share.

My sister lets out a long whistle. "That's the universe working big-time. Think of all the pieces it had to move to get you two together on that mountain."

"Hannah," I groan.

"Noah," she groans back. "Why can't you accept this as the gift that is is?" She's always talking about harnessing the power of the universe and teaching it to conspire *for* me. All that woo seems to work great for her, but when it comes to me, I think the universe is holding a grudge.

"Because I feel like I'm having the world's longest panic attack?" Even as I say the words, my chest tightens, and my throat starts to close up. All week, I've been trying to keep it together and think of Victoria as just another co-worker. Like Sophie. Like every other person I've worked with at these camps.

But that's not working. Every time I see Vic, I'm pulled back to the time when we were so close that we told each other all of our secrets. When we spent every evening together, sharing our dreams and fears. When I thought nothing could ever tear us apart.

That closeness I felt with her? I've never felt it with anyone since.

And when she fell into my arms at the waterfall? When she sat in her pajamas in the dark and told me about her big fear of never being good enough? I wanted to fold her into my arms and never let her go.

"You should talk more," Hannah says. "I think you two still have a lot of things unsaid."

Understatement of the decade, I think. But what I tell her is,

"That feels wildly unprofessional." I pace under the tree, wishing there was an easy solution here that didn't involve digging up lots of hurt feelings. I mean, should we talk about what happened between us? Probably. Should we talk about it here, secluded in the woods where we have to continue to get along and not want to use each other for bear bait? Definitely not.

"Here's what I think," she says, and I can tell from her voice that she's shifted into problem-solving mode. "You need to rip this Band-Aid off and lay it all on the line. Tell her how you felt then, how you feel now, and stop waiting for the right time. Because, spoiler alert: there is no right time. There is now, and there is too late."

When I don't answer, she says, "Don't push her away, Noah. You have to break that habit."

"I don't push people away," I grumble.

"I love you, but it doesn't take a pro to see that you keep everyone at arm's length. You surround yourself with people who will only be around for a short while—like these kids at camp. I know they adore you, but you need deeper connections with people who can love you the way you deserve and have your back when you need it."

"I do have friends, you know." Kind of. Does trivia night with my fellow counselors count?

"You have co-workers and acquaintances," she argues, "and maybe one person who has a spare key to your house." She sighs, and her voice softens. "She's not Dad."

The words hit hard. I pace a little farther from the tree, halfway hoping to lose the phone signal. But I can still hear Hannah's voice clear as a bell. She's right, of course. She's always right.

"It's safe to let people get close to you," she says. "Not

everyone will leave. But when they do, it's because of them. Not you."

"This is not why I called you," I tell her, feeling like my baby sister has surgically removed my heart and is now studying all of its nooks and crannies for answers. She's all about studying data, but I'd prefer she wasn't scrutinizing mine.

"Some people will leave you," she says. "Some is not *all*."

"Have you seen him lately?" I ask her, desperate to shift her focus.

"We were supposed to have lunch last weekend, but as usual, he didn't show. Texted me the next day and said something came up." She sighs. "I just expect that will always be the case, and on the rare occasion that he does keep his word, I just consider that a pleasant surprise. Like winning a couple of bucks on a lottery ticket."

"I'm sorry," I tell her. She puts up a tough facade, but I know how much it still hurts to get ditched by our father because someone more interesting came along. Whether it's his co-worker's party or the new woman he's dating, it never gets any easier.

"Don't be," she says. "I keep leaving the door open for him. My decision, all the way. A small piece of me keeps hoping he might change, but he never does." She lets out another weary sigh. "But think about what I said, all right? Not everyone is as careless with our feelings as Dad."

"I know." And logically, I do know that every person on the planet can't be like him. But for all these years, I've felt like the only people I could depend on were Hannah and my mom.

And Victoria—until she pushed me away.

"I need to go," I tell her, feeling that knot forming in my chest again. "We have a planning meeting before lunch."

"Not everyone gets a second chance, Noah. And besides, what do you have to lose?"

"Okay, I love you. Talk to you later," I say, the words rushing out. "Bye."

She says something else that sounds like "This isn't over," as I end the call. My chest is filled with butterflies, and my head's buzzing with a hundred different thoughts. But one question Hannah asked that struck me hardest is the one with the most terrifying answer.

What do you have to lose?

Nothing, I think. *Or maybe everything.*

Chapter Thirteen

"At least we have showers," Sophie says. "This is way better than some of the other campgrounds we've used."

The campground that Noah reserved for us is in a state park just a fifteen-minute drive from the institute. Surrounded by dense woods, it feels secluded even though it's just a mile off the main highway. The kids are already paired off and choosing the spots where they want to pitch their tents before we head out on this afternoon's short hike. So far, this exercise feels like a logic problem from grade school: if your group has eighteen kids, three adults, and twelve campsites, how long will it take to set up a tent before a hungry bear comes looking for a snack?

Noah keeps telling me that black bears won't eat me, but I still have my doubts. They have pointy teeth, after all, and those aren't made for scarfing down blueberries.

According to Sophie, this outing is one of the kids' most anticipated traditions. The institute provides tents and camping supplies, and the kids bring their own sleeping bags. Our plan is simple: first, we set up camp, then we go on a short hike through the afternoon. Then it's dinner and a little free time, and at dusk, the instructors will meet us to do an evening stargazing program. Tomorrow, we break down camp, do a half-day canoe trip, and then get back to the institute before dinner time. Sophie makes it all sound so easy—if I follow her lead, I'll be fine.

Probably.

Noah's making the rounds with his campground map and a clipboard as the kids choose their sites. He's already marked off three sites on the perimeter for the adults—Noah, Sophie, and I will each have a tent to ourselves and will be positioned in a triangle around the kids so we can monitor them. Everything with Noah feels like a tactical formation.

When everyone has chosen, Noah and Sophie demonstrate how to set up a tent. A few of the kids have done this before, but those who haven't are watching with rapt attention, like they're going to be tested on this later. I've never set up a tent in my life since my idea of camping is staying in a two-star motel with no complimentary breakfast.

You can do this, I tell myself. *Camping is fun. Let yourself have fun.*

I watch carefully as Sophie and Noah extend the poles from Sophie's dome-style tent and snap them into place. *Easy-peasy, kids!* While they slip the poles through the fabric and stake them into the ground, I try to focus on the sequence of steps and not on the delicious way that Noah's forearms flex as he snaps those poles together.

Once Sophie hammers the last stake into place, they declare it done and slap a high-five in true camp spirit that earns a cheer from the kiddos. Noah flashes his megawatt smile, and when his gaze rests on mine, it sends an electric current straight through my belly and down to my wobbly, traitorous knees.

Ugh. *Get it together,* I scold myself. But I can't help it because Outdoor Survivalist Noah is even hotter than Protective Noah.

The kids scatter to set up their tents, and soon the air is filled with shouts and laughter. Sophie goes around to help troubleshoot while I head back to my campsite and try to hold Noah's demo in my brain. If the kids can do it, I can do it. This part, mercifully, is not rocket science.

Twenty minutes later, I'm surrounded by bits of fabric and thin metal poles, and clearly I'd have a better shot at completing a complex equation that describes the behavior of black holes than assembling this tent. None of the pieces connect the way they should, and what I've managed to piece together looks like an elaborate modern hat someone would wear to the Kentucky Derby.

Meanwhile, the kids closest to me are hammering their tent stakes and tying on rain flaps like they were born in the wilderness. Never have I felt so inadequate. Layla waves to me when she catches me studying their moves, and I give her a big thumbs up and shout, "Nicely done!"

Turning back to my tent, I yank a corner of the fabric into position and it pops free and smacks me in the face.

Noah and Sophie had his tent together in under ten minutes. Why is this so difficult to wrap my head around? I can stage houses so even the most outdated ones look inviting. I can negotiate prices with investors, juggle contractors, and make the most demanding clients happy. I did the demolition in the house I shared with Theo myself, knocking down walls with nothing but a sledgehammer and low-level rage, for Pete's sake. But now this crummy one-person tent is going to be my undoing.

I ball my hoodie up and shove it over my face, letting out a muffled scream.

"Hey there," Noah says, because of course he's suddenly right by my side when I'm about to fall apart at the seams.

"Need a hand?" As he surveys the debris field that is my campsite, he has the audacity to look amused.

My shoulders slump. I was finally starting to feel like I fit in here and was getting the hang of this whole wild, wonderful outdoorsy thing, but this tent is throwing my high hopes in my face. It's telling me that I don't belong here on the mountain—not hiking, canoeing, or sleeping in a tent.

But this is where I am, and the only way out is through.

"I really wanted to get this one thing on my own," I tell him. "You made it look easy."

"It's not always," he says. "For starters, though, I'd suggest setting up a little farther away from that poison oak."

I stare at the plant where he's pointing and sigh.

"It's okay to ask for help, you know." He shoves his hands into the pockets of his hiking pants—which naturally fit him like a glove—and lifts a brow. "I promise you won't burst into flames if you do."

"If you're wrong about that, I'll start a wildfire." I know he's teasing, but he's right. "In the Griffin house, asking for help meant you were weak," I explain. My parents were experts at making demands—but for them, asking meant being needy. I didn't want to be weak, but didn't want to be a demanding jerk either. It was easier to just do everything myself—because that way, the only person who could fail me was *me*.

He steps closer, so we're toe-to-toe, and brushes a lock of hair from my cheek. "Victoria, in a million years, I'd never describe you as weak. You're one of the strongest people I know."

I swallow hard, leaning into his touch.

"You don't have to be amazing at everything," he says. "You're plenty amazing, just as you are."

My heart flutters against my ribs and I blink back tears. No one's told me that before. Not ever. And I never realized how much it would mean to hear those words.

A peal of laughter erupts from somewhere behind us, breaking the spell. Flashing me a tiny smile, Noah picks up a couple of poles and snaps them together, then motions for me to grab the biggest piece of fabric.

"To be fair," he says, "these older models are extra tricky."

"You don't have to say that. I know I'm woefully out of my element."

He smirks. "Isn't that part of the idea of summer camp?"

"For the kids, sure."

Those tiny creases reappear at the corners of his eyes. He slips the rod through the loops in the fabric, wiggling it through a stubborn part as he guides the pieces together. And just like that, this lump of nylon and aluminum is starting to take shape. "You want to get the other side?" he says.

I repeat his movements on the other side of the frame, careful not to pinch my fingers as I wrestle the pole into place. He holds it steady, and then hands me the rubber mallet that we use to pound the stakes into the ground.

Next, I let him help me tie on the rain flap, even though I remember how to do this part. It's not supposed to rain tonight, but this is classic Noah—always prepared for anything.

"You're all set," he says. "Achievement unlocked."

"I might have to curl up like a cat to fit inside that thing." Somehow it looks smaller now that it's put together properly. "How is it possible to fit two people in one of these without being twisted up like pretzels?"

His brow lifts as a bit of pink creeps into his cheeks, and now I'm thinking of being tangled up with him and feeling all those chiseled muscles pressing against mine. This is bad. Very bad.

A whistle splits the air, and Sophie yells, "Gather 'round, campers!"

Noah turns to where the kids are gathering, but before he heads toward them, he flashes his deadly smirk and says, "Two people fit just fine."

THE TRAIL IS WELL-MAINTAINED, wide enough to walk two abreast. Birds chatter in the evergreens that tower above us. The rhododendron and laurel are heavy with blooms, their broad leaves dappling us in shade. Noah's in the lead again, but this time I'm in the middle of the group, with Sophie at the back. Layla and Priya are on either side of me, telling me all about the research project they're working on this week. Talking about it lights them up and makes me wonder: when's the last time my work made me feel excited to dive in? When's the last time I felt passion for what I was doing?

I was great at my job in real estate—it was a kind of problem-solving that comes naturally to me, and it was satisfying to help people find their dream homes. But did it light me up? No. Did it make me excited to get out of bed each morning? Not really. It made me feel like I was successful, though, like I'd found something I was good at and could make a living with. After ending things with Theo, I realized I'd been telling myself that I was happy—that I *should be* happy—because I had a good job, could save money, had made my parents proud.

But I wasn't proud of myself. I was afraid to think too hard about what it meant if I stopped doing the work that made my parents proud of me. Who was I if not the scrappy real estate agent, the successful daughter with the solid ten-year plan and the healthy 401(k)? Who was I, if I wasn't chasing down my next big milestone?

Deep down, I'd felt like an imposter for a long time. After college, I'd run back home from Charleston and taken the path my mother wanted me to take. I'd kept telling myself *Fake it till you make it*, but that just left me feeling…well, fake.

I've been operating on autopilot for so long that I lost track of what I want most. It's buried deep somewhere in a corner of my heart, under the crushing weight of everyone's expectations. But being here is showing me how I might be able to lift that weight.

"You have to come visit me in Atlanta," Layla says to Priya. Ever since she found out that Priya's aunt and uncle live in her hometown, the two have been cooking up plans to see each other after camp.

"My parents have scheduled my whole summer," Priya tells her. "After this, it's soccer camp. Then it's engineering camp, and then violin camp. My mom says it's important to be well-rounded." She rolls her eyes. "Even though I don't like sports and I'm tone-deaf."

"Yikes," Layla says. "The only other one I go to is theater camp. But my parents are sending me to Japan for two weeks in August to visit my grandparents."

"I'd love to do theater camp," Priya says. "But my mom would never let me."

"I'll sneak you in," Layla says. "Just skip soccer camp and come stay with me."

"My mom would kill me," Priya says. "For real."

"She's on another continent!" Layla says. "She never has to know."

"My parents are in Italy for the summer," Priya tells me, a sad note in her voice.

"Well, I'm really glad you're here with us," I tell her, and she gives me a genuine smile that makes me wonder how often she hears those words.

"And we're really glad you're here," Layla tells me.

"Yeah," Priya echoes. She plucks a small white flower from the trail and sticks it behind her ear.

"Why's that?" I ask.

Layla shrugs. "You make it seem like you don't have to be good at everything to still be amazing."

I'm stunned speechless. Here I thought these kids would be cataloguing my failures, thinking my being here was some colossal joke. I've been so fixated on what I'm doing wrong that I hadn't imagined what I could be doing right.

Maybe I've been doing that even longer than I can remember.

They've moved on to telling me a story about Derrick getting poison ivy in an unfortunate location when we come to a set of steps leading up. Just like the other trail, these are made from weathered railroad ties and look like they've been here for a hundred years. My thighs are burning by the time we reach the top, where there's a small clearing in the laurels. I pause to catch my breath, taking in the panoramic view from the top of the ridge. It's gorgeous up here, with the deep greens of the trees in the gorge below and the bright blue sky above. Noah's standing with the kids from the front of the group, gathered on a wooden platform. Priya and Layla gasp and hurry toward it, chattering with delight. I'm still trying to catch my breath when Sophie comes up behind me with the last few kids. They all scramble down to where Noah stands and Sophie gives my shoulder a nudge.

"This is the best part," she says. "Get ready to have your mind blown."

I follow her to where Noah's gathered the kids, wondering what on earth is about to happen on that platform.

Then I see what has everyone so captivated.

I've been to the Smokies before, and I've seen some stunning panoramic views of the mountains. But this takes my breath away. To our left, the mountains undulate like waves, shades of blue and green that seem unearthly. There's a scattering of puffy white clouds, and the sky feels impossibly wide. I turn slowly, taking in the endless bursts of white and pink from the laurels, and when my gaze rests on Noah, he's grinning like he's just discovered that these mountains exist.

But then he steps to the side and my chest tightens with panic. My heart falls straight down to my toes and I squeeze my eyes shut, hoping that my brain is playing tricks on me.

But it's not.

Because just beyond Noah and the platform is a narrow bridge that looks like it's made from fishing line and two-by-fours. Beneath it is a gorge that looks ten miles deep.

Noah's going over the rules—no jumping on the bridge, no horseplay—and I'm considering scribbling my last will and testament on a napkin in my backpack.

"Is this an in-and-out trail?" I ask Sophie.

She smiles. "Nah, it's a loop. We only get to cross once, so take all your photos now."

I swallow hard. There goes my idea of waiting here for them to circle back.

"This used to be a swinging bridge," Sophie tells the kids, stepping off the platform. "But now it's updated with reinforced cables and wood beams."

That sparks a dozen questions from them because they're fascinated. A tiny bridge strung from one mountaintop to another? They're here for it. Sophie and Noah are tag-teaming this moment, their excitement contagious as they go on and on about how we're a hundred and twenty feet from the ground, on a bridge first built eighty years ago that took two years to complete. The kids are soaking this knowledge up like little sponges, but I don't want to hear any more about engineering today. Yes, this is a construction marvel, but my brain keeps picturing that bridge in *Romancing the Stone*, the one made from vines and scrap boards so narrow that Kathleen Turner couldn't even get her whole tiny foot on them, and my heart is pounding so hard it hurts.

Sophie leads the way, and the kids start crossing with her, and how on earth does this bridge not snap like a pencil under their weight? I'm shuffled closer to Noah by all the eager moving bodies, and pretty soon, there are just five kids standing between me and Noah, and my untimely exit from this mortal plane.

Priya looks over to her right, where I can see straight down to the river below. Next to her, Derrick yanks his lucky hat from his head and shoves it into his back pocket. Priya's eyes widen and Noah tells her, "Don't worry. It's perfectly safe."

I have serious doubts about that, but I can see from this angle that the bridge is not made of vines and scrap board. It's built from cables as thick as my forearm and massive wooden beams with steel bolts big enough to hold a ship together.

Layla grins at Priya as she takes her hand and says, "It's okay. We'll help each other."

Noah smiles at them and says, "Y'all got this," and something inside me melts at the way he so easily offers this gentle encouragement.

The girls peek over the chest-high rail, and then Priya's shoulders relax and they take a few more steps.

"You good?" Noah asks me.

I nod, but my feet have rooted to the earth. My heart is at a full gallop now and I want to curl into a ball.

He arches a brow like he can see right through me, straight to my shivering heart, but he doesn't push. I want to do this on my own, without his help. Because I'm a grown woman, and I should be able to cross a bridge, even if it's a mile above the safe, solid ground. It's just a matter of putting one foot in front of the other—a fact that my brain logically knows, but my body refuses to believe.

Probably, this is an apt metaphor for several parts of my life.

I swallow hard, because I don't want the kids to see me standing here terrified, freezing like a rabbit. Fear is contagious, and I don't want to ruin this moment for them when they're being so brave and full of wonder.

"Go ahead," I tell Noah. "I'll come over last." This is our protocol, after all. One adult comes after all the kids, making sure no one feels rushed or left behind. On the other side of the gorge, the first kids over wave and shout. A few are still crossing, some lingering to peek down and soak in the view.

Was I ever that fearless? When did I stop believing that I could do anything I could dream?

Taking another deep breath, I feel my chest expand the slightest bit. The last two kids start across, and now I'm alone on this side of the gorge.

Noah's standing near the middle of the bridge, no doubt waiting there just in case any of the kids get nervous. So far, none of them are. It's just me whose knees have turned to Jell-O. When all the kids have crossed to the other side, I realize that he's hanging back because of me. So I take one step onto the bridge, and then one more. He looks at me and smiles—a real one, like the one that tugged at my heart on the night we met— and it feels like this will be okay.

Still gripping the rail, I focus on Noah's warm gaze, the relaxed line of his shoulders, his lips as he mouths the words, *You've got this.*

And then I make the horrible mistake of looking down. Below us, a river winds through the trees like a thread. My heart hammers against my ribs and I sink down, stopping before I'm on my knees.

"Whoa," Noah says. His voice is gentle, quiet. "You're okay."

My hands grip the rail so tightly that my knuckles are white. When I look back at Noah, he's taking slow steps toward me. His lips are moving, but my ears are ringing so loud that I can't hear his words. Each time he takes a step, I feel the vibrations ripple through the bridge, into my hands and feet.

This is a fear I didn't know I had. It doesn't make sense, because I've stopped at scenic overlooks. I've stared off the side of a mountain, and I've driven across bridges over inlets that stretch to the horizon. This shouldn't be that big of a deal.

But my pounding heart tells me that it is.

"Hey," Noah says. He's only about ten feet away now, but he seems to understand that the footsteps and the vibrations are making this so much worse. "It's okay," he tells me, keeping his voice calm and quiet. "I promise you're safe, and I'll help you."

I nod, though I don't agree. None of this feels okay.

"You want to hear some fun facts about this bridge?" he asks, his tone light.

I snort. "Not really, Valentine."

He bites back a smile, no doubt thinking that having me irritated at him is better than being terrified. "It has a weight limit of four tons. It can hold at least thirty people safely, and it was reinforced with more steel cables about ten years ago. You could ride a buffalo over this thing."

"Super," I wheeze. My brain helpfully supplies me with an image of this bridge snapping in half and I'm sinking to my knees again.

"The distance across is shorter than the distance from your

cabin to the dining hall," he says. I know he's trying to help, but I heard Sophie when she told the kids it was just over a hundred feet across. Right now, it might as well be a mile.

I look past him to where all the kids are now staring, and a wave of embarrassment nearly knocks the wind from my lungs. Why can't I just put one foot in front of the other the way that they all did?

"Vic," he says quietly. "Do you want me to come over to you?"

I shake my head, biting my lip.

"What can I do?" he asks. "What do you need?"

Again, I shake my head, because I honestly don't know. Lately, everything feels off. I can't get a handle on what I want anymore. I don't trust myself to know what I need. My skin feels too tight and my brain feels scrambled, and now my whole body feels like concrete.

"You got this, Victoria!" Priya yells. Next to her, Layla gives a loud whistle and throws her hands in the air.

"You can do it!" another kid yells. And then another. And then all the kids are chanting my name, shouting out encouragements, and something in my chest loosens.

I've never felt so many people rooting for me in all of my life. Sophie, Noah, these kids who barely know me and don't want a single thing from me—except to have me join them on the other side.

My heart feels like it cracks wide open, and I take another step toward Noah. He smiles—that secret smile that's only for me—and I take another step.

Behind him, the kids keep cheering and calling my name, and Sophie's clapping right along with them.

"That's it, Vic," Noah says, his voice still low and steady. "You got this. Just a few more steps."

I inch toward him, but it still feels like I'm trying to wade through cement. I take a couple more steps and my foot catches on something. When I look down to check, I see the gorge down below, and seeing the sheer amount of air between me and the ground makes my gut churn.

"Hey," Noah says. "Look at me. Don't look down."

I close my eyes, gripping the rail. Every muscle in my body has gone rigid and moving my feet again feels like an impossible task. I want to tell him this, but before I can even put the words together, I feel the bridge vibrating again under my feet. I squeeze my eyes shut tighter, wishing I could make all of this go away, and then I feel a hand wrap over mine.

When I open my eyes, Layla's standing in front of me. She's somehow pried my hand from the rail and is holding it in hers.

"Holding hands helped me," she says, and my heart somehow finds a way to crack open even more. She gives me a firm nod and squeezes my hand, and there's no way I'm staying rooted here now.

Across the gorge, the other kids are still shouting their encouragement and Layla smiles. "It's scary for a minute, but then totally worth it, right?" she says, and my chest loosens. I take one step, and then another, and Layla starts telling me about her project again. Using some kind of complex equation they learned to figure out if we have another planet in the solar system, hiding in plain sight. I understand about a third of what she's saying, but it has me thinking about rogue planets instead of hundred-foot drops, and pretty soon we're past the halfway point and Noah has started walking backward, keeping his eyes steady on mine.

My legs move more easily, and by the time we get within a few feet of the other side, I have one hand on the side rail and am almost walking fully upright again. The kids' shouts are louder now, and as soon as Layla leads me off the bridge and onto the platform, they all erupt in cheers.

Sophie pulls me into a hug. "I'm so sorry," she whispers. "I had no idea."

"It's okay," I tell her. "Honestly, neither did I."

Noah claps his big hand on my shoulder and says, "Knew you could do it, Vic."

I nod as he squeezes my shoulder, and before I realize what's happening, I've wrapped my arms around him in a bear hug. My cheek's pressed against his chest, and the thumping of his heart is as soothing rain on a rooftop. His body relaxes as his big arm tightens around me, and what's left of this wall between us crumbles into dust.

Chapter Fourteen

NOAH

After dinner, we're all gathered around the campfire to make s'mores and I'm still kicking myself. If I'd known Vic was so afraid of heights, I would have planned a different hike. Six summers, and it has never occurred to me to ask the incoming campers if they have any phobias that I should take into account when planning activities. Clearly, Roxy and I should update the *Get to Know Us!* questionnaire that goes out to every kid—and to everyone hired as staff.

Victoria would have known to ask. Just like she figured out that not every kid wanted to play *sporty-sports*. She always sees much deeper beneath the surface.

Across from me, Victoria's practically glowing. Her hair's soft from the humidity and there's a streak of dirt on her cheek, a few scratches on her arms from the shrubs. Her broken-in boots are scuffed and muddy, and when she smiles, she shines brighter than the firelight.

My plan today was to bring the kids on a hike and show them a place filled with wonder; to roast marshmallows over the campfire and tell creepy stories. Are we doing those things? Yes.

But the entire time I've been thinking of Victoria. Her playful smile, her long, lean legs, the bright blond curls that keep coming loose from that messy bun and falling along the lovely curve where her neck meets her shoulder. All I want to do is take her hair down from that bun just so I can see the way the light catches it as the sky turns golden and the sun dips below the ridge.

The incident on the bridge hit me like a sucker punch. When she fell into my arms and let me hold her until her heart stopped racing, everything clicked into place. She was afraid on that bridge, and she trusted me to help. And for that moment, with her arms squeezing me tight, she didn't care that everyone was watching us. I wanted to cheer and throw my fist into the sky.

I also wanted to fold her in my arms and kiss her until she forgot all about that stupid gorge and the eighty-foot drop.

But I couldn't do any of those things because the kids were all watching and there's no way on this earth that I could make any of those actions look like they came only from friendship and run-of-the-mill camp camaraderie.

And that's all we can have here: friendship and camp camaraderie.

My brain knows this, but my body doesn't like that plan one bit. It wants to be as close to her as it can get, preferably with limbs tangled and her full bottom lip caught in my teeth, her breath catching in her throat as she says my name like a prayer.

And I know she feels the same.

Two weeks. In two weeks, we can have more.

I repeat those words over and over as I watch her sitting with the kids, giving tutorials on the proper ratio of chocolate to marshmallows in the perfect s'more, and how the secret ingredient of crunchy peanut butter makes them out of this world.

But what's really out of this world is the way that she ended up here, falling into my lap like the greatest gift I never could have predicted. She's radiant in the light from the campfire, a big smile plastered on her face, her eyes crinkling at the corners with genuine delight. She says she feels out of her element here, but it sure doesn't look that way to me. She looks like she belongs here—with all the other parts of the forest that are wild and spellbinding.

Next to me, Ethan says, "Don't you think so, Noah?" and it takes me a full three seconds to realize he's talking to me because I'm watching Victoria lick chocolate from her finger and when her big blue eyes meet mine, I think my heart might implode with the next flash of her tongue.

"What was that?" I ask him.

He gives me an epic eye roll and says, "Never mind."

"Okay, everybody," Sophie says, standing. "Do your last-minute pit stops and whatnot and meet me back here in ten so we can walk over to the amphitheater together. Dr. Sanjay and Dr. Cassie have a cool program for you."

The kids scatter like marbles, some headed to the restrooms and some going back to their tents. That leaves me, Sophie, and Victoria to clean up after s'mores and dump some water on the campfire. Victoria yawns and Sophie says, "You going to make it, champ?"

"You bet," Vic says. "Meteor shower, here we come."

Her enthusiasm is adorable, but her eyelids are heavy. She looks like she could fall asleep right now and when her lips pull into a sweet smile, I feel completely undone.

When the kids get back, we all walk over across the campground to the amphitheater. It's a big circle carved out of the mountain, steps and benches made entirely from stone. There's a fire pit in the middle, but we won't be using that tonight. Dr. Sanjay and Dr. Cassie are already here with their telescopes set up at the center of the ring. They tell the kids to sit in the first couple of rows, so Victoria, Sophie, and I sit in the back where we can still hear the presentation but don't have to pay rapt attention.

This is one of those camps I would have adored when I was a kid. I loved science—anything to do with digging in the dirt or looking at the stars. But I was terrible at studying and memorizing facts and details. It was so loud inside my brain that all the names and formulas got lost in the noise—but put me outside with hands-on work, and I was golden.

College was like that, too. Writing papers was easy, but memorizing facts for tests was a killer. Victoria had endless patience with me, helping me devise better ways to study. She had a solution for every problem back then.

Well. Every problem but one.

It's nine-thirty and the sky is already as dark as the bottom of a well. Up here, we're five miles from the nearest town, nestled on one of the lower ridges. It's a prime location for stargazing because the higher ridges around us block almost all the light from the nearby towns, and once Dr. Cassie turns off the lights along the walkway and steps, we're in total darkness.

Once my eyes adjust, I can make out the shape of the Milky Way glittering above us, a ribbon of stars across the velvet black of the sky.

"Wow," Victoria whispers. "This is amazing." The wonder in her voice tugs at something in my chest. Next to me, she sits with her long legs outstretched, hands planted just behind her hips.

"I used to love coming here as a kid," I tell her. "This part of the mountains was one of Dad's favorite camping spots."

She turns to look at me and whispers, "Oh, Noah." I don't

have to look at her to know she's giving me a sad smile, the kind where one side of her mouth just barely tilts upward. "When's the last time you saw him?"

"A couple of summers ago. He's divorced again, and seeing someone new I think. He calls me out of the blue sometimes, asking to meet up, but it always falls through. A few months ago we were supposed to have lunch, but he never showed. Called me three days later and said his friend had invited him on some big-deal fishing trip and we could try again soon." I snort, combing my fingers through the grass. "I sat in that tiny restaurant all afternoon, thinking he'd blow in eventually, with some wild story that would explain his delay. I haven't heard from him since."

"I'm sorry," she says. "You deserve better than that."

I shrug. "Every time he calls, I tell myself not to get my hopes up. We make plans, and he's all in until his friend invites him to a fancy party, or some work colleague gets tickets on the fifty-yard line." I've lost count of how many times he's flaked out on me. "I'm used to it," I tell her. "I'm the guy people stay with until someone better comes along, remember?"

"Noah," she says, her voice low. "That's one hundred percent false."

"It's a pattern," I explain. "Since as long as I can remember, all the way back to second grade, when Sally Ann Burton asked me to be her boyfriend and then dumped me the second Trevor Elliot kissed her on the playground." That familiar ache is back in my chest, as persistent as a ticking clock. "Friends in high school. Every woman I dated for more than a month. Pretty soon it was everyone."

Her hand finds mine in the darkness, and that tiny gesture is enough to make my pulse kick up again. Her thumb slides against my inner wrist and I'm certain she can feel it, too.

"After that I just expected everyone to leave eventually," I tell her. "It was easier to keep people at a safe distance and not get too close." And then Victoria came along, and it was easy to be close to her. I was in love with her before I knew what hit me, but I was terrified that she'd leave me, too. I told myself that I kept my feelings secret because I didn't want to ruin our friendship—but really, I was just trying to protect myself so I wouldn't be shattered when she left me.

"Well obviously this Sally kid made a fatal error," she says. "I'm sure second-grade Noah was a catch, too." She gives me a good-natured smile, her foot bumping against mine. "Because you are, Noah. You're the most genuinely good person I've ever known."

I lean back, staring up at the stars twinkling above us. Dr. Cassie's down at the center of the amphitheater, still talking about a comet that's headed our way this fall, and how it's supposed to be the brightest one in three decades.

"For the record," Victoria says, her voice a whisper, "I made a fatal error, too." She squeezes my hand, and the heat from her touch zips down to my toes. "I didn't want things to end between us," she says. "I never wanted to leave you."

I clench the fingers of my other hand in the grass, wishing I could pull her close, whisper into her ear all these truths that I've been hiding from her for so long.

"I panicked," she says. "I didn't want you to take that trip with Samantha. I wanted you to choose me, but you chose her instead. And it just hurt too much to be near you, knowing that you didn't want me the way I wanted you."

"Vic," I whisper, squeezing her hand. "I always wanted you."

Her eyes widen in the dim light. "Then why didn't you tell me?"

An ache tugs deep in my chest. "I didn't dare let myself think you might feel the same. Because I couldn't stand to watch you leave me, too—when someone better came along."

She blinks at me, lips parted like she's trying to find the right words. Applause erupts around us, and I realize that the program's over. Vic's gaze flicks to the kids, who are already jumping to their feet, and then she gives me a look that makes those tight coils around my heart loosen.

It's a look that says, *We're not done here.*

Chapter Fifteen

VICTORIA

oah Valentine has scrambled my brain. I'm supposed to be focused on these kids and making sure they have three weeks of amazing summer camp that they'll never forget. I'm supposed to be making sure they're safely shuttled from location to another, that their skinned knees are bandaged and their food allergies aren't forgotten, and all I can think about is Noah: his devastating smile, his eyebrows that are so emotive it hurts, and the tender way he looks at me.

I always wanted you, he said.

I never saw it back in college, and now I know why: because I didn't think it could be true. I'd been trained to see my flaws front and center, and assumed everyone else saw them, too.

It's long past midnight, and the kids are finally asleep. It's been raining steadily since Sophie and I made the last round an hour ago, when the last of the kids' flashlights had snapped off. Satisfied that everyone was in for the night, Sophie went back to her tent and I went back to mine. And I haven't been able to stop my racing thoughts since.

After all the activity today, including my panic attack on the bridge, I should be sleeping like a brick. But the moment my eyes closed, all thoughts went to Noah: the soothing rumble of his voice on the bridge, the warmth of his embrace, the deep green of his eyes as they searched mine.

And then, what he confessed under the stars.

The rain's heavier now, and my tent is leaking like a sieve. Every few seconds, a raindrop splatters on my cheek, and now I'm aware of every drop that's falling inside. My sleeping bag's covered in a thin sheen of water, my pillow damp. By morning, everything in this tent will be soaked, including me.

Awesome.

My phone reads 1:37 am. My body's exhausted, but my brain won't let go of these thoughts of Noah Valentine. When I close my eyes and count backward from a hundred, I don't even make it to eighty before I'm thinking about him again—how he clutched my hand in the grass by the amphitheater but it felt like he was holding every part of me. The way he whispered in my ear and I could feel it deep in my chest, down to my toes.

How he smiled so sadly when he told me about camping with his dad, and how he lit up when he told me why this camp was so important to him. How his breath hitched when I slid my hand over his, and how he laced his fingers in mine as if we were holding a secret together.

A raindrop splatters onto my face. And then another. And another. It's like Mother Nature herself is trying to wash those thoughts of him away, but it's not working.

No earthly force can wipe Noah from my mind.

My options are few: I can lie here all night, praying I don't wake up with a cold, or I can go sleep in the Tahoe. I might wake up feeling like a pretzel, but at least I'll be warm and dry.

Another fat raindrop splatters on my cheek.

Grumbling, I wriggle out of my sleeping bag and unzip the

door of the tent. I grab my rain jacket and shove on my hiking boots, and as I tie them I think of Noah holding my foot against his thigh that night in the shoe store. On my first day here he wanted to make sure I had what I needed.

Because it was so obvious I was not prepared for this trip.

And not prepared to see him again.

It must have been so awkward for him, too. But his first move was to take care of me.

The rain blows directly into my tent as I scramble to get out of it. Flashlight in hand, I walk softly around the back side, away from where the kids are sleeping. I pause long enough to make sure no one else is awake and outside their tent, and then head towards the small paved lot where the vehicles are parked. It's maybe fifty yards from where the tents are, so not too far from the kids.

Once inside the Tahoe's passenger seat, I proceed to enact a modern retelling of *The Princess and the Pea* and try each seat in every position I can think of: semi-reclined in the front, slumped against the window like a sack of flour, curled up knees-to-chin on the back seat. Finally I settle for lying on my back with my knees up and feet flat, like I often lie on my sofa at home.

But this Tahoe is no sofa. The seats are hard and a seat belt buckle is poking into my hip. Rain's pelting the roof and I'm still fixated on Noah and that jolt of electricity that shot up my arm when he squeezed my hand in the dark.

With each deep breath, I try to push him out of my mind. Stop thinking about the way things ended, the sorrow that I felt when he told me about Samantha, and the hurt that came when I realized he'd slipped away.

All of that old hurt has come rushing back—but also that feeling of missing him that had burrowed deep down between my ribs and hidden for so long that I thought I didn't feel it anymore.

But I do feel it. Now more than ever.

This isn't the place to have an explosion of complicated feelings though, because we still have a week to go here. These kids need the best camp ever—not two adults making things weird and cooking up a tension that no one can name but everyone feels.

I spent my entire childhood that way, and it's no fun. My parents operated as if difficult feelings would just vanish if you pretended they didn't exist.

Spoiler alert: they don't.

I don't want to ignore all these feelings I have for Noah anymore, but I have to be a professional here. I have to do my job well and give these kids my all.

Thunder rumbles overhead, and a chill hits me so hard my teeth clack. I climb out of the car again to search the cargo area for something warmer than my fleece. Light floods the parking lot when I open the lift gate, but I see what I need. Noah, planning ahead, stashed extra blankets, water, and snacks in the back compartment of each vehicle.

Just in case, he'd said.

"Thank you, Noah," I mumble as I unearth the two wool blankets. "Bless you and your over-preparedness." I might feel like I'm sleeping on a rock, but at least I'll be warm. I grab a bottle of water and close the gate, then fold myself into the back seat again. I've just managed to burrow under the blankets and get myself somewhat cozy when a tap on the window makes me nearly jump out of my skin.

Noah's standing outside the car window, his hand held up in a wave.

When I open the door, he says, "Hey, is everything okay?"

"Sure," I say, as if finding me this way isn't one bit unusual.

His brow lifts in that way that says he doesn't believe me for a minute. He climbs inside, and for a moment, he's illuminated by the light inside the car. He's wearing his plaid flannel pants and his rain jacket, a thin tee shirt underneath. Rain drips from the ends of his hair, the tips of his eyelashes.

"You want to try that again?" he asks.

"Okay, fine," I say. "My tent's leaking. I couldn't sleep."

He frowns. "You won't be able to move tomorrow if you sleep in here."

"I'll be okay," I insist, though he's not wrong.

"Vic," he says, his voice gravelly. "Tomorrow's going to be a long day. You'll be miserable."

No, I think. Miserable is losing someone like him because you're a big fat chicken.

"I'll manage." My shrug feels more like a shiver.

"This is silly," he says. "We'll switch tents."

"My tent has a pond in it by now. So unless you brought a snorkel with you, that option's out."

He lifts a brow. "Then sleep in my tent. There's plenty of room."

"Omigod. No." The thought of sleeping next to Noah is too much. Squeezed against all of that hard muscle with only a little flannel between us? My heart might actually explode.

"What are you so afraid of?" he says, his voice low.

"What if someone saw us?" I say, my voice trailing off. "Sophie or one of the kids—" I shake my head because this is dangerous territory. He knows as well as I do that anyone who saw us sharing a tent would immediately think we were breaking the number one rule.

And they might not be wrong.

We'd both be fired. His camp days would be over. And I could kiss any future job with the program goodbye.

"Is that all?" he asks.

He says *all* like it doesn't mean *everything*.

I bite my lip, wishing my heart wasn't thundering in my chest again. Thankfully, the interior light has clicked off, so he can't see the heat rising in my cheeks.

"Look," he says. His voice sounds so close to my ear, but I know he's still on the other side of the car, his hand resting by the door handle. "You need sleep. I have a warm, dry tent. I'm your colleague right now, offering you a safe place to spend the night. That's all."

Of course, he makes it sound like the logical solution. Still, I can't help but fear the worst.

"What happens if someone sees us?" I ask.

He shrugs. "We tell them the truth. That you got a D-minus in tent set-up and I took pity on you and saved you from drowning."

I smack him on the shoulder, and he snorts.

"Let me worry about that," he says. "Part of my job is to take care of my staff, okay? So let me take care of you."

His words fall like warm hands on my shoulders. When was the last time I let someone truly take care of me? Even if it was just offering a soft place to land?

"Okay," I say. "But you have to wake me before it's light out."

"Well, obviously. If we sleep in, we miss Sophie's ranger coffee and campfire donuts."

"I'm serious, Valentine."

"So am I. Those donuts are to die for." He gives me a playful smirk as he opens the door, and I follow him out into the night, trying to quiet that voice in my head that's screaming *This is the worst idea in the history of bad ideas!*

We turn our flashlights off as we approach his tent. The rain's falling softer now, and the campground is quiet. Noah unzips the tent flap, and when I'm convinced no one is watching us, I climb inside after him.

Technically, it's a two-person tent. Apparently, that classification assumes you'll be super cozy with the person you're sharing it with because we're already tripping over each other. Noah unzips his sleeping bag and spreads it out so we can share. As he sheds his rain jacket, I settle in under the extra blankets and try to ignore the flex of his biceps and the way his snake tattoo curls around it. He keeps the flannel pants on, along with the thin tee shirt that's stretched taut over his muscular frame.

It's criminal that he can look so alluring in an old tee shirt and pajama pants, his hair soaked from the rain.

When he slides under the covers next to me, his lip ticks up in a tiny smile, and my whole body lights up.

"Isn't this better, Griffin?" he says, his voice a low rumble. "Warm and dry. Not at all like a pretzel."

"Are you waiting for someone to give you a medal?" I roll my raincoat up until it's mostly pillow-shaped and curl up on my side, facing Noah.

The last thing I see before I close my eyes is his deadly smirk and that dimple that haunts my dreams.

He's silent for a long while, lying on his back. Just when I think he's asleep, he says quietly, "Listen, about the bridge. I'm really sorry. If I'd known you were afraid of heights, I would have planned a different hike." His voice has a sad edge to it, like he's been thinking about this for a while. And knowing Noah, he has.

"It's okay," I tell him.

"You don't have to say that. It can be not-okay."

I breathe in the faint scent of woodsmoke, listening to the quiet thump-thump of my heart. "I didn't think I was that afraid of heights. I don't know what was different today. I just froze."

"I still feel bad about it," he mutters. It sounds like he's biting off the rest of the sentence. There's more he isn't saying, and I wish he would let those words out, too.

"Don't," I tell him, a little too sharply. "You have no reason to." Something twists in my chest, and I wonder if we're still talking about a bridge.

"I don't have anything else like that planned," he says. "After the canoe trip tomorrow, everything else is low-key."

I remember this from the schedule, of course, but he says it like the words might be a balm. Like he's trying to protect me and put me at ease. It's typical Noah—he might have changed in some ways in the last six years, but not in that way. He's still looking out for me.

"I didn't do what I wanted to," he says, his voice a low rumble.

"What do you mean?"

He turns toward me and sighs. "When we were on the bridge. I wanted to be the one to take your hand and give you what you needed."

The words strike me dead-center. "Oh," I breathe.

"I thought you wanted me to keep my distance. To give you space. But that's not what you wanted, was it?" His voice is so tender I want to fold myself in his arms.

I swallow hard because I'm not sure what happens if I admit this truth. But I have to be braver. I can't keep bottling all these feelings up, pretending they don't exist.

"No," I said. "It wasn't."

He reaches for my hand under the blankets, lacing his big fingers in mine. "I knew what you needed, but I did what you asked." He slides his thumb along my palm in a way that makes my heart flutter. "But you've never liked asking for help."

I nod, feeling a lump in my throat.

"I won't make that mistake again," he says, eyes wide in the dim light. "Because that summer, I thought you wanted space, then, too. But I was wrong, wasn't I?"

I swallow hard. Then whisper, "Yes."

His big hand squeezes mine, and it's taking everything in me not to dive under this blanket and remove every scrap of fabric that's stopping all of his skin from touching mine. No one's ever come close to knowing me the way that Noah does. Over the years, I tried to tell myself that other guys did, but that was a lie that I told myself to make losing him hurt less. All of these feelings I have for Noah? They're tangled and complex. They didn't diminish over time, and now that we're here together, I can't keep lying to myself and telling myself they aren't real. What I feel for Noah is deeper than anything I've ever felt for anyone else, and I don't want to tamp it down anymore.

I want to climb on top of him and kiss him until we both come apart.

But we can't do that here.

I think of Roxy, who got me this job. The kids, who deserve a summer camp that only has kid-drama and not drama from two adults who have to sort out their own complicated wants and their complex past that's riddled with mistakes, missteps, and wounds that are hard to name.

I think of ice cold water, pounding rain, hungry bears, itchy sports bras—anything to take my mind off Noah Valentine and his big warm hands and sexy scruff, his molten stare that still makes me feel like I'm the eighth Wonder of the world.

He always seems to know what's in my heart. I can't hide anything from him, which means he has to know how I'm feeling right now: elated to be so close to him again and devastated because I can't yet tell him all the truths I've been holding back and touch him the way I want to.

I lie quietly in the darkness, willing my breaths to be deep and even. I may not be able to sleep, but I can at least fake it for his sake. In the stillness, I feel his heartbeat in the palm of his hand, slowly falling into rhythm with mine.

Lord have mercy. This is going to be the longest night in the history of the world.

Just when I think he's asleep, he turns over, so he's facing me. In the darkness, I can barely see the furrow in his brow, the intensity of his stare.

"I have so many things I want to say to you," he says. "Starting with this: I never should have taken that trip with Samantha. I was head over heels for you, and it completely terrified me. I'd convinced myself that you didn't have feelings for me, and then the moment you showed me you did, I froze."

He brings my hand to his lips. "I felt like I had to be the good guy and follow through with that trip with her because backing out meant I was like my dad. But doing that hurt you, and that was never what I wanted."

"It's okay," I whisper, because somehow it is. "I should have told you how I felt, but I was embarrassed because I thought you were in love with someone else." Someone prettier, more adventurous, more fun. Seeing all of the photos of them together on his social media had just underscored how very different she was from me. And my brain conflated *different* with *better*.

"It's not okay," he says. "All that time, I was afraid to tell you how I felt because I thought you only wanted to be friends. And

I didn't want to blow up our friendship because it meant everything to me."

"I've never been good at this," I whisper.

"Good at what?"

"When feelings get complicated," I explain. "Back then, I didn't know how to say what I needed, didn't feel like I could ask for what I wanted. And what I wanted most was you."

His teeth graze my knuckles, and my heart bangs against my ribs. I want more of him—here, now, and always.

"It's still hard for me to talk about my feelings," I tell him. "I get overwhelmed and choke. Sometimes, that just means I hold everything inside." In the Griffin house, it was out of the question to discuss uncomfortable feelings like embarrassment or hurt because my parents saw that as weakness. I was supposed to *suck it up. Forget about it.* When something hurtful happened and made me cry, my mom would stiffen her jaw and tell me, *Straighten up your face.* To me, that meant pretending it never happened.

I've done a lot of pretending over the years. But I don't want to anymore—especially not with Noah.

"I get that," he says, his voice gravelly. "But you can always tell me how you feel. The only way you'll hurt me is if you lie to me."

My chest tightens as he moves closer, his knees brushing against mine.

"Please don't hide from me," he says.

I didn't think I'd been hiding exactly, but as soon as he says the words, it feels true. I've been hiding parts of myself, and that might be the same thing.

"You've always made me feel safe," I tell him, sliding my free hand along his jaw. "Like it was okay to be my weird little over-achieving, insecure self."

"It's more than okay. You get to decide who you want to be. Not your parents, not your ex, not your friends, and not me, either." He holds my hand to his lips, and I nearly combust. "You can be as weird as you want, Griffin. It only makes me like you more."

I snort out a laugh. "You say that now."

"Try me," he says, and I can feel his lips curve into a smile.

His foot slides over mine, and I feel another tug low in my belly. There are so many points of contact now—his thigh against my knee, his lips on my inner wrist. When I shiver again, it's not from the cold.

"Hiding my feelings for you is my biggest regret," he says. "I don't want to keep any more secrets from you."

"Same," I whisper.

"Can we just chalk the past up to being stupid kids?" he says.

"We did do some stupid things back then, didn't we? Mixing Jäger bombs with truth or dare, Fall Break on that sketchy riverboat that caught fire and nearly sank. It's a miracle we survived at all."

He grins and nuzzles my hand, his lips moving against my wrist, and it ignites something deep in my chest, this wanting that won't go away.

Mercy, how I don't want anything else between us.

"I have a proposal," he says, his voice doing that sexy-rumble that makes the little hairs on my neck tingle. "Let me take you on a proper date. In one week, when we're off this mountain."

My heart hammers in my ribcage, so loud I'm certain he can hear it. "What would we do on this date, Valentine?" I say.

He makes a sound deep in his throat, low and gravelly, and it nearly unravels me.

"Telling you would spoil the surprise," he says. "But we have a lot of lost time to make up for. Wouldn't you say?"

His knee nudges between mine, just barely, and my heart flutters like a bird.

"A lot," I agree.

"I'd like to see where this goes," he says. "I think we owe it to ourselves, don't you?"

I reach over and run my fingers through his hair—so soft, like a rabbit's fur—and he makes another contented sound that makes me feel like a match that's been struck. And just like that, my resolve is gone. I twist my fingers in his hair and pull him toward me. His mouth crashes against mine, and I can't help myself. His lips are soft, his movements achingly slow, and the rough scrape of his jaw sends a chill down to my toes. His fingers slide along my cheek as he nips at my bottom lip, and all I can think is *Yes. This. Finally.*

His fingers trace my collarbone, and when his lips move to my neck, I slide my hands beneath his shirt and feel the heat radiating from his chest. Those hard muscles feel even better than I'd imagined, and when his hand squeezes my hip, I feel certain he could make me explode like a star.

I'm dying to touch him everywhere, to feel all of his skin pressed against mine.

But we can't.

I pry myself away from him and scramble to sit up. "Omigod," I blurt. "I'm so sorry."

He lifts a brow and says, "Good lord, why?"

"I should go," I tell him. "I don't trust myself around you."

He gives me a devilish grin that makes my heart do a barrel roll. Being with him feels so right, but this is the absolute worst time to be thinking of all the ways I want to touch him and all the places I want him to kiss me. No, not want. *Need.*

It's obvious he wants me to do all those things and more—and that intense hunger in his eyes is not helping this situation.

"I'm serious, Noah. I should leave. Right now. Before I get us both fired."

"Stop," he says, taking my hand again. "Roll up your giant blanket and stuff it between us. I'll stay on my side of the sleeping bag. I promise."

"It's not you I'm worried about."

His eyes flicker with mischief. "I'd love to hear more about that later. Maybe you can tell me on our date." He tucks his hands under his cheek and nods toward the space next to him.

I bite my lip, knowing I should leave. Because it's the professional thing to do. The right thing.

But it's definitely not what I want, and that might be the scariest part of all. Thunder rumbles in the distance, and he reaches for my arm.

"Stay," he says. That one word, so quiet and tender, tugs at my heart. I think of that moment on the beach years before, how I left him without a word, and I can't make myself do it again.

He shoves the blanket between us, a flimsy barrier that's merely symbolic. When we're finally settled under the covers, him on his back and me curled toward him like a comma, I close my eyes and concentrate on the sound of his breaths, the pattering of rain on the tent.

Another glimmer, I think, feeling the warmth spread through my chest.

SOMETIME LATER, I wake up and realize that Noah's arm is draped over my side, his big hand splayed over my hip, my blanket barrier long gone. He's sound asleep, his breaths coming deep and even. His body's locked tight against mine, so snugly that all of his hard parts are pressed into my soft ones. I know I should move away and shove that blanket back between us, but

I can't make myself do that. It's too nice, this feeling of his hips tucked against mine, his broad chest so warm against my back. I don't even want to go to sleep anymore—instead, I want to catalogue all the points of contact, the way it feels to have him so close. I want to etch all of these feelings into my memory so I never forget.

His hand tightens on my hip as he pulls me closer, and I wish I knew what he was dreaming right now.

One more week, I tell myself. Seven days on our best behavior.

Starting now.

Chapter Sixteen

NOAH

When my phone's alarm wakes me, I realize that I've wrapped myself around Victoria like a coat. My arm's tight across her chest, one leg draped over hers, and there are so many other parts of us touching that it short-circuits my brain.

Because it feels even more amazing than I imagined, and I'd give my eye teeth to lie here all day with her.

When she begins to stir, I quickly disentangle myself.

"Sorry," I whisper, as she turns to face me. "Apparently, I'm a snuggler." I'm not sorry, though, because if I could spend the rest of my nights tangled up with Victoria, I absolutely would. Judging by the sweet half-smile tucked at the corner of her mouth, she wouldn't argue.

"It's okay," she says, stretching like a cat in a sunbeam. Then she seems to realize where she is, and her eyes widen with alarm.

In one flutter of her lashes, the spell is broken. She's throwing off the blanket, fumbling to find her boots. Her hair's barely in its ponytail, and it takes everything in me not to pull it down the rest of the way and run my fingers through it as I draw her back down into these blankets.

No, no. *No.*

"I need to go," she whisper-yells, throwing on her rain jacket. She's a tiny tornado, half-crawling and stumbling around the tent as she tries to gather her things and not step all over me in the process. She's doing all she can to avoid touching me completely. When I reach out to steady her, she pulls away and topples onto her backside, landing right by my shoulder with an exasperated, "Ooof!" She rolls away as if touching me would actually set her on fire and then lets out an adorable, frustrated little huff as she rights herself again.

She looks frazzled, avoiding my gaze. This would be funny if it wasn't making me feel like I did something wrong.

"Are you okay?" I ask.

"Of course," she says, thrusting my boot onto her foot. Her cheeks turn pink.

"I don't believe you. Come here." When I move closer and lean in to kiss her, she shoves her finger against my lips to hold me at bay.

"Freeze, mister," she says, her voice low. "Bad idea."

"Whoa," I say, reaching for her hand. "Slow down and talk to me."

"We have to get it together," she says, eyes narrowing. "This never happened."

My chest tightens. That sounds like regret.

She sighs, rubbing the bridge of her nose. "I meant what I said, Valentine. We definitely have unfinished business, and I'm all for unpacking it when we're off this mountain. But for the next week, we have to be on our best behavior. No touching. No moony eyes. Act like colleagues and nothing more." She points her finger at me in that bossy way that makes me want to tackle her and bite it. "Better yet, act like you can barely tolerate me."

I snort. "I do not make moony eyes."

She gives me an epic eye roll. "Yeah, okay."

I grin. Maybe I moon a little.

Vic is still on a tear. "Sophie's going to know something's up if you don't dial it back a notch. Or five."

"And you think you don't make eyes at me?" I say, edging toward her. "You look at me like I'm a double scoop of ice cream on a blistering summer day." Not that I mind one bit.

She frowns and chucks my boot at me. "I'm serious, Valentine."

I stifle a laugh because she's so dang cute when she's all riled up. "Okay," I tell her, holding my hands up. "Whatever you say."

She huffs like she doesn't believe me and unzips a corner of the tent flap.

It's still dark out, but just barely. I find her other boot, which was somehow under my side of the sleeping bag, and hand it to her. While she struggles to get it on, I peek outside. All the kids must be still asleep—there's no movement at their tents. I can't quite see all the way to Sophie's tent, but I don't see any lights or hear any sound besides the chirping of the morning birds and Vic's heavy breathing. But there's the barest bit of orange touching the sky, like tiny tongues of flame.

That means we don't have much time.

"I'll go out first, just in case," I whisper, because someone might be lurking outside my range of sight.

She nods, and I slip out of the tent and do a quick survey of the campground. I've just decided it's clear when I spot movement in the trees, a flash of bright blue twenty yards away.

Sophie. She sees me and waves, and then heads toward me.

I duck my head inside the tent, holding my finger to my lips. Victoria's eyes go wide.

"Sophie's coming over," I whisper. "I'll distract her so you can get out."

Victoria bites her lip and nods.

I slip out of the tent, zipping the flap behind me, and stride towards Sophie. "Morning," I say, heading her off. "Sleep okay?"

"Yeah," Sophie says. "The rain put me right out. You?" Her eyes are bright, her smile wide.

"Fine," I tell her. "I was just about to make some coffee but must have left my mug in the car. Take a walk with me?"

"Sure," she says. "I think the firewood's in your car, too."

"Right you are." I check my jacket pockets when we're a few steps farther from my tent, hoping my keys are still there. Mercifully, they are.

Sophie starts talking about breakfast, and I hear giggling and chatter coming from inside a few tents. We're almost to the parking lot, but Vic needs to get out fast—before any kids are up and about.

"You're in big trouble," Sophie says.

"What?" I blurt. We're at the cars now, and I'm fumbling with the key fob to get the doors unlocked. I glance back at my tent, half-expecting to see Victoria frozen like a deer.

"You forgot to put the s'mores stuff away last night," Sophie says. "When I woke up this morning, two crows were helping themselves to the marshmallows. When I went after them, one flew off with the whole bag."

"Ha!" I snort out a laugh that sounds completely alien to my ears. Sophie must think I'm even more of a doofus than usual. Or else she knows something's up. I open the back gate of the car. "Sorry about that," I tell her. "You want to start the fire and let Vic and me unload the coolers?"

"Sure," she says with a shrug. "You feeling okay?" Her brown eyes narrow as she studies my face. I think of ice-cold whitewater, mischievous crows, anything but Victoria—because suddenly I'm convinced she's right and Sophie can read my mind.

"Yeah, fine," I tell her. "I'm just useless before coffee. You know that."

Behind her, Victoria slips out of my tent like a ghost. She looks around quickly, then straightens and strides off toward the bathhouse like nothing is out of the ordinary.

Sophie nods. "Tell me about it. I brought some cold coffee just because I can't wait for boiling water over a fire. I've got one in the cooler if you're desperate."

"I'd owe you big time," I say, and that seems to satisfy her. The furrow in her brow disappears as I hand her a bundle of firewood.

When I glance over Sophie's shoulder, Victoria is gone.

AFTER BREAKFAST, we pack up the campsites in record time. We'll have to lay everything out to dry once we get back to the institute, but that's better than having the kids pack up at a snail's pace after a full day of canoeing. A busy morning of breaking camp and loading cars should be plenty to keep my mind off Victoria.

But it's not.

All morning, I've been trying to forget how perfect she felt curled against me. So far, I'm failing at that task. As a result, I double-salted my oatmeal so it was barely edible, tripped getting out of my tent and nearly brought the whole thing down on top of me, and then tried to start the car with my house key.

Victoria's short-circuited my brain without even trying.

Sophie's going on and on about ideas for the dance that we're throwing for the kids in a few days, and all I can think about is the way Victoria tugged at my hair and pulled me against her, crushing her lips against mine. It left me completely unraveled and dying for more. Each time I look at her, she makes this startled face like she can't forget it, either.

She was right, though. We can't do that here. Roxy would have my hide if she found out, and the College of Charleston would fire me in a heartbeat. I just need to hold myself together until camp is over. And I can do that because I know Vic feels the same. When I whispered *one week*, she smiled, blue eyes glowing with promise. When I said *date*, she said *yes*.

Once the cars are full of kids and camping gear, we caravan over to the spot where we'll pick up our canoes and launch them into a lazy branch of the French Broad River. With no whitewater, this stretch is wide and calm—an ideal spot to take the kids for an easy paddle. And that's exactly what today should be: easy.

Near the water, two twenty-something guys are waiting by a van with a trailer. They've already unloaded our canoes and piled a bunch of life jackets nearby. The put-in is in a finger lake —we'll paddle around here for a few minutes and get everyone comfortable, and then we'll head downstream for a few miles to our pick-up point at another finger lake. The young guys introduce themselves as Jerome and Skyler and look like they've already spent every day this summer on the river. Jerome's a tall Black guy with big brown eyes and a wiry frame that you get from swimming and paddling. Skyler's a shorter white guy with shaggy blond hair, already sporting a tan line from a tee shirt.

While Jerome and Skyler give the kids a safety talk and paddling lesson, I see the first problem: There are seven canoes, but we reserved nine. They've subbed in one single-person kayak that looks just slightly bigger than a pool noodle. That means three kids per canoe, just as we planned. But now, instead of Sophie, Vic, and me each having our own canoe, two of us will have to share.

Victoria's watching the paddling demo with an intense focus. I can't decide if she's never picked up a paddle or if she's determined not to look me in the eye until camp is officially over.

I bite back a smile, relishing the idea that she can't stop thinking about us, either.

"I should probably take the kayak," Sophie says, mostly to me. "You'd have to fold yourself up like a pretzel to fit in that, and I'm guessing Victoria might not want to pilot her own boat."

"In the interest of not drowning," Vic says, strapping on her life jacket, "I would agree." She smiles wryly.

"Not that I don't think you could do it," Sophie tells her, raising her hands in that way that means surrender. "It's just tricky to handle that kind of kayak if you're not used to it, and then there's the whole rollover factor—"

"Yeah, I'm good with having a boat buddy," Victoria says, pursing her lips. "I know my limitations."

My heart twists as she says that because this woman should never impose limitations on herself. And as soon as we're alone for real, away from these kids who are slinging paddles around like hockey sticks, I'm going to tell her that until she admits that it's true.

Sophie claps her on the shoulder and says, "You got this, lady. I bet if you ask nicely, you can sit in the front and let Noah here do all the work." Sophie shoots me a wink, and the paranoid part of me thinks that somehow, she knows.

Victoria's eyes widen as if she's having the same thought. Her cheeks turn a delightful shade of pink as she quickly ducks her head and fidgets with her life jacket for the hundredth time, as if she's somehow missed one of the three adjustment straps.

I'm a jerk for enjoying watching her blush like that, but I can't help it. Seeing that heat bloom in her cheeks and spread down to her collarbones makes me think of all the creative ways that I could coax that out of her when we're a million miles from this place.

I should just go ahead and dunk myself in the ice-cold river because my body already feels like it's on fire, and sitting in a little canoe with her for the next few hours is going to be torture.

Sophie whistles loud enough to hail a cab all the way from Asheville, and the kids start climbing into their canoes, eager to get going on their adventure.

"Come on," I tell Vic. "This'll be fun." Judging by the way she arches her brow, she's not convinced.

AFTER SOME PRACTICE paddling and steering, the kids make their way downriver at an easy pace. Sophie's in the lead, nimble enough in the kayak to keep turning around and coming upstream when she needs to lend encouragement. Victoria and I are in the back, keeping an eye on the stragglers. Perched at the bow, Vic looks ethereal—like one of those carved maidens on the prow of a galleon. Her hair's in two braids, falling just below her shoulders, and each time she turns her head to speak to me, the sunlight catches the gold of her hair, and I feel like I'm staring at the sun.

I'm at the stern because that's where the more experienced paddler should sit. It's the steering position, and it makes logical sense. It also means that for the duration of this trip downriver, I'm staring at Victoria's back, tracing the line of her sculpted shoulders, the delicate curve of her neck, the way her hips flare out from her waist.

Just like I predicted: torture.

I try to focus instead on the pace she sets, the *thwack* of her paddle as it slaps the water, occasionally sending a spray of cold water across my face. After a while, she takes off her jacket, revealing a tank top with the world's tiniest shoulder straps. I sigh, hoping she'll hit me with a big wave of water soon because now I can see a constellation of freckles on her shoulder blade that I want to trace with my tongue.

Six days left. One hundred and forty-four hours. Then no more pretending.

"You must do this all the time," Vic says, and I'm snapped out of my fantasy fast enough to have whiplash.

"Do what?" I ask. Apparently, my brain has stopped working entirely.

She looks at me over her shoulder and smiles. If I could burn that seductive image into my memory so it would last forever, I'd trade my soul to do it.

"Canoe," she says, arching her brow. "Are you getting heatstroke back there?"

No. What I have is so much worse.

I scoff at her teasing. "It's not hot enough for heatstroke."

"You're being weird, Valentine." She's more relaxed now that everyone else is focused on the river. Most of the tension has left her lovely shoulders, but I hate that there's any at all.

"You just caught me daydreaming," I tell her, lowering my voice. "Can you blame me?"

She turns her head just slightly, and the tips of her ears turn pink.

Her paddle hits the water with an indelicate *thwack*, sending a splash of water over me. That one might have been intentional.

From a few yards ahead comes a shout, followed by laughter. Two canoes have drifted closer to each other, and the kids are splashing each other with their paddles.

"Easy!" I call to them. "Watch for the rocks!"

Six heads swivel toward me and then turn back to the water. One more tiny splash, and then the kids are back on track. This section of the river is calm but still has spots where the rocks stick up like the worn teeth of giants. Aside from the occasional hollow thump of a collision, the kids are doing a good job of steering and staying on course.

I paddle harder to close the gap between us and the kids so we're just a few yards from the last boat. More shouting erupts as we come around a bend in the river, and I soon see why: one of the canoes has veered too close to the riverbank on our left.

"Hey y'all," Victoria shouts. "You need a little help?"

Layla and Priya, at bow and stern, are trying to push off the bank while Derrick, in the middle, paddles on the other side to pull them away. But they're snagged by a downed tree limb. I steer us over so we're between their canoe and the bank, where a canopy of low limbs hangs just above our heads.

"We'll give you a shove," I tell them. "Get ready to paddle away from shore." They nod because they learned this maneuver from Jerome and Skylar earlier this morning. "Now!" I tell the kids, and Vic and I push their canoe away from the bank. They paddle hard, and in a few moments, they're free, full of laughter and high-fives.

Vic uses her paddle to push a brushy limb away from her face while I dig mine into the shallows to pry us away from the bank. It's all rocky soil here, thick with mountain laurels and scraggly bushes. The foliage is so dense you can barely see daylight through it—just the occasional glint of the silver-white trunks of the river birch.

"Push hard against the shore," I tell her, and she nods as the muscles in her shoulders flex in that way that pulls my gaze like a magnet. I give us another hard shove as she bats at the low limb again. When we come out from under it, the leaves tickle my neck and something drops onto my shoulder—probably a branch—but when I move to brush it off, it falls into my lap. I see two eyes blinking at me, the flick of a forked tongue—and then the whole world tilts on its axis.

I yelp like a dog smacked with a rolled-up newspaper and feel my heart pound in my throat. There's not much that I dislike about being in the woods, but snakes are at the top of the list. Even the non-venomous kind, like this one. Black scales, checkered belly, round eyes—this snake is harmless. But it's five feet long, as big as my forearm, and my lap is the last place I want it to be. Because even rat snakes like this one get bitey when they're surprised.

Victoria's eyes widen as I leap to my feet. I'm not being mindful of where my weight is, or worried about looking like a fool as I flail my arms and try to get this enormous snake away from my most tender bits.

In slow motion, Victoria stands and reaches for me, shouting, "Wait, freeze!" and makes the unfortunate choice to move her weight in the same direction I do. Our sudden shift tips the canoe and sends us sprawling into the water.

My head goes under, and I feel a shock of cold as my feet find the bottom. When I straighten, I realize that it's only chest-deep here. Victoria's standing a few feet away from me, the canoe upside down next to her.

She blinks at me like she can't believe this is happening, and I search my body for the snake, certain it's either slithered up my shorts or wrapped itself around my neck, ready to finish drowning me the second it gets a chance. A chorus of shouts cut across the water, and Sophie calls in the distance, telling the kids to stop paddling and drift.

I holler to Sophie that we're okay and give her a wave. The snake pops out of the water by the canoe and climbs onto it with its freakishly strong serpentine muscles and I have a full-body chill that rattles my bones. With her paddle, Victoria slaps the water by the snake, encouraging it to abandon the canoe and head to the riverbank instead.

When I turn back to her, she's biting her lip in a downright delicious way that I'll remember for the next hundred years. I imagine she's about to blow like a teakettle, but then she sputters out a laugh that's like sunbeams breaking through storm clouds. Heat blooms in my chest and there are tears in her eyes as her body quakes with laughter. She gasps and lets out an adorable little snort and says, "I didn't think you were afraid of anything, Valentine. Holy bananas."

I shake my head because there's a lot that I fear. Like messing things up with her and never seeing her again. Never hearing this laugh after next week, never again feeling the softness of her lips and her hands tangled in my hair. The way she says *Valentine* in that light, teasing tone—like she did all those years ago.

"Afraid is a strong word," I say instead. "But I feel the opposite of fondness."

She grins as we right the canoe and Sophie hollers to us again, telling us there's a shallow place just ahead where we can climb back inside.

"This explains so much," Vic says, teasing. "Like how you always covered your eyes during that scene in *Raiders of the Lost Ark*."

I shiver because poor, poor Indy. So many snakes.

"And why you refused to watch *Anaconda* with me," she says.

"That was a legitimately awful premise for a movie," I argue.

"It was hilarious!" she cries, still doubled over. "Wait, didn't your sophomore roommate have a python?"

"Found the dang thing under my pillow one morning," I mutter. "I hardly slept a wink that year."

She covers her mouth. "How did I not know this about you? All this time I thought you just didn't like them. Like, in that way that you despise hairless cats and flip-flops."

"Ugh. Equally awful."

"I'm sorry," she says, straightening her face and holding her hand over her heart. "I'll protect you from the deadly serpents. I promise." She grabs our floating water bottles and puts them back in the canoe, trying to hide her grin while I wring the water from my cap.

"That monster could have swallowed me whole," I argue.

"Yes, behold the fearsome Carolina rat snake," she says, pointing toward the bank where the snake in question lies sunning on a rock. "You're lucky to be alive." She purses her lips again, enjoying this entirely too much.

But her laughter's contagious, and that knot that's been lodged in my chest for years is gone.

"Come on, Indy," she says, one hand on the canoe. "Let's get you back to safe waters. Here, there be dragons."

We guide it toward the shallows, where the water's only knee-deep. I get in first and then hold it steady as Victoria climbs in. We paddle hard to catch up to the kids, who are drifting toward a bend in the river where Sophie's waiting. Layla's voice rings across the water as she leads her boat in a spirited rendition of "Islands in the Stream," which I try not to take as a sign that we're so transparent that everyone can see what's growing between us. Layla and Priya belt out the chorus like they're on Broadway, and honestly, this song has never meant more to me. When we catch up to the group, Victoria pauses to wring out her tank top. It's still plastered to her curvy frame, along with her hiking pants, and I'm never going to get this image out of my head.

Because Victoria Griffin, even when she's soaked to the skin with her hiking clothes clinging to her, and her cheeks smudged with silt from the river, is still the most beautiful sight I've ever seen. She keeps saying that she feels out of her depth here, but that's not how it looks to me. The way she smiles, the way she lights up here—it seems she's still discovering all the ways she can fit in the world, like maybe she's still surprising herself.

She's always been whip-smart and strong, but when she showed up here two weeks ago, she seemed deflated, uncertain. Like she'd been knocked down hard enough to lose her confidence.

But now she's practically glowing with aplomb.

It's easy to imagine all the ways we could fit together. I'm letting myself believe what she said about wanting to unpack everything between us after next week, and finding what might come after.

And I really, *really* can't wait to see what comes after.

When we're just a few yards from the group, Sophie calls out, "You good?"

"Yep!" Victoria yells cheerfully. "All good." She's still grinning when she turns to me, a genuine smile that lights her up from within, and that cold river water has done nothing to put out this fire that's raging under my skin.

One more week, I tell myself. *You got this.*

Chapter Seventeen

VICTORIA

For six more days, Noah Valentine is off-limits. I shouldn't stare at him, I shouldn't touch him, and I definitely shouldn't imagine kissing him again.

So far, I'm failing at all three. Tonight at dinner, his knee brushed against mine under the table and when we locked eyes it was hot enough to burn that room to ash. One simple touch made me replay everything that had happened in his tent and imagine all the ways we might pick that up later. Off the mountain, of course.

But still. Boundaries. That's why I called Gwen right after, because she's become an expert on boundaries and I need her to tell me I'm being reckless and impulsive, and help rein me in.

When I tell her about the camping trip, she sighs and says, "Tell me about that kiss again. And don't leave anything out this time."

The kids have a half-hour of free time before we start movie night. I'm pacing under the cell phone tree, which is still the best spot for privacy—though it's not the best place to convince myself that I can get through these next few days without losing my mind over what might come after.

Specifically, what happens with Noah.

"Was there tongue?" Gwen says, her voice deepening. "Was it just as hot as you imagined?"

"I can't do this," I tell her, looking around to make sure there's no one lurking in the bushes. Only Sophie and Noah know about the cell phone tree, but they're the last people who need to hear any snippets of this conversation. We've got twenty-four minutes of free time before the movie starts and I need a game plan to get through the rest of this session because my intrusive thoughts are in overdrive. "I don't know what I was thinking," I tell her. "It was irresponsible."

"You're being too hard on yourself," Gwen says. "It's summer camp. Have fun. You're allowed to relax a little, too, you know."

"It's camp for the *kids*," I argue. "No fraternizing. That rule was super clear." That was a crisp line in the sand, and I danced right over it when I went into Noah's tent last night. If anyone had seen us, it would have been a disaster. I've imagined having to explain myself to Roxy a thousand times, and I hate that sinking feeling that settles in my gut whenever I think about it. It's that nauseating feeling that goes hand in hand with failure. And Roxy's the last person I want to let down.

Was the kiss amazing? Better than. But that's beside the point.

Gwen sighs, and I know she's twirling one of those big loose curls of hers in her thumb and index finger, like she always does when she's deep in thought. "If you're asking me to shame you, it's not going to happen."

"It's not that," I answer.

"Then stop punishing yourself," she says. "You don't deserve it."

"I'm not," I mutter.

"Aren't you?" she says. "People make mistakes. It's how we grow. Not that I'm saying kissing him was a mistake."

My heart leapt into my throat when Noah suggested getting together when camp was over—but is that feasible? He's settled, with a home near Charleston and a job he adores, and I'm rolling through life like a tumbleweed. It doesn't feel like the right time.

That ever-helpful little voice in my head pipes up to say, *But what if it's the only time?*

Is there ever a right time?

"He wants to date," I blurt. "When camp's over, and we're back home."

"Oh my gawd," she gasps. "Did he actually use the word *date*? That is so freaking cute." She inhales sharply. "Wait. You sound worried."

"I'm just afraid it's not real," I tell her. "What if it's just a summer camp crush?"

"Does it feel as simple as a crush?" Gwen says.

I pick at the bark on the big blue-green evergreen limb that hangs over me like a canopy. "Maybe I'm just feeling…this way…about Noah because we're here in the camp bubble, where everything's fun and magical and the real world is a million miles away. Along with our history."

She hums like she doesn't believe that for a second. "Or maybe," she says, "you don't want to risk your heart again yet. That's fair, you know, after he-who-shall-not-be-named. But don't pretend your feelings aren't real, Vic."

"I like this job," I tell her. "I love working with the kids, and I'm even getting used to being in the woods." I slide my fingers over the rough bark of the fir tree. "I want to do something different with my life, and this is all so inspiring and exhilarating —but it makes me wonder if I'm confusing those feelings with how I feel about Noah."

She hums. "I don't think I follow."

"I feel like I'm falling hard for him—but is it because it's him, or because he's part of this exciting, magical place? Or what if he's feeling something similar and leaves me again when he decides that what we have isn't magical, but completely mundane? And what happens when camp is over, if we start dating, and then this job works out and we're working together —" I stop myself before I say anything more, but the worry makes my gut churn and I don't want to think about how that could end.

Because mixing my work life with my dating life? I already tried that with Theo—and that ended in a dumpster fire.

"Okay, first," Gwen says, "This sounds like more than any crush I've ever had. And second, I need to come clean about something."

Before I can answer, she plows right ahead. "What you said the other day about Noah ghosting you and how he stopped texting after you told him you wanted him to leave you alone."

"I never told him that," I correct her.

After a pause, she says, "I know you're going to hate me for this, and you have every right to, but before you murder me, please know that I did what I did out of love."

"Gwennie," I say. "What did you do?"

She lets out a heavy sigh. "I texted Noah from your phone that summer. I pretended to be you and told him to leave you alone. Then I deleted the message so you'd never see it. And then I blocked his number."

"Gwen!"

"I'm sorry!" she cries. "I was so mad at him for hurting you.

You were heartbroken and he was off galavanting with some other woman and sending you photos like it was nothing, making you watch him fall in love with someone else—and I just couldn't stand seeing how much it crushed you." She huffs. "I wanted to fly across the ocean and punch him in the nose, but I settled for sending an angry text. Or three."

"I can't believe you did that." My gut churns.

"I know. I'm so sorry." She groans. "I guess I thought that if he really loved you like he said he did, he'd man up and come see you in person and resolve things. Or else he'd just disappear forever and spare you any more hurt feelings. But I shouldn't have interfered, and I should have told you this long before now."

I lean against the fir's massive trunk, feeling the air whoosh right out of my lungs.

Noah didn't ghost me after all. Now what he told me at the beginning of camp makes sense: *I thought I was doing what you wanted. You said to leave you be.*

"I'll do whatever it takes to make this up to you," Gwen says. "I feel terrible."

"It's okay," I tell her, because it will be.

"You deserve all the love the world can send you," she says. "Don't shut it out, okay?" Her voice fades in and out a little, and I take a step farther from the tree. I caught the most important words, and they're hitting me square in the heart. "Vic?" she says again. "Did you hear me?"

"Yeah," I tell her. Tears prick my eyes because I know she's right—about all of it. "I should go," I tell her. "I have to do snacks for movie night." Noah and Sophie are setting up the projector in the lounge, and I'm in charge of popcorn. And now it feels like, once again, the world has turned sideways and I've lost my footing.

"Love you, babe," she says. "I'll see you soon. And I'm rooting for you here. I always am."

Just as I end the call and step away from the tree, my phone beeps with a missed call and voicemail that came yesterday, no doubt delayed by our spotty signal. Curious, I play the message. There's a lot of static, so I listen to it twice to make sure I didn't mishear the words—because surely I did.

But I didn't.

The message is from Diana Chase, former partner at Rayanne's real estate firm and her biggest rival—until she moved to Pensacola. Diana's voice sounds razor sharp, her words concise as always. She heard I left Rayanne's firm and wonders if I'm interested in joining hers. She asks the question like she's just asking me to meet for lunch—like it's not the kind of leveling up I'd dreamed of for my career. It's a big idea to leave hanging in a voicemail message, but that's right on-brand for Diana Chase. The phrase *Time is money* was made for her. She was doing well when she left Jasmine Falls, but now that she's been selling multi-million-dollar homes on the Florida coast for a couple of years? She could probably retire already, in her late forties. But Diana's a shark, and she likes the thrill too much to retire. I shadowed her for years, hoping I could learn her kind of poise and closing skills.

For her to ask me now seems almost too good to be true. Because working with Diana Chase? That's a game-changer. A career-maker. An offer I'd be crazy to pass up.

So why am I not more excited by the idea?

Her call is from yesterday, just before noon. It's nearly seven now, which isn't too late to call her because Diana Chase doesn't take time off. I'm not certain she even sleeps. But the movie's starting soon, and I need to help get everything ready for the kids.

I also need to get my thoughts together so I don't sound like a frazzled mess when I talk to her.

So I text her a quick reply, but it's too eager and there are too many exclamation points. Diana Chase does not use exclamation points. Frowning, I delete it and write another, settling for gracious and concise, asking if we can chat in the morning or on Tuesday. Then I read it a dozen times to make sure there are no typos or over-excited punctuation, and hit send.

I wait for a moment, pacing under the tree, making sure it goes through. Satisfied that it did, I shove my phone into my pocket and head toward the admin building, where one of the lounges will soon be transformed into a movie theater. I've only made it a few feet when my phone buzzes with a text.

Great, Diana writes. **How's Wednesday at 10 am?**

Perfect, I reply. **Looking forward to it.** I head back to the tree, just in case, waiting to see the check mark that means it's gone through.

Same, she replies.

Something churns in my belly and I can't decide if it's excitement, or nervous energy, or a different feeling I can't quite name.

THROUGH THE LAST half of *The Martian*, I'm trying hard to forget about waking up with Noah's arm draped over my waist. I can still feel the weight of his hand, the way he held me close against his chest. I could have stayed that way for days.

He laughs at a line in the movie, *I don't want to come off as arrogant here, but I'm the greatest botanist on this planet,* and even from my chair a few feet away, I can see those adorable creases at the corners of his eyes. When he turns toward me, he smiles just enough to make his dimple pop, and it tugs at a spot deep in my chest.

There's so much I still need to say to him, and none of it can be said here at camp. I'm trying to be honest with him about my feelings, but the truth is that I don't quite know how to put all these swirling thoughts into words. I just know that I've missed him so much it hurts to breathe—and I don't want the end of camp to be the end of us.

The logical part of me is building a case for taking this job with Diana. It would mean building up my savings account and getting back on my feet. It would be the smartest career move I could ever make.

But it would mean leaving Noah again and abandoning this new path that shows so much promise. It's only been two weeks, but I love working with these kids and seeing them grow self-confidence. It's something I didn't have at their age, and somehow helping them discover their strengths is healing a part of me, too.

I hate that these things I want are at odds with each other. I don't know how to choose.

Chapter Eighteen

VICTORIA

Three days later, I still can't get Noah—okay, more precisely that *kiss*—out of my mind.

At breakfast, he's alone at the staff table, sipping that awful coffee with a straight face as he studies his binder of notes. When I sit across from him, he gives me a tiny smile, but his gaze is hot enough to turn this cafeteria into cinders.

"No Sophie this morning?" I ask him.

He takes a bite of breakfast burrito and shakes his head. "She's finishing up a call with the admins."

I steal a strawberry from his plate and he lifts a brow. "There's a whole pile of those on the buffet, you know," he says, teasing.

"Yeah, but it's way over there." When I take a bite, his eyes drop to my lips, and an honest-to-goodness shiver runs down to my toes. "Besides," I say. "This one tastes better."

Under the table, his leg slowly brushes mine in a way that feels indecent. "It looks delicious." Noah gives me a sly smile, one that says he will not be on his best behavior even before camp is over, and that job with Diana is looking less tempting by the second.

When Sophie plops down next to me, her plate loaded with fruit and scrambled eggs, I nearly jump from my seat. "So we have a surprise visit from admin," she says. "They're coming tomorrow and will leave the next day."

Noah's brow lifts as he turns to her. "I thought they were skipping this year."

Sophie shrugs. "Changed their minds, I guess." She takes a bite of toast, her brow furrowed. "They'll get here by lunchtime tomorrow so they can see part of each class, then they'll hang around for the evening activities. I'll do the tour, if you two don't mind handling the afternoon games." She looks flustered, which is unusual for her.

"Is everything okay?" I ask.

"Yeah, it's just annoying that they didn't give more notice," she says. "But we'll adjust."

Of all of us, Sophie's the one who's most married to schedules and spreadsheets. She claims to like surprises, but only if they don't disrupt the flow of her plans.

"Usually someone from the home office visits each site at some point during the summer," Noah tells me. "They were supposedly skipping us because everything here is the same as it has been the last few sessions, and they have less staff to travel now."

"Also Roxy wants you to call her ASAP," Sophie tells me. "It sounded time-sensitive."

"Okay, sure." When I glance at Noah, he gives me a reassuring smile. Does he know something I don't?

My heart flutters as I remember the job that Roxy said would be open soon. First it seemed like an unlikely stretch for me, but now that we're nearing the end of the session, I want it even more. This camp has reminded me that I'm stronger than I gave myself credit for.

Plus, I'd like a reason to turn down Diana's offer. And a solid job with the College of Charleston, right in Noah's backyard? Heat blooms in my chest as I think about it. This is not a camp bubble—these feelings are real. I don't know how we'll navigate working together while dating, but now that it feels like a real possibility, I want to try.

Sophie leaves me alone in her office, where I can use the land line to call Roxy. She answers on the third ring.

"How's it going?" I ask her. "I've wanted to text you about a hundred times, but I have to stand under this one tree in just the right way…"

"That's okay," she says. "I know how remote it is there."

"I know we're not really a million miles from everything. It just feels that way sometimes." From the office window, I can see a group of kids outside with their class, heading toward one of the big radio telescopes.

"How are things going?" she asks.

"Honestly, this place is amazing. And you were right—the kids are awesome." I babble on about all the things I'm loving about camp, and when I finally take a breath, there's silence on her end. "Roxy?" I ask. She's quiet for a moment, and for the first time, I think this might not be the good news and job offer that I was hoping for.

"I need to ask you something," she says, her voice dropping an octave. "And I don't know how to ask you in a way that isn't awkward, so I'm just going to say it. Is there something going on with you and Noah?"

My heart leaps into my throat. The whole world freezes.

"What?" Even that one word sounds strangled, like it's been squeezed from a guilty person.

She sighs. "First, let me say that I'm not trying to shame you or embarrass you. I wanted to talk to you first, and hopefully this conversation goes no further than us, this morning."

The room feels as hot as the surface of the sun. My stomach is in knots, and it's hard to breathe. "What's happening?" I squeak out.

"Sophie just uploaded a big batch of photos to the website," she says. "They're from the weekend camping trip—which looked like an incredible time, by the way. The kids look deliriously happy." She heaves another sigh, and I can hear her clicking the mouse by her computer. "But there are a couple of photos of you and Noah where you both seem close enough that it could raise eyebrows."

I shake my head, racking my brain and trying to pull up any moment where we touching in public—did someone see us in his tent together?

"I'm hoping this is nothing," she says, "and if we look at these together, then you can tell me I'm imagining things, and then I don't have to talk to the director and we can both get on with our day." She takes a quick breath and says, "Can you access your email right now?"

"Yes," I tell her. I feel like I've swallowed a stone, but I log in to the staff computer and navigate over to my inbox. There's a chime as Roxy's message comes through. When I open it, I see the photos that she's attached. She's still talking as I study them.

The first photo is from days ago, when we were hiking near the waterfall closer to the institute. The students in the foreground are all beaming—it's the moment they came off the trail and saw the towering falls and the pools below. But there, in the background, on the rocky slope at the end of the trail, Noah is helping me down, his hands around my waist. The memory of that day is burned into my brain. I'd slipped near the bottom and crashed right into him. Sophie snapped this photo at the precise moment when my hands had landed squarely on his chest, and he'd gripped me tight... and didn't let go. I have to zoom in to see our faces, but the intensity is hard to miss.

The second photo was taken at the bridge, after Layla had helped me across. When Sophie took this photo, she was focused on the students grinning in the foreground, arms around each other. But in the background, Noah's holding me in a tight hug after I collapsed against him, full of terror and relief. I zoom in for a closer look, but I remember this moment down to the last detail: my hair was a wind-whipped mess, and I was shaking like a leaf. He'd come over to check on me and I'd thrown my arms around him without even thinking. To most people, we'd just look like two friends. The look on Noah's face, though—it's full of love.

I let myself stare for a moment, focus on the tiny creases at the corners of his eyes, the crooked smile and the lone dimple.

Noah can be hard to read, but that expression leaves no room for doubt. Despite what I told Gwen, this doesn't feel like a camp crush—when I'm with Noah, my heart is full. I can't ignore these feelings I have for him anymore, and I don't want to. My heart's telling me to go for it and take him up on his offer because I'm falling for Noah Valentine—hard.

A smile tugs at my lips, despite the worry that I'm in hot water with Roxy.

"I can explain these," I offer. "In one, we'd just crossed over that bridge that's like a million miles off the ground. I was terrified, and one of the kids held my hand to help me across. Noah was worried, and he came over to make sure I was okay. What you see is me after a panic attack and him trying to help."

"Okay," she says, but I'm not sure she believes me. Right

now, this is Roxy my boss, not Roxy my friend. The thought stings, but I press on.

"In the other one, Noah was helping me down a slippery part of the trail. I lost my footing and crashed right into him." I take a breath and aim for levity. "I see how that could look… unprofessional, but I swear it's me being clumsy and him trying to save me from myself."

A pause. I brace myself for the worst.

"All right," she says, sounding matter-of-fact. "So nothing you need to disclose here? Because they're dead serious about the no-fraternizing rule, and if that's happening, then we need to have a different conversation."

This is the moment where I should tell her. I know it, but as the seconds tick by, I feel more anxious, more afraid, and more uncertain. I don't want to get Noah in trouble, and I don't want to let Roxy down. But I also don't want to feel this embarrassment and shame. The people-pleaser in me is caving in on herself because all of this feels like I'm being dressed down for doing something wrong—and *bad*.

"Noah and I are old friends," I tell her, settling for mostly-true. "We went to college together."

"What?" she says. "I met all your old college friends. I never met Noah."

"He was in my pre-Roxy era," I explain. "It's a long story that I'll tell you over a bottle of wine sometime. But we were very close, and then we had this falling out and never talked again. It was stupid. But he was my best friend."

She chuffs. "You mean your pre-Roxy best friend."

I chuckle at her teasing, so grateful to hear it. "Obviously."

"Huh," she says. "You're like as opposite as two people can be."

I smile at that, because she's not wrong. "I know. It's wild.

And of course, I had no idea he'd be here. I was just as shocked as he was. And, I imagine, as you are." I take a deep breath, feeling better about telling her at least part of this. I don't like hiding things from Roxy, and I know I should come clean about the feelings. But I don't know what all of these feelings mean yet, and I don't want to make this situation worse than it already is. Mountains out of molehills and all of that. "We haven't seen each other in years," I tell her. "And I guess we just got a little carried away. I'm sorry if it looked inappropriate, or if it put you in an awkward position. We're just really close friends."

She lets out a huge breath. "Thank goodness," she says, "I was afraid I was going to have to explain this to the director and start hiring replacements."

My heart squeezes in my chest, because there it is—the worst case scenario. The one that would blow everything apart.

"I took these photos off the site, and it's not any kind of blatant display," she says. "Probably most people wouldn't even notice, but of course I did, because it's you."

"So you're not in trouble?" I ask.

She snorts, and now she sounds like Roxy my friend again. "Oh, please. I've had to deal with way worse staff problems than this. But just keep in mind that the parents looking at the photo site don't know your history, okay? It sucks, but sometimes we have to hold ourselves back a bit because the context is missing. Even innocent gestures can be misinterpreted, and before you know it, you're in an HR firestorm."

I sigh. So much missing context. Can a picture capture everything that's happening between me and Noah? Then another thought occurs to me, and it's like being punched in the gut.

"Is this why the admins are coming tomorrow?" I ask, horrified by the thought of my every move being analyzed. If I obsess over every word and every move I make, I'm just going to seem more awkward and suspicious.

"No," she says. "It's purely coincidental. I'll be driving up with Julie, who's the assistant to the director. We're just coming to check in and show one of our donors what the more remote camps are like. People make big donations when they see the camps in action, and this donor is a big fan of astronomy."

"Oh," I breathe. "Okay." I feel a little of the tension ease, because I don't think Roxy would be untruthful about this—which makes me feel even worse for not being a hundred percent honest with her.

"It'll be fine," she says. "And you get to hang out with me for a day."

"Sweet. Girl time with my bestie."

She laughs at that, and I decide right then that whatever is happening with Noah has to stop completely—at least until the camp is over. I don't know what happens next, but it can't happen here. I won't jeopardize Noah's job, ruin a chance I have at a full-time position here, or create a difficult situation for Roxy.

"I've got to run," she says. "We've got a stomach flu situation at the home campus, and I might need my hazmat suit."

"Ugh, Roxy."

"I know. See you tomorrow, babe."

When I hang up, my whole body feels wound tight, ready to explode. I curse myself for nearly wrecking everything.

And this lie? It feels like a boulder sitting on my chest. But it's not as heavy as the other lie—the one I've been telling myself for six years.

That I was over Noah Valentine.

Chapter Nineteen

NOAH

I'm adding a mile to my jog this morning, hoping that it will take my mind off of Victoria. Ever since the tent incident, it's been impossible to think of anything else. And now that the admins are coming for a visit, I need to be focused on the kids. The activities. The site tour.

Anything but Vic and the way she's turned my heart inside out. The way her hands feel on my chest, the way her full bottom lip feels caught in my teeth? Yeah, I'm not even going to go there. Better add another mile. Because she's right: we never should have let that happen here. I have to shift my focus back to camp, where it belongs.

Whatever's happening with Victoria will have to wait.

Three more days.

Easy-peasy.

I turn up the volume on my earphones, concentrate on the rhythmic slap of my sneakers against the pavement. No more thoughts of Vic and what comes after. No more thoughts of how perfect her body felt curled against mine. My job is this camp, and these kids—and they deserve my full attention.

But the minute we're off this mountain, Victoria will have every scrap of my attention.

I swear I hear her calling my name, even over the pounding of the music. My brain pops back into overdrive, planning the most creative ways I can show her what she means to me the second we're alone for real. I frown, legs pumping harder, as if I could ever outrun all these thoughts of her.

"Noah!" I hear again, this time louder, and my stupid brain needs to get the memo already. *No more fantasizing about Victoria. Period.*

My name rings in my ears again, and then I feel a hand on my shoulder.

I stumble and catch myself before I hit the pavement, then pull the earphones from my ears. Victoria bends over at the waist, breathing hard. Her hands grip her thighs, squeezing, and that is the last image I need to have burned into my brain right now.

"Jesus," she pants. "I'll never understand why people love to run so much. I feel like I'm actually dying."

"What's wrong?" I ask. With her cheeks bright pink and her hair so unruly, she looks like she's trying to outrun a wildfire.

It's also sexy as hell.

"We need to talk," she says, her voice ragged. Her hands are planted on her hips as she leans back, face toward the sky. This draws my gaze down her body, exactly where it does not need to be, and I consider jumping into the nearby pond just to get my body under control. Because her flushed cheeks combined with all that panting is going to make me combust.

"Not here, though," she says. "Can we meet in the office in a little while? Sophie's going on a supply run, so we won't be interrupted."

"Okay," I say. "Sure." Whatever she wants to talk about so

urgently can't be good. Especially if she needs to plan a time and location when we can be alone.

She nods, biting her lip, and I can't take much more of this. I want to scoop her into my arms and pin her against the nearest tree and kiss that pouty lip of hers until her heart's pounding as hard as mine is.

"What's wrong with you?" she barks. "Why do you look like you just ate a ghost pepper?" She's staring at me with that adorable little furrow in her brow that I want to smooth out with my thumb.

"Nothing," I reply. "I was just running too hard."

She frowns like she doesn't believe that for a second. "I have to make a phone call in a few minutes, but what if we talk right after? It's important."

"How about in half an hour?" I offer. That's time enough for me to run one more lap and then take the coldest shower in the history of the world. I'm going to need every drop of this ice-cold mountain water just to get my heart back to its baseline rhythm.

"Perfect," she says.

Before I can say anything else, she heads off toward the main building, shoes pounding the pavement like it did her wrong, and I'm left feeling like a house on fire.

THIRTY MINUTES LATER, I find Victoria in our office inside the admin building.

She's leaning against the desk, smiling and nodding as she cradles the phone to her ear. When she sees me, she gives me a quick wave and holds one finger up—*Give me a minute.*

Turning my back to the big bank of windows in the conference room, I study the framed prints in the hallway—

modern photos of the Horseshoe Nebula and the Helix Nebula, which I learn from the caption are the result of dying stars. I'm transfixed by the swirling red and green gases, streaks of color as bright as auroras against the vast black of space. It's hard to imagine that this beauty comes from something as it dies.

The door behind me opens and Victoria says, "Okay, I'm done. Thanks for waiting."

"Of course," I say, following her back into the room. "Good news from home?" I close the door behind me, and she sits on the small sofa at the back of the room. Because it's more like a loveseat, I sit in the chair next to her.

I get the feeling that she needs some space to tell me what's on her mind.

"That was a work call," she says, tucking her hair behind her ear. "Or, potential work, I guess."

"Was that Roxy? Did something full-time come up?"

Her brows pinch together. "No. Another real estate office made me an offer. But that's not what I wanted to talk to you about."

"Are you going to take it?" I ask. Her answer means everything. And the way she glossed over it? I don't know how to take that.

She waggles her finger at me. "One crisis at a time, Valentine."

"Crisis?" I ask, because apparently, I'm now a parrot.

"Roxy asked me if something was going on between us," she says. "She swears the admin visit isn't about that, but I'm freaking out. She sent me photos."

"Wait. What?" My heart drops straight into my stomach. "Okay. This is not what I was expecting." If the admin staff gets a whiff of fraternizing, then they'll fire us both in a heartbeat and I can kiss this camp gig goodbye—permanently.

"Yeah, this is not how I expected to start my day, either," she says.

I rake my hands through my hair, trying to stay calm. "What did you tell her?"

She sighs as if she has the weight of the world on her. "I told her that we're old friends. But a couple of photos went up on the site, and Roxy saw them." A blush rises in her cheeks, and she tugs on the ends of her hair, a habit I remember all too well. It means she's nervous and anxious. Scared.

I want to fold her into my arms and tell her it's going to be okay—but that's the impulse that created this problem.

"The photos were nothing terrible," she says. "I mean, it's obvious that we're friendly and close, but it was nothing beyond that. It just raised a flag for Roxy because she's got this ridiculous sixth sense about people."

"Jesus," I breathe.

"We have to take a step back," she says. "I think we have a lot to sort out, and I have a bunch of feelings to untangle, but the point is that we have to be one hundred percent professional, and we haven't been. My life already feels like a train wreck right now, and I don't want to screw this up, too."

I nod, resisting the urge to take her hand in mine. "You're not screwing anything up with me," I reassure her.

She blinks at me in confusion. "I mean the *job*," she says. "Roxy vouched for me, and here I am breaking the one big rule. I don't want to let her down, or ruin this camp for the kids."

Her words hit me like a knife in the chest. Of course she's worried about the work, not me. She's concerned about her reputation, her future with the program. She's not worried about how we fit together after camp is over.

"And then there's your job," she says. "You've been doing

this for years, and I don't want to wreck that for you, either. I know how important it is for you."

I nod, swallowing hard. Although she's right, these are not words I want to hear.

"I just don't want to ruin all of this," she says. "I've missed our friendship so much, and being here has helped me see that. I was hoping we could have that again. If you wanted it, too."

"Friendship," I say, straining to keep my voice even. "That's what you want?"

"I hated the way things ended between us," she says. "I hated that things were unresolved for so long."

"That doesn't answer my question."

She stares at me for a long moment, like she's working through a complicated math problem.

I lean closer, daring her to deny what's written all over her face. Daring her to deny that she wants more than friendship between us. Because that kiss? It didn't feel like the end of something. It felt like the beginning.

"You want me to be your friend?" I ask her. "Nothing else?"

She practically leaps to her feet, pacing in front of me. "I'm not sure of what I want anymore. You said it yourself—camp time is compressed. Things happen fast, and they feel more intense. I think we need to hit the pause button and think harder about what happens next. Don't you?" She tugs on the ends of her hair, a dead giveaway that she's feeling torn. "I just feel like everything in my life is turned upside down right now, and it's all happening so fast, and—" she pauses, letting out a weary sigh. "Making decisions in the heat of the moment is never a good idea."

My heart feels as heavy as a brick. I thought we were on the same page—that she wanted to see where this might go, too. She seemed so certain when we were on the camping trip: by the waterfall, at the campsite, after the bridge.

But something has changed. Now she's saying that she hasn't been feeling at all what I've been feeling. She just wants closure. To smooth out the rough patch of our history and then say goodbye. My stomach's twisting into a knot. This feels just like that night on the beach in college, when she kissed me like it was our last night on Earth and then ran from whatever she was feeling and refused to talk to me.

Before I can put any of that into words, she presses on. "When the admins are here, we have to be icebergs," she says, back to her nervous pacing. "Pretend like you can barely tolerate me. And I'll do the same."

When her gaze flicks back to mine, it's stern and calculating. That look means there's no room for negotiation. She's decided what she wants, and it's not me.

"Can you do that?" she says, her voice softer, but still insistent. Twisting that knife in my chest.

"Icebergs," I repeat. "Whatever you say." The words hang heavy between us and my heart sinks like a stone.

Chapter Twenty

VICTORIA

Roxy grins at me. "I gotta say, the wilderness looks good on you." Her style is chic meets quirky—today, it's a short knit skirt with harness boots and a navy blouse dotted with tiny pink elephants. Her red hair is pulled back into an updo that's held in place with a couple of copper hairpins that she bought at a craft fair we visited last summer.

I pull a leaf from my hair and snort. "It took a little getting used to."

"Never took you for the outdoorsy type," she says. "But I stand corrected."

A few weeks ago, I would have argued that I was better suited for one of her indoor positions. Now I'm not so sure.

I'm not certain about a lot of things anymore. And maybe that's just fine. Maybe I don't have to have everything figured out all the time, despite what that negative voice in my head tells me. Maybe it's time I let go of my lofty expectations and give myself some grace.

We're sitting on the patio by the cafeteria, where the kids are finishing lunch. So far I've managed to avoid Noah since after breakfast, when Roxy arrived with her assistant Julie and the donor, Mira. Soon they'll tour the facilities and see how the fancy telescopes work, but right now they're inside chatting with some students.

"Mira seems cool," I say. She's got a smile that makes you feel right at home and shakes hands like she's meeting her new best friend. Her mostly gray hair is cut into a sleek bob and she has little creases at her eyes that come from years of laugher. Plus, she paired a button-up blouse and tailored pants with bright magenta sneakers—and that made me like her instantly.

"She's great," Roxy says. "She's a retired surgeon and has a soft spot for space camps because her late husband worked for NASA. She's a major donor for the university—has a dorm named after her." She sips her coffee and waves toward Julie and Mira. "She's taken an interest in us, and her donation could fund our camps for a decade—and allow for expansion to some other remote sites and hiring more staff."

"Wow," I breathe. "Now I regret telling her that goofy joke earlier. She's even more VIP than I suspected."

"Are you kidding?" Roxy says. "She loves a good space pun. She told me you were a delight."

Inside, Noah and Sophie are doing their post-lunch announcements, the signal for all campers to head for their classrooms.

"Time for the grand tour," Roxy says, checking the time. "I'll catch up with you in a little while."

"Great," I tell her. "Have fun."

"This is one of my favorite parts of the job," she says. "I love showing people how awesome our staff is and letting them meet happy students. And the fact that you're here makes it that much better."

"Thanks for bringing me on board," I tell her.

"Hey, you're the one that bailed me out," she says, slipping her sunglasses back on. "Your being here means less college-staff drama, and that, my friend, is priceless."

I swallow hard, hating that I haven't been entirely truthful with her about Noah. I don't know if telling her would make things better or worse, but I hate that this secret is hanging between us.

WE ARE ICEBERGS. I have to keep reminding myself of our agreement because, of course, I can't avoid Noah completely.

Roxy, Julie, and Mira have been here for three hours and forty-seven minutes, and even though they've been all over the site and have only spent approximately thirty-three minutes talking to me, I still feel like they're scrutinizing my every move, looking for any evidence that I'm doing something inappropriate with Noah. Or that I don't belong here.

I'm not sure which is worse.

"Did you hear me?" Noah says. "Vic?"

He's standing near the top of the ladder and once again, he's caught me staring. I swear I only meant to spot him (safety first!), but as he reached toward the ceiling to tape the extension cord into place, my eyes snagged on the thin strip of tan skin at his lower back that was exposed right above his belt. The way those jeans are clinging to his muscular body is criminal. My hand is gripping the leg of the ladder with far more force than necessary.

He looks down the ladder at me and a lock of dark hair falls in his eyes. "You okay down there?"

"Yep," I sputter. "All good." I hand him the two-foot wide

paper star and he secures it into place on the tiny hook in the ceiling.

"Sophie went all out with the space theme," I say.

"Decorating is one of her superpowers," he says, adjusting the star so it's just right.

"Look at us, getting these stars aligned." It's a lame attempt at levity, and it falls completely flat.

"Yeah," Noah says. "If only everything could be fixed with tape and power cords." His tone is cool and professional, just as it's been ever since we talked yesterday. Even though he's doing just as I suggested, it feels like he's freezing me out.

I hate that feeling.

He climbs down the ladder and his hand brushes over mine as it slides down the rail. He ignores this touch completely, but the heat from his hand sizzles along my skin, his fingers leaving a path of sparks in their wake.

His face reveals nothing, as still as the moon.

This is agony. I want my fun, teasing Noah back. I want all of his warmth and charm, all of his hopeful glances and secret smiles.

"Listen," I blurt. "About yesterday."

"What about it?" he says, untangling the bundle of white fairy lights. He frowns, trying to find the end of the string.

I sigh. He's not going to make this easy.

"I misspoke. I probably came off cold, and I didn't mean to. This whole situation just has me panicked." I grab the other end of the strand and try to free it from the mass of lights, but every move I make gets them more tangled. "I'm trying to do the right thing here for both of us. But maybe I'm kidding myself. Maybe I should just suck it up and do the thing I'm good at and stop reaching for something else," I tell him. "Take the job in Florida and stay in my lane." The words taste bitter in my mouth.

He frowns. "What job in Florida?"

"That call yesterday. A real estate agent I knew back home offered me a job with her new firm in Pensacola."

His brow lifts in that way that means he's part surprised and a little hurt. "Is that really what you want? I thought you were done with real estate."

"She's a huge deal. Working for her would make my career." We fumble with the lights, and when his hand brushes over my arm, his gaze snaps to mine. "I feel like I should do it," I grit out. "I mean, Diana can be hard to work with—*The Devil Wears Prada* has nothing on her—but at least that's a job I know how to do well." I shrug. "Plus, it would solve my money problems. It's the smart move."

"But it's not what you love." His tone is cool.

"It's a top real estate firm," I tell him. "I'd be foolish to turn down a boat load of money."

He sighs, raking his hand through his hair. Just when he starts to speak, he bites his lip, like he's holding back a tidal wave of thoughts.

"What?" I ask.

He leans closer, pinning me with his gaze. The disappointment in his eyes guts me. "I think you're giving up on this too soon. It's like you're looking for reasons to go back to the work that makes you feel hollow."

"That's not fair." I can feel the blood rising in my cheeks, because he's not entirely wrong. Diana's the safe choice, the devil I know. If Roxy were to offer me a full time job with the camp—and that's a massive *if*—then it's still a leap that I'm not sure I'm ready for. There's safety in the familiar, even if *familiar* doesn't light me up.

He shakes his head. "Someone's dangling this shiny thing in front of you, but it's a distraction. It's not the thing you need."

I grit my teeth, tugging at the lights and feeling nothing but tension. He huffs as I pull him off-balance, and we both move our arms above our heads in opposite directions, the little bulbs tinkling in the space between us. We're trapped in a web of lights now, getting more tangled by the minute.

"How would you know what I need?" I snap.

His brow lifts. "Because you *told* me, Vic." His voice is calm, but stern. "You told me you wanted something that brings you joy and gives you purpose—something that excites you. Why do you think you don't deserve that?"

"It's not that simple," I say. "I can't keep waiting for something that might not happen. What if this is the best offer I get?"

"What if something better is right around the corner?" he says. "Or right in the palm of your hand?"

Heat creeps into my cheeks because he's not just talking about a job anymore, and now I see I've done the very thing I wanted to avoid: I've entangled my feelings for working here with my feelings for Noah. Now it's hard to imagine one without the other—and it's difficult to say which has the tighter hold on my heart.

And both feel like a risk I'm not quite ready to take.

He tugs on the strand of lights, pulling me closer. "You're selling yourself short. Settling for something that isn't what you really want. It kills me to watch you do that."

I tug right back, but there's a knot in the bundle of lights left between us. "I'm not something you need to fix, Noah."

"This isn't about fixing." He steps closer, his eyes smoldering. "You can do so much better. You *deserve* better." His jaw tenses as he stares down at me through those ridiculously thick lashes. I'm close enough to smell that spicy-woodsy scent that's all Noah, to see the faint freckles across his cheeks. Being this close just reminds me of lying next to him in his tent, so close that I could see that adorable crooked smile in the moonlight.

He's not smiling now, but his pupils widen as if he's thinking of that moment, too. And the kiss that came after. His lips part, just barely, and his brows pinch together as his eyes burn into mine.

My heart hammers in my chest. It's infuriating how he can make words that seem so demanding sound so protective.

"This summer has been amazing," I tell him, which is absolutely true. "The kids have been a joy. It's been exactly the kind of break I needed from all the chaos in my life, but it's time to get back to reality."

He frowns, that muscle in his jaw tensing. "This hasn't felt real to you?"

"Summer camp is this weird dreamlike state," I tell him. "It's an escape from your regular life, where you can remake yourself into a different version of who you are for a little while. But when it's over, you go back to your regular life." I give him a small shrug. "It's felt real in the way that dreams feel real—just before you wake up."

His head dips closer to mine. "Who says you can't have everything you dream of?" he says, his voice low and gravelly. "Who told you that lie, sweetheart?"

My heart squeezes as he wraps the strand of lights around his hand, pulling me off-balance so I stumble right into him, my palms flat against his chest. Tears prick the corners of my eyes as I think of all the times I've been told to manage my expectations, all the times I've convinced myself I wasn't trying hard enough, being brave enough, being good enough. How many times have I held up this facade, projecting this image to everyone that I was fine while crumbling on the inside? How many times did I compromise what I wanted—with my job at Rayanne's firm, my engagement to Theo—instead of believing something better was waiting for me?

"Noah," I begin, my voice barely a whisper.

"Listen," he says, "I'm not going to pressure you for an answer. But I want to make one thing crystal clear." His voice is doing that sexy-rumble that turns my knees to jelly. "It might be completely selfish, but I don't want you to go. Partly because I think you're settling for something your heart doesn't want—but mostly because I want to go on that date with you." He pauses and shakes his head. "That's a lie. I want to go on lots of dates with you, Vic. And I don't think I'm alone in that feeling." His gaze locks on mine and that electric feeling is back, zipping along my skin and making my heart flutter like a bird.

"Timing was always our problem, wasn't it?" I ask him.

He lifts a brow. "I'm not sure I'd agree."

I think back to that night on the beach, when he'd returned my kiss so fiercely, like he might never get another chance. I've replayed that night a thousand times, wondering how it might have gone differently if we'd done that sooner, in a moment that wasn't overshadowed by fear.

I feel like I'm back in that same position, choosing this path because I'm afraid it's the best job offer I'll get. That this move will fix what's broken in my life.

But what I want most is staring me right in the face, with epic eyebrows and a crooked smile that promises all the adventure I've longed for.

I don't get to have both.

"Hey, what's all this?" Roxy says, and I jump backwards. Her voice is chipper, but her brow is arched in that way that means she's taking in this scene and hasn't missed a single detail. Like the blush that's creeping up my neck, the way Noah's hand has caught my arm to steady me.

I step away from him like he's been struck by lightning and blurt, "Just me being clumsy in a battle with the Christmas lights."

If Roxy's brow lifts any higher, it's going to fly right off her face. She knows that I'm neither clumsy nor capable of lying. "Right," she says, her gaze flicking to Noah. "Can I help with anything?"

"We're just about done," he says, his voice as smooth as honey. Does nothing rattle this man? "Vic, you want to do the honors?"

I blink at him. It's as if all thoughts have fallen right out of my brain except for one: *What you want most is staring you right in the face. What if you let yourself have it?*

"Flip the switch?" he says, nodding toward the dozen paper star lights that hang from the ceiling.

"Sure," I breathe, walking over to the power strips by the windows. When I flip the power switch, Roxy gasps as she holds her fingers to her lips, her grin impossibly wide.

Next to her, Noah's scanning one side of the room to the other, checking our work.

"Amazing," Roxy says, and it is.

The whole room is filled with strings of twinkling fairy lights. The star lanterns, made from brightly-colored paper, fill the room with pools of light, their intricate patterns of punched holes now visible. The walls in this room are painted a rich navy blue, so even though it's not quite dark outside, the effect is stunning. Noah told me earlier that the stars are Sophie's—they have to stretch the activities budget pretty far, and they rarely have anything left over for decorations. So Sophie brings her own from home. This year, Noah brought the thousand yards of twinkling lights, plus all the gear needed to hang them without damaging the room.

They have this down to an art, and I can't help but be a little envious of them for finding this vocation that means so much to them.

"Sophie told me there are special cookies," Roxy says.

"This bakery in town is incredible," I tell her. "They make sugar cookies with some secret ingredient that are to die for—I ordered five dozen so we all have a few extra."

"That's my girl," Roxy says. "Always sniffing out the best treats." She glances at Noah and my face burns like the surface of the sun.

"And they're airbrushed to look like the planets," I tell her, hoping all this talk of cookies might refocus her attention and stop my hammering heart. "Little pieces of art that are almost too gorgeous to eat. Almost."

"How's the visit going?" Noah asks her. "Is Mira head over heels yet?"

Roxy grins. "She's like a kid in a candy store." She glances around the room once more and shoves her hands into her skirt pockets. "I figured she'd be happy after a quick tour, but she wants to see every inch of this place. She wants to sit in on the classes tomorrow and even asked to check out the dance. So we're staying one more night."

"That's great news," I say, but my stomach churns. That's twenty-four more hours that we'll be scrutinized, and I'm exhausted from trying to manage all of these feelings that keep coming up. Gwen used to tell me that I shouldn't tamp down my feelings because it's like trying to push a beach ball under the water—no matter how hard you shove it down, eventually it'll spring back to the surface. And probably smack you right in the face.

"For sure," Roxy says. "I'm glad we got to visit. Perfect timing."

If only, I think, glancing at Noah. With us, there's no such thing.

Noah smirks at her. "The fun's barely started, though. You haven't heard me deejay."

Roxy rolls her eyes. "Please tell me that you let Sophie manage the playlist. I've told you a thousand times that you can't dance to Led Zeppelin."

Noah snorts in defiance, resting his hands on his hips. "Challenge accepted."

"We want the kids to come back, you know," she tells him. "And bring their friends. We don't need to scare them off with your quote-unquote *dancing*."

"You're breaking my heart, Roxy." His gaze flicks toward me and a lump forms in my throat.

She grins and then nudges my arm. "You okay, Vic? You look like you swallowed a bee."

"Great," I tell her. "A-okay." I give her two thumbs-up, like a total dork, because apparently my awkwardness has been dialed up to eleven.

She purses her lips. "Okay, then. I'll leave you to it and see you later for activity time."

Once she's out the door, I busy myself with untangling the last of the lights. Everything I say to Noah seems to make things weirder between us, and I don't know how to fix it.

I am so not fine. I'm completely falling for him and refusing to think about what that means. I'm pretending I know what I'm doing here on top of a mountain with a bunch of whiz kids. I'm lying to my best friend and acting as if Noah and I aren't breaking the biggest rule in the camp's rule book, and I am failing at playing it cool.

I am light-years from fine.

But until Roxy leaves, I have to pretend that I am.

Chapter Twenty-One

NOAH

A wall has come up between us again, and I'm not sure I can dismantle it. All I know is that I don't want Victoria to slip out of my life again. Whenever she talks about that job in Florida, her voice sounds strangled and this tiny muscle below her eye twitches and I know precisely what that means: she's frustrated and feeling trapped.

She had that same look when she burst onto the balcony the night we met. She was running away then, too—and truthfully, so was I. Something in me recognized her as a kindred spirit and together we learned how to lean on each other. I'd never trusted anyone enough to lay my vulnerable parts bare, but Victoria was compassionate and easy to trust.

And she can do anything she wants when she sets her mind on it.

Now, for example, she's across the room mirroring Layla and Priya's dance moves. We're four songs into my space-themed playlist and she and Sophie jumped right in to break the ice. They're grooving under the glittering star lights like this is the best night ever, and it's about the cutest thing I've ever seen.

There are a dozen reasons I don't want Vic to take this new job, why it's so obvious that she *shouldn't* take it, but it's not my decision to make. I need to give her space, but distance is the last thing I want between us.

It feels like she's slipping away. Again.

By the end of this week I'm going to be a babbling wreck of a man. And that thought triggers one that squeezes my heart like a fist: *what if, when camp is over, I never see her again?*

"Nice costume," Victoria says, coming to stand beside me. "A classic." She studies my suit, a slim-cut black one that's a little too hipster for me but is perfect for a Man in Black.

I squeeze the cartoonish green rubber alien that's riding in my breast pocket in place of a pocket square. It squeaks as its eyes bulge, earning a laugh from Victoria. Her smile yanks me back in time to that Halloween party where we first met. Two new college students fumbling through their first autumn in a new city, looking for that little niche where they belonged. We'd always fit well together, right from that first night. From that moment forward, she'd always had my back and I'd had hers—and I forgot what it was to be lonely.

Ever since our talk yesterday, she's been pulling away from me. And that loneliness is creeping up behind me, stalking me like a storm cloud.

"You're exceptionally sparkly," I tell her. I shove my black Ray-Bans up into my hair and take in the details: a silver jumpsuit that hugs her curves and shines like a disco ball, a hot pink wig, big heart-shaped sunglasses, purple lipstick that is way more appealing than it should be. And a headband with what looks like a stylized antenna—she's like a space invader from a 1950s flick.

"Satellite of love," she deadpans, those purple lips pursed in a smirk.

"Deep cut," I tell her. "Nicely done."

"Sophie helped me. I didn't realize I'd need a space-themed outfit for the dance. She said she always brings a couple because she can't decide until the day of."

"Roxy left that part out of your contract, huh?"

She shrugs. "I might have skipped over some parts of that packet she sent me. It's okay, though. I like a challenge. And a chance to wear a hot pink wig."

All around us, the kids are chattering and wiggling around in some delightfully wacky outfits of their own. The dance is a tradition here, so the kids bring costumes they make at home. Some are simple, like little green aliens and astronauts—and some are so elaborate it blows my mind. Ethan's dressed as a rocket ship, complete with a cone-shaped hat and streamer-like flames, and Layla's wearing a long dress that's painted like the Milky Way.

"I can't believe we pulled this off," Victoria says. "This looks even more amazing than I thought it would. The movies were such a great idea."

Behind her, there's a projector showing a reel Sophie put together of clips from a bunch of space-themed movies. There's a little bit of everything, from *Guardians of the Galaxy* to *Mars Attacks!* to *2001: A Space Odyssey*. The clips play silently while my special dance playlist booms through the speakers in the corners of the room. This lobby is now a wonderland filled with twinkling lights, paper star lanterns, and sugar-fueled tweens. A small lounge just around the corner is set up as a chill-out room where the kids can go if they need a quiet space, with dim lights and no music.

So far, the kids are having a blast.

"Have you seen Roxy lately?" I ask Victoria.

She shakes her head, and in that instant I see the tension

settle back into her shoulders. "Not since dinner," she says. "She's coming soon, though. Apparently, Mira's super excited about the dance."

"Come on guys," Sophie says from behind us. She grabs each of our hands and pulls us to the center of the room where the kids are dancing. "Let's see your moves!"

The kids cheer as we come closer, pulling us into their circle. David Bowie's "Star Man" is blaring through the speakers, and Victoria laughs as Sophie takes her hand and twirls her around. Something tugs at my heart, and I realize that I desperately want to be the one holding Victoria's hand and spinning her across the floor, under these brilliant twinkling star lights.

I've fallen so hard for her, all over again.

She looks so happy here, doing these goofy dance moves with the kids. I don't have to look hard to see the moments when she gets out of her own head and lets herself relax and just *be*. I want her to have that feeling all the time—to know that she's perfect just as she is.

Song after song goes by, and we stay on the dance floor. The kids are all wiggling around like little excited electrons and soon Victoria and I get shoved right against each other. When we collide, her hands land on my chest, right below my collarbones. My hands go instinctively to her waist to steady her, and her eyes widen. An electric current zips along my skin and my mouth instantly goes dry.

She drops her hands as if she's touched a hot stovetop. I know she's worried about what Roxy and the other staff might see, and I hate that we have to keep this wall between us. I just want to hold her close and feel the softness of her skin and smell the sweet citrus scent of her.

We're jostled again, and I'm regretting putting the frenetic "Intergalactic" on the playlist, but also I'm not. Because I'll happily let Victoria collide into me any day of the week, as often as she likes.

When she spins back my way, I say, "I'm going to check the other room and make the rounds."

"Oh!" she sputters. "I should—"

"Stay," I tell her. "They love having you out here with them."

She takes another look around just as Layla and Priya appear, each grabbing one of her hands and pulling her into their circle. Victoria smiles, and already I miss having that particular smile directed at me.

Slipping out of the mass of dancing kiddos, I head across the room to the snack table and grab a cup of water before ducking into the chill-out room. A few kids were resting in here earlier, but now they're back in the main room watching the movie clips and occasionally being pulled into dances. Out on the adjoining deck, two boys are pointing up at the sky, discussing the planetary alignment they learned about this week.

When I head back inside, Roxy walks up beside me.

"This is amazing," she says. "Y'all have outdone yourselves."

"We might have gone a little overboard with the decorations," I reply. "But the kids dig it."

She nods, watching the kids shift into another line dance. They're mostly in sync, and it's completely adorable. Victoria and Sophie are right there with them, Sophie leading the moves and Victoria laughing as she tries to keep up.

"How's the session going?" Roxy asks me.

"Great," I say, "Maybe the best one ever." It's hard not to stare at Vic as she wiggles her hips and waves her arms around her head. She's the master of goofy dancing, and the kids love it.

I love it, too.

"How's Victoria doing?" she asks. "She getting along okay?"

"We're lucky to have her. The kids love her." *You love her*, that voice inside me says. *You always have.*

Roxy nods, as if waiting for more.

"I mean, she had an adjustment period, like anyone would. But Vic's great at this. She's got this way of pulling everyone together without putting any pressure on them, you know? She doesn't want anyone to feel left out, but she doesn't want to make it a big deal, either."

"She's good at that."

Victoria laughs, now apparently in a dance-off with Layla, whose sparkly galaxy dress is rippling around her as the kids clap and cheer.

"Making people feel like they belong is one of her superpowers," I say. "And she doesn't even realize it."

Roxy gives me a tiny smile—one that says she sees everything.

As if summoned, Victoria comes over to us, pushing her hair behind her ears. She's practically glowing, with her cheeks flushed and her pink hair wild from all the movement and the humidity. She grins and that tug is back, low in my belly and impossible to ignore.

"Y'all have a sneaky vibe," she says, a bit out of breath. "What are you whispering about over here?"

"Your killer dance moves," Roxy says with a wink.

Victoria gives her a teasing eye-roll. "Yeah, okay. I'm a little out of practice." She does the cutest little shimmy and says, "The tweens are teaching me to be cool again. What else you got?"

"How you put everyone at ease," I say. "Make them feel seen. Make them feel like they belong."

She turns to me then, her lips parted in surprise.

"Noah was just telling me what a huge asset you've been," Roxy tells her. "I mean, obviously, I knew that would be the case, but I like to be proven right. And then hear about it in great detail."

"These kids would be missing out if she weren't here," I say, and my chest tightens at the thought. Because I'd be missing out even more. "She makes everyone here feel like they matter."

Victoria blinks at me, her eyes glassy. A blush creeps into her cheeks and she turns to Roxy. "It's been really fun. These kids have taught me a few things, too."

"None of that is one bit surprising," Roxy says. "I knew you'd be a good fit here." She glances toward the main entrance and waves to Julie and Mira, who are smiling as they survey the room. "I should get back to these ladies, but we'll catch up later, okay?" She squeezes Vic's arm and heads over toward the others.

When I turn back to Victoria, she gives me a tiny smile. "I can't believe you said that about me."

I shrug. "It's true. You make every place brighter just by being in it. I'll tell you every day if that's what it takes for you to believe it."

Her lips part and that adorable furrow is back in her brow. She looks like she might cry, and it takes everything in me not to pull her into a hug. "Come on," I tell her, giving her arm a nudge. "Next dance is the electric slide."

She follows me back to where the kids are gathered and says, "Okay, Valentine. Time to shake those tail feathers." A sweet smile pulls at her lips and I want to etch this moment into my memory: Victoria, under this blanket of colored stars, looking at me like I'm the best thing that ever happened to her.

You and me together in this crazy little world, she used to say. And I want to badly for that to be true again.

Chapter Twenty-Two

VICTORIA

Long after the dance is over, I'm still thinking about Noah dancing under the twinkling lights in his perfectly tailored suit, his hair wild and his eyes bright. I might never forget that crooked smile that spread across his face as he went all in, doing his enthusiastic version of the Carlton dance that will be ingrained in my memory forever.

And what he said to Roxy about me? I'll never forget that, either.

I've nearly drifted off to sleep when there's a knock on my door—an urgent *tap-tap-tap-tap.* It takes me a minute to understand that is not the tapping of Noah's shoes on the linoleum as he does the cabbage patch, but knuckles pounding against my door. By the time I stumble out of bed, the knock has grown louder and a tiny voice is calling my name.

I open the door to find Layla standing in the hallway, her eyes wide. "It's Priya," she says. "She's having an allergic reaction or something, and she needs help."

We hurry down the hallway as a couple of doors open, the girls' heads poking out.

Inside Layla's room, Priya is slouched on her bed, her back against the wall and her feet straight out in front of her. She looks like a puppet whose strings have been cut. Her face is drawn, her lips tight. Becca from across the hall is sitting next to her, holding her hand. When I rush to her side, her eyes flutter open.

"Victoria," she says. My name comes out like a gasp. She has tears in her eyes, and my heart is pounding like a jackhammer.

"It's okay," I tell her. "What happened?"

There are three other girls in the room—two more than there should be—staring at us with wide eyes. One of them looks close to tears. Layla's bed is pushed against Priya's, piled with pillows. A laptop sits open to a movie and next to it there's a scattering of candy wrappers and partially-eaten snacks.

"Becca," I say, snapping back into action. "Go get Sophie and tell her to bring me the first-aid kit." She nods and hurries out of the room.

When I turn back to Priya, her brows pinch together as she says, "I must have eaten something I wasn't supposed to." Her lips are swollen, and there are small red splotches on her neck and arms. I quickly catalog every snack we put out during the dance. We knew about Priya's peanut allergy and have been very careful about food we brought onto the site. The kitchen staff knew about it, too.

"Do you have your EpiPen?" I remember from our student files that she brought two with her.

She squeezes her eyes shut like she's in pain, and my heart bangs against my ribs. That first aid class I took before camp started covered how to use the pen, so I can do it if I have to.

"I'm not supposed to waste them," she says. "It has to be an emergency."

I don't want to scare her, but I want her to understand this is serious. "Sweetie, this is a time when you need it," I tell her.

Her lip trembles.

"It's okay to be afraid," I tell her. "But we've got this."

"I don't want to," she says, shaking her head. Her breathing is a little labored, and the swelling and red blotches are concerning. She needs the injection. "I've never done it myself before," she says. "This only happened once before, at home."

I hold her hand. "I'll help you, okay?"

She squeezes my fingers tight and says, "I hate needles."

"Me too," I tell her. "The good news is that this is a small one, and it only takes a second."

"Here's her EpiPen," Layla says, rushing over.

I think through the steps I learned in the first-aid session, then pop the cap off the pen as Priya squeezes her eyes shut again.

"On three, okay?" I ask her. "Right here." I touch a spot on her outer thigh, right below the hem of her sleep shorts, and she nods.

I count to three in a hurry and jam the pen against her skin, hearing the loud click of the autoinjector as Sophie bursts into the room with Becca.

"We were just watching a movie on my laptop," Layla tells Sophie, "And then she started wheezing."

Sophie looks at me and I give her a quick nod. She's got the portable phone from the lounge in her hand. Her expression's calm, but I can tell she's blasting through her mental checklist.

"Priya," I say. "How do you feel now? Is it still hard to breathe?"

She shakes her head. "Getting better now," she wheezes.

"Any idea what you ate?" I ask her. "Or how much?"

She points toward the beds, where food wrappers lay

scattered by the laptop. "We just pooled our snacks," she said. "Thought they were all safe."

"It's okay," Sophie tells her, giving me a weary look. "You just rest a minute." She pulls me toward the door and lowers her voice. "I'll go get Roxy. You stay here. We need to take her the hospital. The EpiPen is only a temporary fix."

I nod, shoving my hands into my pockets so no one sees them shaking. "Okay."

But this is very much not okay. When I take a closer look at the bed, I see a plate with two partially-eaten cookies that I ordered from the bakery and a knot forms in my chest. The most important part of this job was to keep these kids safe—and I failed.

SOPHIE HELPS Priya into the back seat of the rental car and then climbs into the driver's seat. Roxy nudges my shoulder and says, "Good job in there. I'll call the land line with any updates, but I expect we'll be there overnight."

I nod, still clutching the portable phone from the cabin. Roxy waves as Sophie eases out of the parking lot and onto the gravel road that winds down the mountain.

I don't feel like I've done a good job here. I feel like I've barely been hanging on, and tonight was the last straw. I'm way out of my depth, and this is my fault. If those cookies caused Priya's reaction, I'll never forgive myself. I was so careful when I placed the order, so explicit with my instructions. I thought I'd figured out how to do this job, and I let myself get comfortable, let myself feel like I belonged here. I was distracted by Noah and this tidal wave of feelings, and now I've made this colossal mistake.

The perfectionist in me is raging, her argument simple: if I was good enough for this job, for these kids, I wouldn't have made this error.

"Hey," Noah says, giving my shoulder a nudge. "How about I make us some tea." He's changed into a white tee shirt and jeans, his hair wild from raking his hands through it.

"I need something way stronger than tea," I mutter, knowing full well that option isn't on the table.

"Well," he says. "Under normal circumstances, I'd be able to help you with that. But since we're at a kids' camp, I can offer you tea, juice, and hot chocolate with tiny marshmallows."

"Fair enough." I follow him into the boys' cabin, but go no further than the lounge area and kitchenette, which is the mirror image of the girls' cabin. Everyone's asleep again now, or at least in their rooms. We did a final check before Sophie rushed Priya to the hospital, because of course some of the kids had heard us and asked what was happening.

While Noah fills an electric kettle and searches for the cocoa, I collapse into one of the two wooden chairs at the dining table. When he sits across from me, his knee bumping against mine, I don't have the strength to move away.

Or maybe I just need to feel that tiny connection.

"Listen," he says. "This is not your fault."

I blink at him, shaking my head.

"I know that's what you're thinking," he says, "because you have that line between your eyebrows that's deep enough to grow potatoes."

"But it *is* my fault," I counter. "Obviously."

He cocks his head to the side in challenge.

"In her room. The girls were eating the cookies I got at the bakery. I saw them on the plate." The words come out in a rush, a painful confession.

"But you told the baker about all the allergies we have here."

"I sure did. They assured me no peanut products, no tree nut products." I rest my face in my hands. "I shouldn't have taken a chance."

The kettle whistles and Noah fills our two mugs with hot water and cocoa powder. He pushes one toward me when he sits back down, then sprinkles a handful of marshmallows into each mug.

"Even if it was the cookies," he says, "accidents happen. You took every precaution you could." His eyes are steady on mine, daring me to disagree.

"But I brought the killer cookies here!" I shout.

He sighs, sitting back in the chair so that his long legs stretch to fill the space between us. "That's the adrenaline talking," he says. "And perhaps some anxiety. And also that stubborn little part of you that thinks she's never allowed to be human and make mistakes."

I open my mouth to argue and he holds his hand up. "Stop."

What really stops me, though, is the way he has effortlessly summed up my life. Because that's me in a nutshell: a people-pleasing perfectionist who would rather shrivel up and die than be told she's done something wrong—and worse, hurt someone because of it.

"Is it possible," he says, "that she ate something else that caused the reaction?"

"The half-eaten cookies were right there by the laptop, Noah. It doesn't take Sherlock Holmes to—"

"But," he interrupts again. "You said there were other candy wrappers there, too. Every kid here showed up with a bag full of snacks from home. I can promise you that." He stirs his cocoa, the *clink-clink* of his spoon driving the words home.

"Priya's so careful about what she eats," I argue. "She reads the labels."

I'm infuriated that he won't let me wallow in my shame. The punishing thoughts are racing through my brain like jagged bolts of lightning.

"Here's a wild idea," he says. "Why not focus on how great you were with her and how quickly you took charge. We're very lucky you were here to help."

When I give him another doubtful stare, he says, "Sophie told me all about how you saved the day."

"Sophie exaggerates."

He leans closer to me. So close that I can smell that clean cedar-like scent that's entirely Noah. He stares at me hard, his warm hazel eyes both a comfort and a challenge. "Hear me when I say this. That was scary for Priya, and you made it so much easier for her."

Tears well in my eyes, but I can't look away from him when he's staring at me like this, pinning me with words I desperately want to believe and daring me to push back.

"But that's what you do, Vic," he says, his voice a low rumble. "You put people at ease. Even in the toughest moments. You make them feel seen. And loved."

I shake my head, fighting back tears. I do not want to fall apart in front of Noah. Not in this musty room, in a wobbly old chair, in my threadbare pajamas with my messy hair and racing thoughts. "I've been kidding myself with this," I mutter. "I should just withdraw my application and take the stupid job in Florida." Even as I say it, my gut clenches at the thought—because I'd finally let myself believe that this camp could be part of my new path.

And I let myself believe that Noah could be part of it, too.

But mostly, it's because I want them both and I'm not convinced I can have them.

He scoots his chair closer, then slides his hand over mine. "Why do you look for reasons to beat yourself up?" he says, his voice more tender than I've ever heard it. "This is the one thing I've never understood about you."

"The one thing?" I ask.

"Okay, fair," he says, trying for levity. "Maybe it's just the biggest. You're this brilliant, gorgeous, compassionate juggernaut of a human who's completely fearless when it matters. You help people feel comfortable in their own skin. You inspire people to be better, dream bigger. You're the strongest, most resilient person I know, and no matter how difficult things get, you never let them harden you. There's not a single person on this earth I'd rather spend my summer with, and I just wish there was some way I could give you a glimpse of what I see when I look at you. And yet the things you tell yourself—" he shakes his head, "if anyone else said such mean things to you, I'd haul them out into the woods and leave them there for the coyotes to chew on."

I blink at him, feeling something coil in my chest that I can't ignore anymore. "Then why wasn't I enough for you?" I ask. "Back then."

His brows pinch together. "Is that what you think? How could you ever, in a million years, believe that's true?"

My throat feels like it's closing up, but I force the words out anyway. "Because that night on the beach. You let me go. You didn't choose me."

"Victoria," he says, and the sound of my full name on his tongue makes me shiver. The way he drags each syllable out, like he wants to taste them—it turns those butterflies in my chest into a frenzy. "It was never because of you—it was all me. I panicked. I had these complicated feelings and was so afraid of doing the wrong thing." He shakes his head. "When you kissed me that night, I nearly lost my mind because I'd been wanting you to do that forever. But I didn't want to be deceptive. I wanted to break things off with Samantha first, before you and I took it any further." He lets out a heavy sigh. "I thought I owed it to her to go on that trip we'd planned, to keep my word and somehow let her down easy—but that was wrong. I was trying to do the right thing, but instead I wrecked it all."

"What happens if I'm not enough for you now?"

He stares at me, and for the first time I can recall, Noah Valentine is speechless.

Or perhaps, he doesn't have an answer.

"Vic, you're the best thing that ever happened to me. Why are you so afraid to believe that?"

My heart squeezes in my chest. He's the best thing that happened to me, too.

He cups my cheek with his hand, then slides his thumb along my cheek. "Sweetheart, you're it for me. I don't know how else to convince you."

All those feelings and worries I've pushed down are swirling in my head like a hurricane. Do I want this camp job because I truly love it, or because it allows me to be close to Noah? And if things between us were to fall apart, would I still want this job?

The thoughts are just too overwhelming. I want to believe him, but my brain won't let go of this fear that he'll decide he's wrong and I'm not enough after all. It feels like the walls in this cabin are closing in.

"I just want you," he says, taking my hand in his. "That's what I know for sure. The rest, we can figure out together. If you want to take that job in Florida, then I'll move to Florida. I go where you go."

"How can you say that?" I shake my head. "You're making this decision too fast. You're not thinking this through."

He shrugs, sliding his thumb over my knuckles. "I know what's most important to me. I don't need to think about it."

"I need some space to breathe," I tell him. "Some time to think about this."

He draws my hand to his lips and says, "Then take it. I'll give you all the time you need."

His tenderness cracks my heart in half. He deserves an answer and I hate that it feels so simple for him and so complicated for me. As much as I want this to work between us, I can't shake the thought that I'm letting my feelings for him affect how I feel about my next career move.

I hate that my instinct is to run from him. I'm tired of running *from* people when things get hard—I don't want to make that mistake again. Instead, I want to run *toward* my new future because I'm excited about it. Instead of fleeing something out of fear, I want to chase something out of love.

I kept my old job because of my fear of how my parents would be disappointed, fear that I wouldn't find a better job. I stayed with Theo because I was afraid there wasn't someone better out there, or that the life he offered was the best I could hope for.

Now I see how wrong that was, and I don't want to make that mistake again.

My heart wants Noah to be part of that future, but my brain's busy telling me all the reasons it won't work. With all of these thoughts buzzing through my head, I'm certain I'll say the wrong words and wreck us in a way that can't be fixed.

So I need to step back. Slow down. Breathe.

"I can't talk about this anymore right now," I tell him, standing. "I'll see you in the morning."

He nods, following me to the door. "Let's talk tomorrow night. When all the kids are gone and it's just us."

"I won't have an answer by then."

"That's okay." He gives me a tiny smile. "We can talk about anything. Or nothing. That part doesn't matter."

I nod, even though I'm not sure that's true.

Chapter Twenty-Three

NOAH

I ran three miles this morning to get Victoria off my mind—specifically, the look of panic on her face last night when I told her how I felt about her.

It didn't work.

Now my muscles are screaming, I'm a sweaty mess, and my brain still helpfully reminds me approximately every three minutes that Vic is about to leave me.

Again. This time for a job she told me doesn't even make her happy.

It was impossible to sleep last night, because I had about a million things I wanted to say to her—but I didn't know how to say them without sounding completely selfish. She'd told me she wanted to give this a try, to go on a real date together after camp was over. And the idea that she wanted to give us another chance had me feeling hopeful for the first time in ages. I thought she felt the same way I did, but now she's throwing all of that away.

This hurts even more than it did the last time she left.

I need a shower before today's morning meeting with Roxy,

but I need coffee more. Caffeine soothes me, and right now I feel like crawling out of my skin. It's ten minutes before seven and the kitchen staff's busy getting ready for breakfast. Taylor Swift's blasting from a radio somewhere behind the kitchen doors and at least three people are singing along with her, woefully off-key but with admirable enthusiasm. When I slip over to the coffee station by the bank of windows and fill my mug, Victoria steps up next to me.

"Hi," she says. "You get some rest?" She's wearing a green tank top that draws my eye straight to her tanned sculpted shoulders and shorts that make her legs look a mile long. Her hair's curlier, a little wild from the humidity, and all I can think is how soft it would feel against my chest.

"Not much," I admit.

"Me either," she says, taking in my sweaty running clothes with a flick of her gaze—but her eyes take a leisurely path back up to mine. "I need about a gallon of coffee before this day starts."

"Same," I tell her. "Departure day is always hectic. I need all the help I can get."

She bites her lip, and for a moment I think she might say more about last night, about her plans. I want her to tell me that she'd rather explore what's happening between us than settle for a job that sounds great on paper but takes the sparkle out of her eyes. I want her to tell me that she feels the same way I do, that she couldn't sleep because she was thinking about us, and picturing all the things we can do together as soon as we're off this mountain and not in charge of a group of tweens anymore.

I've given a lot of thought to that last one.

Instead, she takes a sip of coffee and flinches. "Ugh. Are we certain this isn't siphoned straight from the pond out there?"

"As long as there's caffeine, I don't care much where it came from."

She smirks at that, because she knows full well I'm picky about my coffee and brought a French press here with me. This was just the faster option.

She pours two more coffees into paper cups and hands one to me. "Roxy called a little while ago to say she and Sophie were ten minutes away and desperate for coffee that wasn't made in a hospital."

As I follow her outside, a buzzing fills the air between us. She shoves the extra coffee cup into the crook of her arm and pulls her phone from her pocket. Frowning, she stares at the screen, at the incoming call from *Diana*.

Diana the real estate agent, with the career-changing job offer.

"You need to take that?" I ask.

She shakes her head as we approach the entrance to the main building, where Sophie and Roxy are waiting.

"I'll call her back," she says, silencing the call. That furrow is back in her brow as she shoves the phone back into her pocket.

"Look," I tell her. "I know it's not my decision and I don't get a say, but I hate to see you settle when I know that you could soar."

Victoria stares at me for what feels like a solid minute, and then her lip trembles.

"I have plenty of other selfish reasons why I think you shouldn't go to Florida," I go on. "But that's the biggest one." I sip my coffee, hoping that might force down the giant lump in my throat, but it doesn't. This feels like one of those now-or-never moments and I don't want to be anywhere close to *never* with Victoria.

I don't know why it's always been so hard to be truthful

about the scope of my feelings for her—maybe because I was just afraid that the truth might reveal a gap too wide for us to navigate. I decide right then and there, lukewarm pond-water coffee in hand, that I'm done holding things back from her. Life's too short, and I'm done keeping my feelings buried so deep. She deserves the truth, even when it comes out messy. After all, the best parts of life are messy sometimes—we have to take ourselves apart and put ourselves back together to fully experience this life and all the beauty and the challenge that comes with it. And there's no one else I'd rather rearrange myself with than Victoria.

Probably, I shouldn't spill my guts here, moments away from a briefing with our supervisor. But I can't hold back anymore. I don't want one more minute to go by where Vic doesn't know how much she means to me.

"I really want us to go on that date," I blurt. "Preferably not in Florida, but I've been hoarding frequent flyer miles and am overdue for an actual vacation. It'll be hot as blazes and I swore I'd never set foot across the state line after that horrific freshman-year road trip that I'm still not going to tell you about, but if that's where you're going, then I'm in." I pause and when her eyes flick to mine, I hold her gaze. "All in."

"Noah," she breathes. Her brow lifts as her mouth falls open and I can't decide if this was a genius move or the most hopeless. All I know for sure is that I don't want her to walk out of my life again—especially if it's because she thinks I wouldn't follow her.

"I know we can't get into it here," I say. "But I just want to make that one thing clear because I meant everything I said last night." She's so worried about doing what's good and right and expected, and I can't blame her for wanting to be professional. But I can't tamp these feelings down anymore, either.

"I'm not sure I see a way that can work," she says. "Even though I'd like it to."

"It's not like you're going halfway around the world," I tell her. But to be honest, even that wouldn't be too far.

She sighs, planting her hands on her hips. "Long-distance is the worst. I wouldn't ask you to—"

"You don't have to," I tell her, stepping closer.

Her expression is hard to read, but I know she has plenty of thoughts about this—I just want her to share them with me. She opens her mouth to answer and the whole world stops as I hold my breath.

"Let's talk later," she says, nodding toward the conference room. "Roxy and Sophie are waiting." She stalks toward the room without another word, and my chest tightens—just like it did on that beach a million years ago.

I can't help feeling like she's pulling away.

"ALL THINGS CONSIDERED," Roxy says, "we were very fortunate." She's sitting at the head of the conference room table, wincing as she sips the cafeteria coffee. "Priya's much better and in good spirits. Her parents weren't happy to hear about the incident, but they're grateful for everyone's help."

Across from me, Victoria bites her lip. Her hair's pulled back in a short ponytail and her shoulders are so tense I could bounce quarters off them. When her eyes flick to mine, a tingle runs along my whole body, straight to my toes.

"And," Roxy says, "I'd like to commend you all for stepping up the way that you did. Especially you, Victoria. Priya told me she's terrified of needles." Across from me, Sophie smiles and gives Vic's arm a nudge.

"And I owe a big thank you to Sophie, for staying in the hospital with us all night and keeping Priya's parents updated."

"No problem at all," Sophie says.

"Was it the cookies?" Victoria asks.

Roxy shakes her head. "Priya said one of the other girls, Jess, brought granola bars that her mom made. Jess didn't realize they were made with peanut butter. Priya only had a small piece, but that was enough to cause a reaction."

Victoria looks stunned. Roxy's still talking logistics and damage control, but Vic looks like she's barely listening, still processing the fact that this wasn't her mistake.

"You all are doing a great job here," Roxy says. "I'm so glad to have y'all as my team. If I'm being honest, I wish I could have you three at all of my summer camps."

When Victoria finally glances my way, I give her a small reassuring smile that says, *See? Told you.* She responds with a one-shoulder shrug.

"I want to talk more about this later," Roxy says, "but today's going to be busy and Noah here needs to head out soon with our fliers."

"So far all flights are still on time," Sophie tells me, passing me a list of flight info for five kids.

"One more change of plan," Roxy says. "Priya's not flying home today. Instead, her aunt and uncle will drive up from Atlanta and pick her up from the hospital this afternoon. Layla's also going to catch a ride with the aunt and uncle. She asked to stay with Priya, and the girls sorted this out and ran it by the parents, who gave us the okay." She takes another gulp of coffee and checks the time on her phone. "Victoria, I need you to take Layla to the hospital and wait there with Priya so you can talk to her family when they arrive. It's important that one of us is there with her today."

"Of course," Vic says, nodding.

"Sophie, you'll still be here to meet parents who are driving in. Noah, this means that you'll have an extra airport run for the later flights. I'd stay and help you, but I have to get Mira back to Charleston by one o'clock today."

"No problem," I tell her. Looks like that talk with Victoria will have to wait until this evening. It's probably better that way, because Sophie will be the only other person here with us on the mountain. Staff always stays the night after the kids leave—and once the last kid gets on a plane and the last parent drives away, camp is officially over.

"Okay," Roxy says, bringing her hands together. "Here's to a smooth, uneventful departure day." She raises her coffee cup in a toast, and we all do the same.

When Victoria catches my eye, her lip lifts in a hint of a smile. It's one of her mysterious smiles that makes her look a little sad —and I can't shake the feeling that it's a kind of goodbye.

Chapter Twenty-Four

VICTORIA

When we all stand to leave, Roxy touches my arm. "Can we talk privately before I take off?" she says.

"Of course." My anxious brain goes right to the catastrophic place, telling me that there's more to the Priya incident than she let on during the meeting.

"Come take a walk with me," Roxy says. "If I sit any longer I'm going to explode. I've got a four-hour car ride ahead of me and I'm full of sugar and hospital vending machine coffee."

I follow her as she heads across the parking lot and starts down the walking trail that loops around the facility.

"I just wanted to check in and make sure you're okay," she says. "I know last night must have been scary."

"Yeah," I agree. "But I'm good. And I'm so glad that Priya's okay."

Roxy nods. "Summer camp's always full of surprises. We hope for the pleasant kind, but now and then something like this happens. I'm really glad you were here and did what you did."

"Thanks," I tell her. "You're right about having a great team, by the way."

She snorts. "Obviously. I only hire the best."

I cringe at that because today I do not feel like *the best*.

"I also wanted to give you an update on this job," she says, picking up her pace. "The college would like to officially extend your position into one that's year-round."

"What?" I ask, because those words are the opposite of what I expected. "Are you serious?"

"You're a great fit," she says. "I told the director he'd be making a huge mistake by letting you slip away, and for once, the big doofus listened to me."

"I don't know what to say," I tell her.

"Say you'll stay on with us. A simple *yes, Roxy* will suffice." She smiles. "We can celebrate properly when we're off this mountain."

My heart pounds in my ears, filling me with guilt because I can't say yes. Not like this.

"I have to tell you something," I blurt. "I haven't been completely honest with you." When I slow my pace, she gives my arm a nudge.

"Okay," she says. "But walk and talk." She walks faster, swinging her arms. "Managing parents sends my cortisol off the charts."

"You asked me about Noah, and I left out some details."

She glances at me, her brow lifted.

"We're old friends. That was true."

"Okay," she says, dragging out the syllables.

"We were close, and I had some complicated feelings about him." My heart's in my throat, but I try to concentrate on the sound of my boots smacking the concrete. "And being here with him has brought some of that back to the surface."

"You still have feelings for him," she says.

"Yes," I admit. "I don't think I've ever felt this for anyone before."

She nods, her expression hard to read. Is it anger? Disappointment? Hurt?

"I think he feels something too," I go on. "But we agreed that we couldn't pursue this here. And we haven't." That job offer is going up in flames, but I don't want it if it means I have to keep lying to Roxy.

She studies me for a long moment and then says, "Oh, he definitely feels something. I see the way he looks at you. Like you hung the moon and every star in the sky."

My heart squeezes at the thought.

"I shouldn't have kept this from you," I tell her. "But I felt like I was breaking the biggest rule, and I didn't want to let you down. And the last thing I want is to get Noah in trouble. This job means the world to him, and he's amazing with these kids."

"He is," she says. "And so are you."

I hold my breath, because it sounds like a big *but* is coming.

She sighs. "Sweetie, you aren't letting me down. Having intense feelings for someone isn't something to be ashamed of. That's not breaking any rules."

I wince. "But kissing him is."

She stops so abruptly that I bump into her. When she turns to me, she's biting her lip. "Vic," she breathes, her eyes pinning me in place. "What are you saying?"

"One kiss," I tell her, keeping my voice low. We're on the far side of the meadow now, which feels like ten miles from everyone. "But nothing more, I promise. We agreed we couldn't cross that line—or, cross any further over it. Not here. And for the record, *I* kissed *him*. So if someone needs to be reprimanded or fired, it's me. Not Noah."

Hands on her hips, she closes her eyes and turns her head up toward the sky. She lets out a heavy breath, and my heart pounds against my ribs. This is it—the moment where she'll fire me and tell me to pack my bags. I've ruined everything, just like I was afraid I would.

"Roxy?" My voice comes out in a squeak. "Say something."

She shakes her head and squeezes her eyes shut. "Sweet baby cheeses."

I wait, but she just starts pacing in a small circle, her lips a hard line.

"I'm sorry," I tell her. "There's no excuse. Just tell me what you want me to do. How can I fix this?"

She blows out a heavy breath. "Did anything else happen?"

"No." I swallow hard, thinking of that night, how I wanted so much more. How I still do.

There's a long pause, and my heart hammers so hard that it hurts.

"Here's the thing," she says finally. "Something like this usually means termination. At a site this small, I'd be losing two-thirds of my staff. Protocol is to send in replacements."

Tears spring to my eyes. I've let everyone down—Roxy, Sophie, all the kids.

"But we're at the end of camp," she says, shaking her head. When she turns to me, her face softens. "That wasn't the greatest move," she says. "But you're not a reckless, thoughtless person. I know you, Vic, and I know you care about these kids and this job. You don't take it lightly."

I nod, choking back tears. "I want a chance to fix this, Roxy."

Her brow furrows. "If you tell me that nothing else happened, and nothing more *will* happen while you two are on site, then I believe you."

"Of course," I tell her. "Nothing else."

She nods. "Then your supervisor Roxy is going to say that

this was a misstep. Everyone has them. We're going to chalk this up to an error in judgment that will no longer be an issue, and we'll move forward." She gives me a tiny nod. "Consider it fixed."

Relief washes over me as I nod in agreement. "Thank you."

"And your friend Roxy is going to insist that you not beat yourself up over this."

I make a sound that's somewhere between a grumble and a growl.

"Look." She turns and puts her hands on my shoulders. "Is this an ideal situation? No. Was anyone hurt? Were the kids affected? Also no. You're human, Victoria. I appreciate you telling me, but I'm not holding anything against you. You're a good person who made a mistake. It happens."

I nod, fighting back tears for what feels like the millionth time this week.

"I'll withdraw my application," I tell her, feeling my heart constrict at the thought. And that's when I realize how badly I want this job.

"Because you kissed a guy?" she says. "No way."

"Roxy," I argue. "I think I should."

She lifts a brow. "Absolutely not. Do you think a man in your position would quit? I'm frankly fed up with women telling themselves *no* before anyone else does. I'm not going to let you do that." She plants her hands on her hips and pins me with her stare. "If you want the job, it's yours. And based on the way you seem to be absolutely glowing up here, I think you do."

I nod, thinking of Diana's offer, and my stomach's in knots again. The job with her could skyrocket my career—it's what I've spent the last several years working toward. When she told me how much I could expect to make in commissions, I nearly choked because holy bananas, that many zeros would change my life completely.

This job with the camp won't come with that many zeros. But what it offers could be so much more meaningful.

I don't want to make this decision out of fear, and right now my overthinking brain has several fears bouncing around inside it. I'm afraid I'll regret passing up the job with Diana. I'm afraid taking this job with Roxy is biting off more than I can chew. I'm afraid saying no might be the biggest mistake of my life. But most of all, I'm afraid of what might happen if I take this chance with Noah and then we fall apart—because that would mean losing everything.

Again.

In the storm of dark thoughts, one bright one floats the the surface: *But what if everything works out just the way you want—and nothing falls apart?*

"Can I have a couple of days to think it over?" I ask.

She nods. "Of course. I'll email you the offer letter with all of the details before I leave."

"Thank you."

"Now," she says. "Your friend Roxy has one more question. Does he make you happy? Because you deserve someone who lights you up like the Fourth of July, and I won't let you settle for anything less."

I smile because bossy Roxy is my favorite.

"I think he could," I say.

"Someday," she says, "I want to hear all the details. But let's have that conversation when we're off this mountain."

"Deal," I tell her. Even thinking of that night at the campground is stirring up the butterflies again.

She nods and starts walking back toward the cabins. Today's one of those perfect days where the sun's filtered through big puffy clouds, and the air is crisp and clear. There's just enough breeze to keep the summer heat at bay.

"For the record," she says, "You're also amazing with these kids. I hope you know how much that means."

This time, I don't argue with her.

WHEN LAYLA and I get to the hospital, Priya looks up from the Octavia Butler book she's reading and gives us a small smile. Aside from the dark circles beneath her eyes, she looks good.

"How are you feeling?" I ask her.

"Better. But I'm so bored," she groans, just as Layla sits on the bed next to her.

"Good thing we're here, then," Layla says.

"Aunt Radha texted me and said they're leaving soon," Priya says. "They said they'd be here by three, but they're always late."

"No problem," I tell her with a shrug. "We've got nowhere else to be today."

She smiles and says, "Thanks for coming back to stay with me." Something in her tone makes me think she's more accustomed to being left by herself. My heart squeezes at the thought.

"Are you kidding?" I ask her. "You don't get to leave under cover of darkness and rob me of a proper goodbye."

Layla digs through her backpack and thrusts a big pink envelope towards Priya. "Open it," she says, her eyes glittering.

Priya's face lights up as she opens the envelope. Inside is a card made from a collage of images: blue mountains, a waterfall, a big golden moon, one of the massive telescopes like at the institute. When Priya opens the card, Layla says, "We made it for you this morning. Everyone signed it since they didn't have a chance to tell you bye."

Priya beams as Layla pulls her into a bear hug and says, "Everybody was so glad to hear you're okay."

There's another tug deep in my chest, and a thought hits me like a bolt of lightning. The thing I liked most about real estate was helping people find a place that became their home—a place where they felt they belonged. And being at this camp, with these kids—it's the same in that way. The classes are cool, and the outings are a blast, but the most meaningful part of being here this summer has been moments like this one: watching two kids who felt like misfits grow more comfortable in their own skin and leave this place feeling like they can belong, too.

This camp sometimes pushed me to my limits, only to reveal moments like this one that remind me of how much good there is in the world. A glimmer, Noah would say, but to me, it's much more.

This job won't make me a big pile of money like the job with Diana would—but right now, I can't imagine working for her and going back to that lifestyle I was so eager to leave. But I can easily see myself doing this work, being surrounded by people like these kids who bring the best parts of me to the surface, where they can grow in the light.

"Picture time," I tell the girls, pulling my cell phone from my pocket. I want to etch this moment into my memory.

"Oh, I almost forgot," Layla says, digging through her bag again. She pulls out a blue ball cap and hands it to Priya. It's dustier now, but I recognize the Ursa Major constellation embroidered with the outline of a bear. The hat Derrick wore nearly every day—the one he nearly lost at the waterfall that very first week.

"I don't understand," Priya says. "This is his favorite."

Layla smirks, nudging her arm. "He said it looks better on you."

Priya blushes as she puts the hat on her head. When I snap the picture, the girls are grinning like a couple of Swifties who just won front-row tickets.

When Layla pulls me onto the bed with them and snaps more photos, I see what Roxy means. Even under the dreadful fluorescent lights of the the hospital, I'm glowing.

I don't need to overthink this job offer anymore. I can embrace my doubts and move through the hurricane of racing thoughts and biting fears because there are moments like this on the other side.

And these moments? They're well worth running toward.

I text the photo of me with the girls to Noah, but he doesn't respond. He hasn't responded to any of the texts I've sent him today, and I'm hoping that's just because he's busy with airport runs and refuses to text while driving. Still, his silence only makes me replay our last conversation, picking it apart for evidence that I gave him a reason to ignore my attempts to talk.

AS I'M DRIVING BACK to the institute, my phone pings with a text message, and I grin, anticipating a playful response from Noah. I can't wait to tell him about Roxy's offer. And my new plan.

But the text is from Sophie.

How's it going there? Did Priya's family show up yet?

Great! I reply, using voice-text. **They were all super nice and left a little while ago. I'm headed back now.**

Sweet! she writes. **See you soon. Party on the patio tonight to celebrate another great session.**

Noah still hasn't responded. After a moment, I send another voice text to Sophie: **How's Noah? Air all the kids in the air?**

All good, she answers. I frown because it both is and isn't.

BACK AT THE INSTITUTE, I find Sophie sitting at the picnic table by the cabins, reading a book that, based on the cover, definitely has some dragons and spicy times. She's so into it that she doesn't notice I'm there until I sit down across from her.

"Welcome back," she says with a smile. "You officially survived camp."

"Feels like it's been longer than three weeks," I tell her, stretching my arms over my head. "And yet also, like we just got here yesterday."

She nods, closing the book. "Feels like that every time. Everything go okay with Priya's family?"

"They were lovely," I tell her. "Concerned, of course, and talked at length with the doctor who treated her. Then they asked Priya a million questions about camp, and once her aunt started quizzing me instead, Priya practically dragged her outside by her arm and swore she and Layla would tell her all the details on the car ride."

In the parking lot, Aunt Radha gave me a rib-cracking hug and thanked me again for staying with Priya. As they all climbed inside the car, the girls were already chattering about their favorite parts of camp. When they waved to me out the windows, I felt like my heart grew three sizes.

"Those two are the cutest," Sophie says. "Friends for life now. That's the magic of summer camp."

"Did Noah make it back yet?" I glance toward the parking lot, where there's now only my car and Sophie's. It's nearly seven, and the sun's dipped below the ridge, leaving the sky a deep periwinkle. The first stars are popping out beneath a sliver of moon.

"Change of plans," she says. "It's just you and me tonight. He had to drive back to Charleston."

"Oh." I try not to sound as deflated as I feel. "Is everything okay?"

"He's fine. Said he needed to help his sister with something urgent that came up."

She glances at me, perfectly penciled brow lifted, and I'm certain she's finally put all these pieces together. My heart squeezes when I think about my unanswered texts—I wanted to talk tonight, but now he's left without a word.

He's pulling away again, and it hurts even more than it did the first time, all those years ago. I pull my phone from my pocket and scroll through the texts I sent him today. It's possible they weren't delivered, and I didn't notice with all the activity at the hospital.

But the messages went through just fine. All six of them, from my breezy **Just FYI, the hospital coffee is WAY worse than our camp coffee,** to my later **Are we in the home stretch yet, because I'm going to need to celebrate with an adult beverage soon.**

All day, I told myself that he was too busy wrangling kids and returning rental cars to reply. Sooner or later, he'd write back with some snappy joke about Derrick's luggage and tell me he was just as eager as I was to have time alone together tonight.

But that message never came.

That nagging voice in my head whispers that it was bound to happen this way, that I was foolish to think whatever was growing between us could survive outside of this camp. I didn't want to let myself believe that he could disappear like this again, but ignoring my texts all day is all the proof I need.

And that proof hurts me way down deep, even more than I thought it would.

"You okay?" Sophie says, her brows pinching together.

"Just tired," I tell her, because the truth is so much more complicated.

She nods as if she half-believes me. "Hungry?"

"Ravenous."

Flashing me a tiny smile, she says, "Come on. The kitchen staff prepped a meal for us. They promised it was both delicious and easy enough for me to cook without incident, and I want to test that theory."

"I'll be your sous chef," I say, following her toward the dining hall. At this point, I'll do anything to get Noah off my mind, even if it's chopping onions and washing dishes.

After we've finished our spaghetti picnic in the dining hall, Sophie says, "So am I going to see you at another one of these camps?"

"I hope so," I answer. "This was nothing like I expected. I seriously considered running away when I first got up here."

"You did have that look in your eye," she says. "But I'm really glad you didn't."

"I wasn't prepared for any of this. But that reminds me— Roxy said that you might be able to help me in that department. She said I should ask you about Pinehaven."

Sophie smiles. "Now that's my real happy place."

IT'S after ten-thirty when I take my flashlight and walk out to the cell phone tree to check for messages one last time. It's been several hours since I last texted Noah, and as I wait under the big fir tree, I hold my breath as my phone lights up with new emails and texts.

I scroll through quickly, but the only texts are from Gwen, telling me to drive safe and call her when I'm on the road.

An owl calls from somewhere overhead, and I pace under the tree, waiting to see if any other messages come in.

They don't.

There's no word from Noah. Not even a reaction to all the texts I sent him earlier today.

I'm floored that this is happening again, and mad at myself for getting my hopes up so high. That voice in my head just laughs and says, *Are you though? Are you really surprised?*

I think of how close we were, how everything seemed to be falling into place. How the offer from Roxy made it seem that all of this would work out. But maybe I was right the first time: maybe I just don't get to have both.

Shaking my head, I type out one last message to Noah so there won't be any confusion this time around.

I get that we're in a weird place right now. I was hoping to talk about things before we left, and I know I haven't been the best at explaining how I feel. I'm ready to talk if you are—but if you're not interested, I understand.

I study the words for a moment, and then I hit *send*.

Because my inner optimist isn't completely dead, I sit under that tree for the next half-hour. I'm waiting to see if Noah will respond, but I'm also listening to the owls calling to each other from the treetops, to the wind as it rustles the leaves. Before this camp, I couldn't tell you the last time I heard those sounds—or, more precisely, when I made time to listen for them.

This place has changed me in more ways than I can count. And even if I leave here heartbroken, I still wouldn't change a single moment.

It's after eleven when I check my phone once more. Still no response from Noah.

I stand and brush myself off, stare once more at this impossibly black sky filled with glittering stars—a billion tiny points of light in the vast darkness. Stars that seem to nearly touch, so close that we've woven them together with stories of bears and warriors—but it's just an illusion. The space between those stars is infinite.

"Message received," I say, shoving my phone back into my pocket. "Loud and clear."

Chapter Twenty-Five

NOAH

Twelve hours earlier.

Departure day is always chaotic, but today is breaking my record.

It started when I woke from a criminally vivid dream about Victoria and me doing a few camp activities that would definitely get us fired. I had to run fives miles before dawn to get those images out of my head, but then we had that meeting with Roxy, and Vic had her hair piled up in one of her messy buns again and my brain went straight to the part of that dream where I'd finally—*finally*—gotten my hands on those unruly curls, pulled her tight against me and kissed her until we were both dizzy.

Not the best thoughts to have during our morning meeting with my boss.

Then I managed to spill my to-go coffee (the delicious kind, from my French press) straight down the front of my shirt while driving the kids to the airport. A massive wreck on the interstate meant we were over half an hour late. Then an emergency bathroom stop for Ethan, who decided to have every kind of dairy at breakfast despite knowing it would spark a revolution in his entire digestive system, added another fifteen minutes to our delay.

Now I'm racing the kids through the airport, where two flights have already changed gates. I check my phone for an update from Sophie and see a text message from Victoria. I don't even have time to read it as I hustle the kids into the line at security, reminding them to empty their pockets and take off their shoes, and also to grab everything at the end of the line because, yes, at least one kid always forgets to grab their shoes and heads off to the gate in only socks.

It happens more often than you might think.

Once the five of us are through security, I begin the real gauntlet: delivering the four kids to their departure gates.

First is Becca, whose flight leaves in thirty minutes. I say a little thank-you to the universe for this tiny airport as we jog over to her gate, where the boarding has begun. She says her quick goodbyes, and once she's on board, we head to the next gate.

And then the next.

Ethan and Derrick are on the same flight out. We're camped at their gate when my phone buzzes with another text. I see that it's Vic at the same moment that Ethan's stomach makes a noise that sounds like a bulldozer.

"Uh-oh," he says and bolts toward the restroom.

Derrick heads to a kiosk behind us and says, "I'm hungry. They have donuts."

"Be back in ten minutes!" I holler after them. This plane is about to start boarding, and I haven't had a kid miss a flight all year.

And I don't intend to break that record today.

I skim Victoria's texts—they're her typical blend of funny and flirty, reaching out to tease me about coffee and let me know that she's staying in touch. Below, there's an adorable picture of her with Layla and Priya. She looks content. Calm.

Utterly gorgeous and lit from within.

I type out a reply, then delete it. I start another and delete that, too. Why is it so hard for me to tell her how I feel?

A garbled voice comes over the loudspeaker and calls for boarding group four. I spot Derrick and Ethan at the kiosk a few yards away, grabbing an armful of snacks and bottled drinks.

I let out a sharp whistle that would make Sophie proud, and both boys turn toward me. "Come on, fellas," I holler. "Let's go!"

They shuffle over to where I'm standing in line with their luggage, next to a woman whose pug keeps sniffing my shoe. Derrick's scrolling on his phone as he walks toward me, balancing the world's biggest bear claw on top of a bottle of soda. As they approach, Ethan says, "I think I lost my boarding pass," and I turn him around and head for the nearest flight attendant. In my haste, I trip over something that feels like a duffle bag but turns out to be that pot-bellied pug that has strayed from its owner, eyes fixed on Derrick's bone-dry, overpriced bear claw.

The dog's fine. He's built like a tiny tank.

I, however, go sprawling towards the floor, zig when I should have zagged, and steamroll poor Derrick, who grunts with surprise as the soda and pastry go sailing through the air. Along with his phone and mine.

I land hard on the floor, wincing as my shoulder reminds me that I am not twenty years old anymore and not made of rubber.

Derrick chases after his soda as the pug lunges for the bear claw. Laughter erupts around us as the dog lets out a victorious snort-yip and scarfs that massive pastry in one obscene gulp. His owner, a twenty-something blond woman in yoga clothes, shrieks as he yanks her off-balance and drives her right into the chest of the man behind her. This catches the eye of the nearest security guard and his German shepherd, both of whom narrow their eyes at us in precisely the same judgmental stare.

Mortified, I scoop up my phone and tuck it into my back pocket as I hustle Ethan toward the flight attendant because we have no time to lose. Derrick holds their place in line, scratching the pug behind the ears.

"Found it," Ethan says, his hand deep in the pocket of his backpack. "False alarm."

I let out a deep sigh as Ethan jogs back over to where Derrick is waiting for him by the gate.

"See you next year, maybe!" Derrick hollers at me, and Ethan gives me a solemn wave.

They amble down the ramp toward the plane with the last of the passengers, and I let out the breath I've been holding for what seems like five full minutes. I take a few ibuprofen to ease the pain that's bloomed in my shoulder, then wait to watch their plane taxi down the runway.

I'm congratulating myself on surviving this gauntlet as I'm walking back to my car, sipping a fresh coffee so deep and rich that it almost makes up for that spill with the pug. I pull my phone from my pocket to check my messages, and then curse so loudly that a gray-haired lady in the parking deck frowns and wags her finger at me.

In my hand is a phone with Captain America on the lock screen. The phone of teenage boy.

"Sorry," I tell the lady, and she *tsks* me as she walks toward the elevator.

I howl at the injustice of it all, but that doesn't erase the fact that the phone in my hand is not mine but belongs to Derrick. I replay the moment of our collision at the gate again and again because I was certain I'd checked this phone before I shoved it into my pocket. Certain I'd checked the time or at least made sure it was mine, because my phone and its case are identical to Derrick's.

The same green case with the grippy silicone texture. We even joked about it that first week, when Derrick had been trying to find a signal and dropped it on the pavement right in front of me. *My mom got me this case because she said it was indestructible even for me*, he'd said. *I've dropped it a million times.*

But as I lay sprawled on the hard airport floor, I assumed the phone closest to my knee was mine. In a hurry to get the boys onboard, I didn't double-check.

And now I'm stuck with a tween's phone that's chock full of silly games and is incapable of speed-dialing Sophie, or loading my email, or responding to Victoria's texts that I'd told myself I'd answer as soon as the kids were all strapped into their seats and headed home.

Meanwhile, my phone is shoved into the pocket of Derrick's jacket, probably already sticky from a candy wrapper and lord knows what else, cruising at thirty thousand feet on its way to Atlanta.

WHEN I GET BACK to the Institute, Sophie says, "Noah, I've been calling you nonstop. What's going on?" She frowns, clearly annoyed.

"Sorry," I say, and then tell her the short version of how I came to have Derrick's phone. I hold it out to her as proof, as if I could make this stuff up. "I'm going to call his parents and see if they'll overnight mine to me if I do the same."

She pushes her braids over her shoulder. "I was starting to worry you'd been in an accident."

"I'm sorry," I tell her again. "It's locked with a passcode."

She smirks, taking the phone from my hand. Before I can even ask what she's doing, she taps the screen a few times and says, "Boom."

"You got in?"

She taps and swipes a few more times. "My little brother's just as predictable. Now I'm disarming the lock screen so you can keep using it."

"I won't need to—"

"Yes, you will," she interrupts. "Because your sister called here four times trying to get in touch with you and needs you to call her ASAP." Handing me the phone, she says, "She's okay, not hurt or anything. But she said it's DEFCON-1, and she's calling in her big favor."

I let out a heavy sigh. Hannah's kept that big favor in her pocket for years.

"Listen," she says. "All the car pick-ups are done. Victoria's still at the hospital with Priya and Layla. So I'll take the second group to the airport, and you can head out early to help Hannah."

"You don't have to do that, Soph."

"I know," she says. "But your sister needs you. I can handle the kiddos, and I'm already done packing up the office. No problem."

"You really are the best," I tell her.

She gives me a friendly shrug. "You'd do the same for me."

· · ·

I CALL Hannah from the landline in the office, and she picks up on the first ring. Her voice is high pitched, and she's talking so fast I can barely understand her. She never, ever sounds this hurried. She's always calm and calculating, planning ten steps ahead.

"Hannah," I interrupt. "Slow down. Are you okay?"

A breath whooshes out of her.

"I'm safe," she says. "I'm not hurt. But I need you to come help me move out of my apartment. I want to empty this place and be out by the time Jason gets back tonight."

"What happened?"

"The *CliffsNotes* version? I found out he's been cheating on me, and I don't want to stay in this place one more minute. But all of my work stuff is here, and I have to get it moved out so I can work from…wherever I land. He'll be back by six, and I want to be long gone by then. Can you please, please come help me get all this crap out of here? I also need you here as my moral compass so I don't do something cuckoo yet appropriate, like fill his bed with fire ants and use his precious record collection to start a bonfire."

"Ugh, Hannah." I rake my hand through my hair, knowing my only option is to go help her. It means I won't get to see Victoria and talk about what happened last night—or explain why I haven't answered her texts all day.

But this is my baby sister, and she needs me. Hannah never asks for my help because she always wants to handle everything herself. I have some theories about why that is—because independent women like her are often the way they are because they're accustomed to people letting them down.

I see that in Victoria, too.

And right now, I can't be one of those people who lets Hannah down.

"I'll be there as fast as I can," I tell her. "If that idiot comes home before I get there, just leave. Wait for me at a coffee shop. Got it?"

She snorts. "I can handle the idiot."

Not the way I want to, but I keep that thought to myself. Jason's not a violent man, based on what Hannah's told me—but he's a manipulative one who'll try to con his way right back into her good graces faster than you can say *heartburn*. And under all that armor, Hannah has a big, soft heart.

BY THE TIME I get down to Hannah's apartment in Charleston, it's nearly five o'clock. Her door's standing wide open, and half a dozen plastic tubs are piled just inside.

"Hannah?" I call.

"Thank goodness," she says, plowing into me like a linebacker. She wraps me in a tight, quick hug and then says. "Thanks for coming. I'll fill you in on everything over an expensive bottle of tequila—my treat—but right now, we need to get rolling. He's always home a few minutes after six, and if I see his face, I'm just going to put my foot through it."

She stomps into the bedroom in her beat-up red cowboy boots, and there's not a doubt in my mind that those words are true.

For the next forty minutes, we pile her most important belongings into her car and mine. When the last box is in the trunk, her cheeks are pink, and her hair's frizzy because the humidity down here stops for no one. Opal the doodle is strapped into her passenger seat, tongue lolling like this is the best day ever.

"You're taking the dog?" I ask her.

Her brow lifts. "Of course I am. She prefers me and Jason can't be trusted with anything that needs more care than a pet rock." The dog barks, as if to confirm. "Plus, he doesn't deserve her."

"Didn't deserve you, either," I say, and her lip ticks up in a smile.

"I'll follow you," Hannah says, because it's understood that she'll come crash at my house. She knows I'm always her soft place to fall.

BY TEN P.M., Hannah's snoring on my sofa, right where she crash-landed after we ate an entire pepperoni pizza and played our *Bridgerton* drinking game with some top-shelf tequila. I consider waking her so we can pull out the sofa bed, but she doesn't move a muscle as I tiptoe around the room, gathering the last of our dishes. A couple of hours ago, she set up her workstation in the far corner of this room, claiming she only needed a laptop and a comfy chair to do her work. I offered to make a space for her in my spare room, which is basically like a study with a treadmill, but she said, "No need for that. I've already got a couple of leads on apartments and will be out of here before you know it."

I drape a blanket over her and switch off the lights as I head out onto the back porch. My house is small, situated in an old neighborhood filled with mid-century style homes. With two bedrooms and an open-plan kitchen-living-dining area, it's plenty big enough for me. It needed some repairs and updates when I bought it, but the thing that sold me on this place was the yard and the screened-in back porch. The previous owners, who loved gardening, created an oasis out back, complete with flowering shrubs, a seating area around a fire pit, and a hammock nestled in the shade. Now, as I collapse into the wicker sofa on the porch, my cordless phone lights up with a call.

"Hi," Roxy says. "I finally got a hold of Derrick's parents and have this phone situation worked out for you."

"Please tell me they're up for overnighting."

"Yes," she says. "I gave them your address, and they said they'd ship it to you first thing in the morning. I got you a prepaid label so you can do the same. I just emailed it to you."

"Roxy, you're the best."

"How's Hannah?"

I peek back inside the house, where she's still motionless on the sofa. "Exhausted, but she's okay. I owe Sophie big time for letting me skip out early."

"Yeah, she's one of the good ones," Roxy says. "But so are you."

I almost ask her for Victoria's cell number. But then I consider the last words Vic said to me and think better of it. If she wants space to think, then I'm going to give it to her. I told her I'd wait, and I meant it. But I wish I could text her right now, just to make sure she got back safely and let her know I'm thinking of her.

"Thanks," I tell Roxy. "For everything."

"Of course. Enjoy your week off, Noah. I'll be in touch soon."

In another week, I'll be at the next camp, this one based at one of the satellite campuses outside of Charleston. I hope that Victoria will be there, too—but now that we're off the mountain and I'm alone on my porch, that possibility seems much less likely than it did a few days ago.

After hanging up, I go inside to check my email. When I pull my laptop from my messenger bag, Victoria's copy of *Ready Player One* slips out and lands at my feet. She was right, as usual

—the story hooked me from the start, and I've been trying to savor it, not allowing myself to read more than three chapters each night. I place it on the kitchen counter and then open my laptop.

Roxy indeed sent the mailing label for Derrick's phone, which I print out immediately.

As I scroll through my inbox, I see another email from her—it's a follow-up that she always sends when a camp is over, just to check in and see what went well and what could be improved. When I open it, I see that she didn't use blind-copy to send it to our staff. My email address is fully visible—as are Sophie's and Victoria's.

I stare at Vic's email address for a long moment.

There's no doubt in my mind that she thinks I'm ignoring her texts, and I don't want her to feel ghosted. Again.

In two days I'll have my phone. I can read those messages I only glimpsed, and I can reply.

But right now, two days feels like an eternity.

I start typing, then delete. I repeat this five more times until I have a breezy, friendly message that's not the hopeless rambling of a man who's fallen so hard he's knocked all sense out of his head.

Because that's exactly what's happened. I've fallen so hard for this woman, I might never recover.

Victoria—

I just wanted to check in and see how your day went. I'm sorry I missed you, but I had to rush home to help Hannah. I was looking forward to talking with you and wanted to at least call. But—funny story—I lost my phone. Or rather, Derrick took mine home by accident (because of course he did), and I have his.

Let's talk soon. I miss you already.

N.

I stare at the words, then add in the phone number of my landline. It's worth a try, right? I finish the last of my margarita and make a plea to the universe as I hit *send*.

Chapter Twenty-Six

NOAH

"But first, pancakes," Hannah says. Dressed in a hiking skirt and a blue tee shirt that says *Abide No Hatred*, she's blowing through my kitchen like a hurricane. Her dark wavy hair is pulled back into a ponytail that swings wildly as she whisks that bowl of batter like it sassed her. After spooning the batter into the skillet, she moves on to manhandling my espresso machine as she attempts to froth milk to go along with the waiting espresso shots. Hannah only has two speeds: sweet, blinking sloth and cartoon Tasmanian devil.

Right now, we're a million miles from sloth mode. She's likely been up for two hours already, based on the disastrous state of my kitchen.

I take the coffee she thrusts toward me and sit down at the breakfast island, which is covered in printouts of apartment listings. She's already gone at them with highlighter and red marker.

"Fuel up," she says. "I thought we could go back over to the apartment and pack up the rest of my things while Jason's at work. Then, we can check out some places that are in my price range. You up for that?"

She says that last part like it's a question, but it's not. These pancakes are a bribe, but I'm okay with it. Hannah needs her own space, and she wouldn't stay here more than a few days even if I offered.

"I mapped out the top contenders so we can do this systematically and don't drive all over creation," she says. "We can bring all of my stuff back here and then take my car to scout these places. I'll drive and you navigate."

I wince as the coffee burns my tongue. "Deal." I hadn't planned to spend my day apartment hunting, but I can't say no to Hannah and her Big Plan. Even after taking a shower hot enough to melt iron, my shoulders are tight with knots and my neck feels like a horse stomped on it. But that won't stop me from helping her today.

She flips a few pancakes in the skillet and nods. Next to her is a plate of charred ones that look like hockey pucks. While she waits for golden brown, I open my laptop and check my email, hoping for a reply from Victoria.

But there isn't one.

I swallow the lump in my throat and tell myself this doesn't have to mean anything. It's barely eight-thirty a.m. Vic likely spent last night at the institute, and she's probably leaving soon to head home if she hasn't hit the road already. Staff always have the option to stay one extra night, but they have to be out early. Probably, email is the last thing on her mind.

Still, my brain wants to go straight to catastrophizing. Spending the day with Hannah is the only way I can hope to keep my mind off Victoria and not obsessively check my inbox every three minutes.

"Bon appétit," Hannah says, pushing a plate toward me. "And also, do you have bungee cords and rope? I think we can get all of my stuff into your truck, but there's a non-zero chance that it could be a *Beverly Hillbillies* situation and we might need to strap things down creatively."

BY MID-AFTERNOON, we've rescued all of Hannah's belongings and ruled out five vacant apartments. Three were a hard pass based on the overwhelming population of college students and their distinct dorm vibes. The fourth smelled like an ashtray and the fifth was a garage apartment that almost definitely had a gas leak.

"This one isn't horrible," Hannah tells me as we poke around a third-floor walk-up with sticky floors and windows that are nailed shut. "But it does smell like cats and burnt cheese."

"That bathroom is a crime scene," I mutter, wincing as she surveys the tiny shower with its pink and yellow tile.

"Do you think that's mold or just dirt?" she asks.

I turn off the light with my elbow as we go back into the bedroom. "You know you can stay with me as long as you want."

"You'll regret that after about a week," she says, her nose wrinkling as she studies the carpet and its various stains.

"Let me make my storage room-slash-office into a spare bedroom." I shove my hands into my pockets, determined not to touch anything else. "Give yourself a few weeks to find a place that hasn't been set on fire or settled by raccoons."

She frowns, heading toward the front door. Marla, the landlady, is waiting outside, smoking a cigarette while her Pomeranian is busy yapping at the neighbor's cat.

"Thank you, Marla," Hannah says, shutting the door behind us. "This is a little small for me, but I appreciate you taking the time to show us around."

"Okay," Marla says with a shrug, scooping the dog into her arms.

As we climb into Hannah's car, she says, "There's one other one out towards Folly Beach. It's stupid expensive, but it's the last one open right now." She shows me the listing, sawing her bottom lip with her teeth.

"You know I'm going to be gone for the next two months, right?" I crank the air conditioning up as high as her old Accord can handle because my shirt's already sticking to me, and I'm hopeful the moving air will blow off all remaining particles of mildew and cat pee. "I'll be moving from one camp to another, with a day off between them if I'm lucky. You'd have the house to yourself."

She sighs, tapping her fingers on the steering wheel.

"You'd be house-sitting. Doing me a favor."

Her brow wrinkles as she chews on her lip. I've almost got her.

"Plus, you can keep my plants alive. I'd very much appreciate that. They're already looking pitiful and the last time I asked my neighbor to water, she drowned my whole herb garden. You know how hard it is to kill mint?"

She snorts. "Okay, fine. I'll baby your plants for you."

"Thank you."

As she pulls into the street, she shoots me a sideways glance that's part teasing and all gratitude.

THE NEXT MORNING, I'm tidying up my spare room-slash-office while Hannah unloads the last of her belongings from my truck. It's nearly ten a.m. when a delivery van pulls up with the package I've been waiting for—my phone.

The battery's dead, so I plug it in to charge while I finish making more space for Hannah. I'll be leaving in a few days to go to the next camp down in Beaufort, so she'll only have to tolerate the sleeper sofa for a few more nights.

When my phone comes to life, I go straight to the text messages. Victoria still hasn't replied to my email, but once I see her texts, I understand why.

First there are the breezy ones.

Hey, you. Hope the airport's being nice to you.

Then: **Did you get some decent coffee yet? My body is rejecting whatever's in this hospital vending machine. This is criminal.**

Then there's the adorable photo of her with Layla and Priya. Big smiles all around, and all I can think is that she looks content, like she's properly fit herself right into this role. This is the message I'd seen at the airport, the one I kept fumbling my response to.

The response I never sent.

Her next reads: **Priya's family is great. I was worried for nothing. I do that a lot, don't I?**

You doing all right out there? I'm heading back to camp now.

Hey, Sophie told me you had to go home early and help Hannah. I hope everything's okay.

And the last one, from 10:46 p.m: **I get that we're in a weird place right now. I was hoping to talk about things before we left, and I know I haven't been the best at explaining how I**

feel. I'm ready to talk if you are—but if you're not interested, I understand.

I cringe as I reread that last message. No wonder she hasn't gotten in touch again. She thinks I've changed my mind about us —because no person who was interested would let those last words go unanswered.

From across the kitchen island, Hannah says, "What's happening?"

"Nothing."

"Nice try. You look like you just learned a meteor's about to strike and turn us all to dust."

I sigh, turning my phone face-down on the counter. "I wrecked things with Victoria. Again."

"What? Explain yourself." She hops up on a barstool and rests her chin in her hand.

I start off with the broad strokes, and then end up spilling my guts and telling her every detail. Her brows shoot up to her hairline when I tell her about the night at the campground, and then she frowns when I get to the part about that last conversation we had after the dance. Hannah's face goes through her entire range of expressions and by the time I get to the text messages, there's a lump in my throat that feels like a rock.

"I should just call her, right?" I say. "Or text her back so she knows I'm not ignoring her."

I reach for my phone, but she grabs my arm. "Okay, stop," she says. "We can fix this."

"We?" I ask.

"Obviously you need some pro tips here. You're so lucky I'm around."

"I think I know how to—"

"Shush," she says, holding her finger up to me. "This

requires more than a text message or a phone call." She taps her finger against her lip in that way that means she's already five steps into a plan. She plucks Vic's well-loved copy of *Ready Player One* from the counter and shoves it toward me. "Thank goodness for your shared interest in nerd-dom."

"What does Ernest Cline have to do with anything?" Before the words are fully out of my mouth, I remember teasing Vic about the sticker she'd put on the back cover with her name and address, how she scoffed and said, *I like to make it easy to have my things returned to me.*

"That first chapter's really good," Hannah says. "I needed a palate cleanser after scouring apartment listings."

I trace my fingers over the sticker, thinking of that moment in the bakery, when I caught a glimpse of what we could be like together when we didn't have these silly camp rules getting in the way.

"We need more coffee," Hannah says, opening her laptop. "It's time for a big romantic gesture."

***

JASMINE FALLS IS one of those small towns that's just so dang cute it feels like it should be a movie set for the most heartwarming, feel-good film of the year. My GPS takes me straight down Main Street, where the town square's all decked out for something called SummerFest that promises a cake-baking competition, pony rides, an art walk, and carnival-style games for the whole family—including the fur-babies.

Sitting at a traffic light lets me soak up all the details—pastel-colored storefronts, a tasty-looking cake shop, a gallery full of bright paintings. I'm curious to see more, but I lost an hour by stopping for fresh flowers, a bottle of shiraz, and two cupcakes from my favorite bakery in Summerville because Hannah insisted I not show up here empty-handed.

The GPS leads me past the outer edge of town, back into the rolling hills and pastureland. In a couple of miles, I turn onto a road that cuts through the forest and comes out by a sparkling lake. I drive past a more developed area, through a section that looks like a park, and come to a spot where the road ends right by two modest-looking bungalows that are side-by side. One's painted white, the other yellow, and look like they could have been built at the same time. Two cars are parked by the white one, but the GPS directs me to the yellow one. When I see the number on the mailbox, I park by the garage and walk up to the front door, flowers in hand.

It's easy to picture Victoria living here. A modest two-story Cape Cod-style house, it has big windows and a flagstone path. It's cozy and welcoming, from the small porch with the blue front door to the flowering shrubs and irises along the split-rail fence by the garage.

I swallow hard as I walk up the steps and ring the doorbell. During the whole drive, I've been rehearsing what to say—and now all of those thoughts fall right out of my head.

After a few moments, I ring the bell again. When there's still no answer, I pound on the big wooden door.

"She's not here," a voice says from behind me.

When I startle and turn toward the sound, I'm met by a woman who looks like a taller, curvier version of Victoria.

"Hi, Gwen," I say. "It's been a minute."

"Noah Valentine." She narrows her eyes and gives me a quick once-over. "It certainly has."

"You don't seem surprised to see me."

Her brow lifts. "I've heard a lot about you lately."

Based on her tone, that's not a net-positive.

"I really need to see her," I say. "It's important."

Gwen plants her hands on her hips and purses her lips, staring me down with a stormy-blue gaze just like Victoria's. I'm definitely not her favorite person right now. Part of me wonders what Vic might have told her, what advice Gwen offered in return. Maybe it's best I never know.

Because that stare says she's calculating how far she'd have to drag my body into the swamp to make it disappear forever.

Based on our location? Not far.

"Slim chance of that," Gwen says, that brow arching again. "Ghosting her isn't winning you any points around here."

"Please," I beg. "This can't wait. I need to talk to her."

"Then I'd suggest trying the phone," she says, her tone matter-of-fact. "Or have you forgotten how to use one?"

"This is an in-person conversation," I offer. "I owe her a lot more than a phone call."

That seems to get her attention.

"She's upset with me, and I understand why," I tell her. "But I swear, I didn't ghost her. Not on purpose, anyway." In the next breath, I become a human firehose, telling her all about Derrick and his identical phone, the ravenous pug and the bear claw, and my embarrassing wipe-out in the middle of airport security.

When I'm finished, she bites back a grin and says, "That's quite a story."

"Ridiculous, but true. I know she thinks I'm avoiding her, and I need to correct that. As soon as humanly possible."

She nods, and I can tell she's thinking about the last time this happened, when I left the country instead of correcting my mistake. Victoria and Gwen are as close as two sisters can be, and there's no way Vic left out any relevant details—definitely not back in college, and most likely not today.

"Let me fix this," I tell her. "Please."

She stares at me for what feels like a full minute, her face like a storm cloud. "Come on," she says finally. "It's hot as blazes out here and you need all the help you can get."

I follow her down the steps and across the lawn to her house, which indeed looks very similar to Vic's—at least on the outside. When Gwen leads me inside, she takes me straight into the kitchen where a tall guy with reddish hair sits at the kitchen bar, studying his laptop.

"Logan," she says, "This is Noah. The ghost."

I cringe as Logan lifts a brow. He's as big as an oak tree, but dressed in a tee shirt and tan pants that look tailor-made and likely cost more than everything in my closet combined.

"He's here to make a big romantic gesture," she tells him.

This time, I don't argue. Victoria deserves all the big romantic gestures.

Logan's brows shoot upward as he gives me a quick once-over. "Ah," he says. "In that case, welcome. Can I get you a coffee? No offense, but you look like you could use one." His lip ticks upward. Apparently he's heard a couple of Noah stories, too.

"Thanks," I tell him. "I'd appreciate it." My heart's still pounding with adrenaline from the rush of driving over to see Victoria.

"Is she coming back soon?" I ask Gwen, already planning where I might wait for her. In that cute bakery on Main Street, maybe. Or stretched out in that cozy hammock I glimpsed by the corner of her porch. Is it weird and stalker-ish to wait for her at her house? Probably. But what if I'm waiting with wine and cupcakes?

"No," Gwen says, pulling her phone from her pocket. "She'll be gone a while."

My heart sinks. *Florida.* Did she take the job and head down there already? Have I missed my chance with her entirely?

No, I think. Because I'll hop right back into my car and drive down to Florida, too. Pineola? Pensacola? Gwen will tell me, and I'll fill myself with coffee and snacks and drive all night if I have to.

Because Victoria's worth it. I should have made that clear to her a thousand times before. I hate that she left camp thinking that I was ignoring her—because of course that's how she'd feel after three days of unanswered texts.

I turn back to Gwen. "Please tell me where I can find her. I know you barely know me, but I'm not some weirdo stalker. The last three weeks have made me see that I'm completely…I mean, your sister's the only—" I pause, trying to still my racing heart and form a complete sentence that doesn't sound hopeless and desperate. "She's the person I love most in the world and I think I might actually die if I don't see her again."

Gwen and Logan exchange a look. So much for not sounding desperate.

"A wee bit dramatic," Gwen says. "But I'll allow it."

"Ah, give the man a break, love," Logan says, giving her a mischievous smile. "Imagine if I hadn't flown back to you, that night you thought I was gone forever." He gives her a devilish wink as he slips an arm around her waist.

She bites back a smile and ruffles his hair. "As if you could have stayed away from me."

He grins, eyes sparkling. "Truth. Now imagine this lad's feeling even a fraction of that."

They hold another long look, and after a few raised brows and half-smiles that I hope are code for *Let's help this poor guy out,* Gwen pulls her phone from her pocket and turns back to me.

"The only reason I'm doing this is because I know she's nuts about you, too," she says. "Has been forever." She takes a step toward me, eyes narrowing like a cat's. "But if you break my sister's heart, I won't think twice about leaving you in the swamp for gator bait."

"I wouldn't expect anything different," I tell her.

"Good," she chirps. "Now tell me your number so I can text you an address."

Chapter Twenty-Seven

VICTORIA

That last half-mile is a doozy," Joan says, peering at me over her reading glasses. She's perched behind the check-in desk at the main lodge, right where she was when I left a few hours ago. She's still watching reruns of *Bones* and sipping from a massive thermos filled with what she calls her afternoon toddy. A sticker on the thermos has an earnest-looking tabby cat wearing a backpack and proclaims, *A life well-lived is spent outdoors.*

I'm starting to agree with that sentiment. Even in moments like this one, when my thighs are screaming for a hot bath with epsom salts and my shoulders ache from carrying my backpack.

Joan checked me into this cabin two days ago, and now she talks to me like I'm her new best friend. Yesterday I brought her a lemon blueberry muffin from a bakery in town and this morning she told me about her favorite hike that starts a few miles from here, just off the Blue Ridge Parkway.

"You were right, though," I tell her. "That view at sunset is incredible."

"Right?" she says, her face lighting up. "It's totally worth that brutal uphill climb." With her pixie-cut dark hair and sparkling gray-blue eyes, she looks barely forty—but told me she's almost sixty. Born and raised in this little corner of Virginia, she's spent her whole life *rambling in the mountains*, as she calls it. She told me she still hikes almost every day, usually early in the morning before starting her shift here at the cabins.

"Thanks again," I tell her. "For the recommendation."

"Anytime," she says, grabbing a guide book from a shelf under her desk. One arm is covered in a sleeve of fine-lined tattoos of flowers and birds, the colors done in muted earth tones. "I marked my favorites in here," she says, handing me the book. "Just bring it back to me when you check out." She's really leaned into this idea of being my local guide. Not that I mind one bit—I came here to clear my head, but also to push myself to get stronger, even if it's only a week until the next camp begins.

Sophie was right about this place—being here is the perfect way for me to gather my thoughts about how I want to move forward. A cozy, private cabin with no wifi has given me just the right amount of seclusion and quiet to make me feel calm again. And in this quiet, I've been able to finally hear that voice deep inside me—the one from the woman who's been knocked down enough that she was nearly impossible to hear.

But not anymore.

"Thank you," I tell Joan. The book's a small pocket-sized guide, with a dozen or more dog-eared pages and generous spots of highlighting. "I'll take good care of it."

She nods as the landline next to her rings with a call. "Have a good night, hon," she says, reaching for the phone.

I give her a friendly wave and head back down the dirt path to my cabin, which is about a hundred yards from this building.

Sophie called it rustic, but comfy. It's not quite camping and is more modern than the room I had at the institute—but I still feel like I'm roughing it a little. The cabin's like a studio apartment, with a kitchen-living room area, a tiny bathroom, and a loft upstairs that sleeps two.

I climb the front steps and unlock the door, already fantasizing about the long shower I'm going to take to ease these tired muscles. Unlike that first week of camp, I'm no longer gasping for air when I hike moderate trails. I'm still slow, but each day outside gets a little easier—and that just motivates me to keep going. Once inside, I kick off my boots, and immediately think of Noah and how he insisted I get a decent pair. I've only checked my phone a thousand times since Sunday night, hoping there might be a text from him.

There hasn't been.

And that fact hurts me even more than I thought it would.

After stripping out of my sweaty hiking clothes, I take a a hot shower—I'll feel these aches tomorrow, but it'll be worth it. Every ache lets me know I'm moving forward, training my body to be stronger and grow more accustomed to the unpredictability of nature—and other parts of life, too.

No matter what happens with Noah, my heart will get stronger, just like all other muscles do when you use them. These three weeks with him and the tween campers have reminded me of the one lesson I'd never learn in the Griffin house: the more you love, the more your heart grows.

And that's always a win.

A little after ten p.m., I'm nibbling on the remains of my microwave pizza, reading Joan's field guide when I hear a loud clatter on the porch. Certain it's one of the sneaky raccoons or bears that Joan warned me about, I grab the nearest big object—a wooden duck decoy from the bookcase—and fling open the front door, ready to holler and stamp my feet and scare the biscuits out of the nosy critter.

When I open the door, I'm stunned into silence, mouth gaping like a fish.

Noah's on all fours by the steps, his leg tangled in the camp chair that was by the door.

"What on earth—" I blurt, just as he looks up and says, "Once again, my timing is perfect."

"I thought you were some wild animal," I say, still holding the decoy above my head like a weapon.

His brow lifts as he smirks. "And your plan was to bludgeon me with a duck?"

I drop my hand and tuck the decoy against my chest like a football. "What are you doing?"

"I tripped over your chair and dropped my phone," he says, standing. "It's pitch black out here." Dressed in a navy button-down shirt and slim-cut jeans, he looks like a guy on a first date, trying hard to make a good impression. His jaw's scruffy with stubble, and his hair's rumpled in that way that begs me to run my fingers through it. And when he smiles, it melts my heart.

"Hi," he says, pushing his sleeves to his elbows. He's so close that I can smell that hint of cedar, and my body instinctively moves toward him.

"I meant, what are you doing *here*."

"Hoping you let me come inside and have that long overdue chat." His eyes are wide, a deep green in the moonlight. His gaze is intense, his smile tender. Will I ever tire of him looking at me this way?

I step to the side, holding the door open. "How did you find me?"

As he slips past me, his arm brushes against mine and sends

a zip of electricity down to my toes. He's been here less than a minute, and my body is already dying to be close to him again.

"I went to your house to return your book. And then Gwen told me you were gone."

"And she sent you here?" My heart hammers in my chest.

He stares at me through those impossibly long lashes. "I asked her very nicely."

Flustered, I go to the sink and pour two glasses of water. When I set them on the counter between us, he catches my hand and holds it as if it's as fragile as a bird.

But it's my heart that's fragile, and he has no idea that he's holding it in his hands, too.

"I needed to explain," he says. "In person." His thumb slides over my palm, and my breath hitches. "I wasn't ignoring you, Vic. I left camp in a hurry because Hannah had an emergency and needed my help. Before that, at the airport, Derrick accidentally took my phone and left me with his. There was this whole thing with Ethan and a half-feral pug—but none of that matters." He waves his free hand in the space between us and steps closer. "Anyway, the last few days have been crazy, and nothing went the way I'd hoped, and I know I could have gotten your number from Roxy, or had Gwen call you, or found some other way to talk to you sooner, but I didn't want to say these things over the phone. I needed to see you." He sighs, lacing his fingers in mine, and it's like two puzzle pieces locking together. "I needed to see your face, and hold your hand, and be in the same space with you."

My heart somersaults in my chest. How did I ever think I could walk away from this man and not feel the ache deep in my bones?

"I don't want to lose you again," he says. "I want to be with you—wherever that is. I know you said you needed some time, and I'm not here to put the pressure on. I want you to take all the time you need and do whatever you need to do, but I also want you to know that I'm here. I want to figure this out."

I feel like a dam that's about to burst. A hundred thoughts race through my brain, but only one of them matters.

"I'm glad you came," I tell him.

He lets out a breath. "Thank heaven, because I thought there was about an eighty percent chance you'd tell me to get lost. After that last text, I thought I'd ruined everything. That you were pushing me away."

"You didn't," I tell him. "And I wasn't." When I slide my hand along his cheek, he leans into my touch, and my whole body hums. "I'm sorry that it felt that way, but I needed to step away for a minute to sort through all of my messy feelings. I'm not always great at that, as you know."

He takes my hand in his and holds it against his chest. "Maybe we can work on that together."

"I'd like that."

"Does that mean you—"

At the same time, I say, "Roxy offered me the job."

He smirks. "Well, of course she did. She knows a good thing when she sees it."

"I told her yes. Because I found my happy."

He grins that delicious grin that I will never ever get tired of seeing. "That's my girl." Then he scoops me into his arms, and I laugh as he spins me around the tiny kitchenette.

When he sets me back down, I tell him, "You were right. But I had to step back to see it. I loved working at the camp, but I needed to know that I wasn't choosing it because of how I feel about you. I was caught up in this whirlwind, and finally felt like I found where I belonged—but part of me was afraid it wouldn't last. Or it would fall apart and I'd lose everything like I did before." I let out a heavy sigh, still reeling from the fact that he's here, standing in front of me. That despite all of my anxious thoughts, he didn't give up. "I couldn't separate my feelings about the camp and my feelings about you, and time was running out, and—you cloud my judgment, Valentine. Whenever you're around, you're all I can think about."

His brow lifts as he slides his arm around my waist. "Is that right?"

I give him a teasing eye roll. "I'm nuts about you," I confess. "And most days I don't know what to do about it."

"I have some ideas," he says, his voice so gravelly it makes the little hairs on my neck tingle.

I give him a playful nudge and he shoots me a cocky half-smile that means we'll definitely revisit this conversation later.

He brings my hand to his lips, planting a kiss on the inside of my wrist. "I get it," he says, serious again. "Sometimes I have to step away to get clear on what I really need, too. But know that you can tell me anything. Always. When you're feeling lost, I'll come with you so we can find the way forward together."

"Fair warning," I tell him. "I get lost. A lot."

"You'll have to try a lot harder than that to scare me off, Griffin."

I smile, looping my arms over his neck.

"I love the idea of getting lost with you," he says, sliding his fingers along my cheek. "I have from the moment we met. And just for the record, I never wanted anything as much as I want you."

He leans down and kisses me tenderly at first—but it only takes a moment for this spark to ignite. He catches my lip in his teeth, his hands squeezing my hips as he pulls me closer. And then my body melts into his, and I feel the pounding of his heart against my chest.

All I can think is *yes. This. More.*

"Wait," he says, pulling away. "I forgot something." He takes a step towards the door, but I catch his arm.

"Where do you think you're going?"

"I brought dessert," he says, his tone teasing. "And wine. And flowers. I couldn't possibly show up to win your heart empty-handed."

"Later." I pull him against me, sliding my hands along his chest. His eyes darken as he steps forward and pins me against the kitchen counter, his hips holding me in place. If his gaze was any more intense, it would burn this cabin to ash.

"I've been waiting for ages to get you all to myself," I tell him, dropping my hands to his waist. "The last three weeks have been both amazing and absolute torture."

He grins at that, one hand finding the small of my back while the other winds in my hair. "Same," he says, his voice low and deep. His hands slide along my skin, as if memorizing every curve, and my heart bangs against my ribs. There's no better feeling than this.

And there's no other place I'd rather be.

"We have a week until the next camp starts," I tell him. "I say we make it count."

He leans closer, his lips moving against my ear. "I'm all yours, Griffin," he says. "But then, I always have been."

He scoops me onto the counter, and I lock my legs around his waist because somehow, he still feels too far away. His eyes pin me in place, and when he bends to kiss me again, I rake my fingers through his hair and catch his bottom lip in my teeth. I could kiss this man for days and still not get enough.

He murmurs my name, his lips moving against my neck, and I am both lost and finally found. When he mumbles something I can't quite make out, I pull his face to mine and tell him to explain because I don't want any more words lost between us.

"I can't wait for our next adventure," he says, eyes glittering with promise.

When he folds me into his arms again, my mind is quiet, and my heart is full—and for the first time I can remember, I know I'm exactly where I belong.

Epilogue

VICTORIA

Six months later

"Y ou're really not going to tell me where we're going?" I ask, though I know his answer.

"And spoil the surprise?" Noah says. "No way, sweetheart."

I can't see him through the blindfold, but I know he's smirking over there in the driver's seat. There's the telltale rumble of cobblestones beneath the tires, and based on how long we've been driving, that means we're in one of the historic districts of downtown Charleston.

"Is this a dinner cruise?" I ask, immediately feeling anxious about being packed on a boat with a bunch of strangers on New Year's Eve. Although seeing the fireworks in the harbor would be amazing.

"Nope."

"Carriage ride?"

He snorts. "Please, Griffin. You deserve better than the

typical touristy stuff. And you know I strive for first-rate surprises."

I grin as he parks the car and cuts the engine. In a flash, he's opening my door and helping me out onto the sidewalk, one hand clutching mine and the other looped around my waist as I find my footing. I can see the tiniest sliver of pavement and grass through the bottom of the blindfold, but I won't peek because Noah's probably been planning whatever this is for weeks.

The man delights in surprising me. And as it turns out, I like surprises when they come from a place of love. And the surprises that Noah cooks up? They're the best.

Well, except for that one with the terrifying bridge over the bottomless gorge in the mountains—but even that one worked out all right in the end.

"About twenty steps on the pavement," he says, slipping his arm through mine. He leads me a few paces down a sidewalk, then turns onto a walkway lined with palmettos that brush against my arm as we pass.

A floral scent hangs in the air, mixed with the comforting woodsy scent that's all Noah. With one hand at my lower back, he leads me up two steps and then pauses as he punches a key code into a door. After two tiny beeps, the bolt flips, and he ushers me inside. My boot heels clack on the hardwood floor, and I immediately feel more at ease. This is no restaurant—it feels like a home. The air is fresh inside and warmer, with a hint of cloves that must be left over from the holidays.

"Now?" I ask, touching the blindfold.

He places his fingers over mine and leans close. His lips move against my ear as he whispers, "Not yet."

Before I can reply, he scoops me over his shoulder into a firefighter's carry and heads up a flight of stairs. My heart hammers in my chest as I shriek in surprise and tug at the hem of my skirt.

"You better not drop me, Valentine," I say between giggles.

He gives my backside a playful smack, earning another shriek from me.

"Have a little faith, Griffin," he says, his voice doing that sexy-rumble that I will never, ever get tired of hearing.

I have nothing to worry about, though. With Noah, I always know I'm safe. The sky could shatter around us, and he wouldn't let me go.

The floorboards creak under his feet, and then I hear the sound of another door opening. A breeze lifts my hair as he sets me back down on my feet. His face is just inches from mine when he slides his fingers along my cheeks and slips the blindfold off.

The first thing I see is his mischievous grin. He's proud of himself, and soon I see why.

We're standing on a small balcony that's decorated with huge potted plants and strings of outdoor lights. With a canvas canopy covering half the sitting area, it's like a little oasis. The houses here are close enough together that you can see straight into everyone's tiny yard, but the plants around us create a privacy screen so we're hidden from view. I'm still taking in all the details when I realize that this isn't just any vacation rental— it's the balcony where we met.

"Noah," I breathe.

"My uncle can't bring himself to sell this place," he says. "He's out of town for the week and offered to let us stay." He gives me a tiny shrug. "New Year's getaway."

"Can't say I blame him. Is that awesome little bakery still right down the block? Because if so, I wouldn't want to let go of this house, either."

"Ah," Noah says, holding his finger up. "That reminds me." He ducks back inside through the French doors, leaving me to soak up the last few rays of the sun. I'd forgotten how this corner of the neighborhood lights up during the golden hour, all the bricks bathed in warm light as the sun sinks below the tree line.

The balcony's had some serious upgrades since I was last here—including a new iron railing, new floorboards, and a small table that comfortably sits two. Long gone are the rickety ladder of the fire escape and the beat-up chairs where we once sat dressed as a reluctant superhero and a cheeky wood nymph. Now, the cute bistro-style table is set with a big bouquet of fresh-cut lilies, surrounded by tea light candles and hanging holiday cacti bursting with blooms. This looks like a photo from a magazine, from the bright-colored rug to the wicker loveseat and the wind chimes.

When he comes back out, he's carrying an open bottle of wine and two stemless glasses, looking effortlessly sexy in his slim-cut jeans and green wool sweater. After all the traveling with camps over the last few months, it's nice to be in a quiet place, just the two of us. Between the kids' camps and overnight stays at Noah's, I've barely spent a night in my own home since the summer. Hannah just found a new apartment two weeks ago, and though I haven't officially moved in with Noah, he's asked me to about a hundred times.

As he fills our glasses, he says, "I considered whisking you away to a more exotic location for our time off. But I needed to discuss something with you, and this place seemed more appropriate for that."

I give him a teasing finger-wave. "If this is another shameless attempt to get me to officially move in with you—"

"Nah," he says with a smile. "We'll get to that part when you're ready. You just say the word." We've talked about our next move several times, but I can't imagine selling my house —formerly my Aunt Bernice's that she left to me. I know I won't live in Jasmine Falls forever, and maybe not much longer, because commuting to Charleston when we're in the off-season isn't the greatest. But I can't quite make myself sell the house yet. I'm not ready to cut ties with my hometown entirely.

He hands me my wine and clinks his glass against mine. "To the new year," he says, holding my gaze. "And to our next adventure, wherever it might take us."

"To second chances," I add.

He smiles and sips his wine. "You know," he says, "When I first met you on this balcony, I was thinking of transferring to a different college."

"Really?" I ask.

He nods, leaning against the railing. Above him, the fairy lights blink on, the sky around us finally turning a dusky purple.

"I never felt like I fit in at C of C," he says. "That weekend, I'd pretty much decided to leave. I was just working out logistics." He leans closer, nudging my shoulder. "But then I met a girl with antlers and adorable freckles who'd spend hours talking to me about stuff that left me curious and amazed—and that changed everything."

"You're serious, aren't you?"

He shrugs. "You get me, Griffin. You saw all my messy parts, my weird parts, and you were still all in. Not everyone gets to have someone like you."

"I felt the same way about you," I tell him. "Still do."

He smiles. "Then I'd say that makes me one of the luckiest."

"That's about the best we can hope for, isn't it?" I ask. "Someone who loves us because of all our messy parts, and not in spite of them."

He clinks his glass against mine again, his eyes a deep green in the fading light.

"I'm really glad you didn't transfer," I tell him, and something tugs deep in my chest as I consider: it's a wonder we met each other at all. And then running into each other at the institute this summer? I'm not a person who believes in destiny, but Gwen would tell me that's the universe working overtime to bring us what we need.

This time, I'm inclined to believe her.

"That party was terrible," I quip. "But it's still the best night I ever spent on a balcony. And I wouldn't trade that for the world."

Smirking, he steps closer and slips his arm around my hips. "We can do better."

Before I can reply, he drops to one knee. He pulls my hand to his lips, and my heart flutters like a bird. His gaze locks on mine, so tender and full of love, and my knees wobble the way they always do when Noah looks at me this way—like I'm the most precious part of his world.

"Victoria Griffin," he says, his voice gravelly. "I've wanted to ask you this a thousand times, and I can't wait one more day." He pulls a ring from his pocket and holds it in the space between us, the fingers of his other hand laced in mine. "You are, by far, the best adventure. And the one that matters most." He gives me a sheepish grin. "Will you marry me?"

I sink to my knees and pull his face to mine. When I kiss him, he folds his arms around me and holds me tight like he never wants to let me go. I kiss him until I'm breathless, seeing little pinpoints of light, and then topple against him and knock him off-balance. He laughs as he tumbles backward and pulls me onto his lap.

"Is that a yes?" he asks.

"Of course it's a yes," I tell him, sliding my hand along his chest. "A thousand times, yes."

He slips the ring on my finger, a modest diamond that catches the light like a star. He loops his arms around my waist and holds me close, his eyes searching mine.

"Happy New Year, sweetheart," he says. "I can't wait to see what happens next."

I'm sure I couldn't predict what that might be, even if I tried—and I'm perfectly okay with that because I know that the future that unfolds with Noah is the best one of all. There will be plenty of messy parts because that's what happens when two lives intertwine—but the messy moments are how you build something amazing together. Something that grows.

Something that lasts.

"I heard you're supposed to ring in the new year doing something you want to do more of," I tell him, raking my fingers through his hair. "Set the tone."

"You say that like you have some ideas," he says, his eyes darkening with mischief. He dips his head, nuzzling my neck in that way he knows makes me melt.

"I certainly do," I answer. When I tug his hair, he growls with impatience, and my heart bangs against my ribs. If I lived two lifetimes, I'd still never get enough of this man.

He slips a hand under my sweater, to the small of my back. "I wonder how similar they are to my ideas."

"Only one way to find out, Valentine."

He's on his feet in a flash, pulling me against him as he laughs a raucous laugh that lights me up and promises that this moment—on one tiny balcony under a vast canopy of stars—is only the beginning.

Exclusive Bonus Content, Just for You!

Want more of Jasmine Falls? Join my author newsletter (it's always free) and get fun extras like bonus epilogues and my short novella **You Got This, Maggie Monroe.** It's a standalone story in the Jasmine Falls Love Stories series, and is only available as a thank you to my newsletter subscribers. So go ahead—add a little something extra to your reading list. :)

Sign up and learn more at lucydayauthor.com.

Like the Book? Please Leave a Review!

Thanks so much for reading *My Star-Crossed Summer*! I hope you enjoyed the story. Please consider taking a moment to review this book on Amazon. Reviews make a huge difference to indie authors like me because they help more readers find my books! (Also, I do a little happy dance every time you leave a review, and that just makes me more excited to write the next book in the series…)

If you liked Victoria and Noah's story, check out the other books in the Jasmine Falls Love Stories series. Each book features new characters and can be read as a standalone. And, as always, the happy-ever-after is guaranteed.

Acknowledgments

First, thank you to my readers. Your enthusiasm always makes my day brighter, and your kind words make me excited to keep writing these stories. You remind me to keep looking for the glimmers (and the meet-cutes!) everywhere.

Katie Pryal, thank you for being my first reader, my wild, wonderful brainstorming partner, and the little voice in my head that nudges me forward on the hardest days. Darci Swisher, thank you for close reads and your excellent advice—especially on this one! Camille Pagán, thank you for creating such a wonderful writing community and for offering so much wisdom and support—you are a lighthouse, and you've helped me more than I can say. To my awesome writers' group (you know who you are!), thank you for the endless support—I'm so glad we found each other. You hold my little feet to the fire, and I love it.

To my friends and family: you inspire me more than you know. Thank you so much for believing in me and encouraging me to chase my dreams. I love you all so much and am so glad to have you in my life.

And finally, to Andrew, my best friend and my most delightful adventure. Somehow you're both my anchor and my soft place to fall. You make my heart grow more every day.

About the Author

Originally from South Carolina, Lucy Day loves sweet tea, summer nights, and big-hearted love stories. She is winner of two IPPY Silver Medals for Romance (*The Almost Lovebirds*, 2023 and *One Sweet Holiday*, 2024) and the Next Generation Indies Award for series fiction (*The Jasmine Falls Love Stories* series, 2024). She started writing in college and wrote her first novel after leaving her job at a web comic in St. Louis. Lucy is a bird nerd who can't live without strong coffee and wide open spaces. She's married to her best friend and when she isn't writing a new love story, she's out walking in the woods, dreaming up her next adventure. She lives in Iowa and is hard at work on her new series.

To learn more, visit lucydayauthor.com.

9 781947 834781